The Purrfect Murder

Books by Rita Mae Brown & Sneaky Pie Brown

WISH YOU WERE HERE
REST IN PIECES
MURDER AT MONTICELLO
PAY DIRT
MURDER, SHE MEOWED
MURDER ON THE PROWL
CAT ON THE SCENT
SNEAKY PIE'S COOKBOOK FOR MYSTERY LOVERS
PAWING THROUGH THE PAST
CLAWS AND EFFECT
CATCH AS CAT CAN
THE TAIL OF THE TIP-OFF
WHISKER OF EVIL
CAT'S EYEWITNESS
SOUR PUSS
PUSS 'N CAHOOTS

Books by Rita Mae Brown

THE HAND THAT CRADLES THE ROCK
SONGS TO A HANDSOME WOMAN
THE PLAIN BROWN RAPPER
RUBYFRUIT JUNGLE
IN HER DAY
SIX OF ONE
SOUTHERN DISCOMFORT
SUDDEN DEATH
HIGH HEARTS
STARTING FROM SCRATCH: A DIFFERENT KIND OF WRITERS' MANUAL
BINGO
VENUS ENVY
DOLLEY: A NOVEL OF DOLLEY MADISON IN LOVE AND WAR
RIDING SHOTGUN
RITA WILL: A MEMOIR OF A LITERARY RABBLE-ROUSER
LOOSE LIPS
OUTFOXED
HOTSPUR
FULL CRY
THE HUNT BALL
THE HOUNDS AND THE FURY

The Purrfect Murder

A MRS. MURPHY MYSTERY

RITA MAE BROWN

& SNEAKY PIE BROWN

ILLUSTRATIONS BY MICHAEL GELLATLY

DOUBLEDAY LARGE PRINT HOME LIBRARY EDITION

BANTAM BOOKS NEW YORK • TORONTO • LONDON • SYDNEY • AUCKLAND

This Large Print Edition, prepared especially for Doubleday Large Print Home Library, contains the complete, unabridged text of the original Publisher's Edition.

THE PURRFECT MURDER
A Bantam Book / February 2008

Published by
Bantam Dell
A Division of Random House, Inc.
New York, New York

ISBN 978-0-7394-9199-7

Printed in the United States of America

Dedicated to
Fred and Doris Duncan,
two remarkable people who know
that Nature provides the nuts;
you've got to crack them yourself.

Cast of Characters

Mary Minor "Harry" Haristeen—Formerly the postmistress of Crozet, she now is trying to make a go of it with farming. She turned forty in August, doesn't seem to mind.

Pharamond "Fair" Haristeen, D.V.M.—Harry's husband is an equine vet, and he tries to keep his wife out of trouble, with limited success.

Susan Tucker—Harry's best friend since cradle days often marvels at how Harry's mind works when it works. The two of them know each other so well that they could finish each other's sentences.

Mrs. Miranda Hogendobber—Miranda observes a great deal but keeps most of it to herself. She's in her late sixties, devoutly Christian, and mothers Harry, who lost her own mother in her twenties.

Marilyn "Big Mim" Sanburne—The Queen of Crozet sees all and knows all, or would like to, at any rate. She despotically improves everyone's lot but is good-hearted underneath it all.

Marilyn "Little Mim" Sanburne, Jr.—She's finally emerging from her mother's shadow, which displeases her mother while it pleases everyone else. Most especially pleased is her new husband, Blair Bainbridge.

Jim Sanburne—The mayor of Crozet, his daughter is the vice mayor; he's accustomed to being in the middle of wife and daughter. Jim is a regular guy, which puts him in sharp contrast to Big Mim, who was born with a silver spoon in her mouth.

Aunt Tally Urquhart—This wild woman, in her nineties, must be a devotee of the god Pan, for she's in her glory when pandemonium reigns. She's Big Mim's aunt and delights in shocking her prim niece.

Deputy Cynthia Cooper—She's smart, in her late thirties, and Harry's neighbor. She, like Fair, tries to keep Harry out of trouble when she can. She likes law enforcement.

Sheriff Rick Shaw—He's the dedicated public servant, insightful but by the book. He wearies of the politics of his position, but he never wearies of bringing criminals to justice. He likes Harry, but she gets in the way.

Olivia "BoomBoom" Craycroft—She was widowed in her early thirties and, being quite beautiful, always trailed troops of men behind her. One of them was Fair Haristeen, who had an affair with her when he was divorced from Harry, whom he's since remarried. BoomBoom can be forceful when necessary.

Alicia Palmer—A great movie star, now in her late fifties, she's thrilled to be back on the farm in Crozet. She's also thrilled that she's found BoomBoom, for they truly connect.

Tazio Chappars—This young architect finds herself in terrible trouble and she can't remember what happened.

Paul de Silva—He's Big Mim's stable manager and in love with Tazio. When she's carted off to jail he's beyond miserable.

Dr. William Wylde—Respected, responsible, and good-natured, this OB/GYN delivered half of Crozet.

Benita Wylde—Will's wife is an avid golfer and learns some painful lessons about life. She rises to the occasion.

Margaret Westlake—She manages Dr. Wylde's office.

Sophie Denham—She is the senior nurse in Dr. Wylde's office.

Kylie Kraft—She is the junior nurse in Dr. Wylde's office and is known for going through men like potato chips.

Dr. Harvey Tillach—This physician loathes Will Wylde.

Mike McElvoy—Every county has at least one building inspector. Albemarle County has two, but Mike is the one who sets everyone's teeth on edge.

Carla Paulson—She's a good-looking middle-aged lady and is building a new house. Tazio Chappars is the architect, and Mike McElvoy is the inspector. This makes for a sulfurous triangle.

Folly Steinhauser—She also built a huge house within the last two years and has learned to detest Mike McElvoy. She's quite rich and not unwilling to challenge Big Mim. Her husband, Ron, is possessive but slowly failing, as he's a lot older than Folly. He misses a lot these days.

The Really Important Characters

Mrs. Murphy—She's a pretty tiger cat with brains, speed, and a reasonably tolerant temperament. She knows she can't really keep Harry, her human, out of trouble, but she can sometimes get her out once she's in a mess.

Tee Tucker—This corgi, also devoted to Harry, has great courage and manages to live with two cats. That says a lot.

Pewter—The gray cannonball, as she does not like to be known, affects disdain for humans, but she loves Harry and Fair. However, if there's a way to avoid a long way or trouble, she's the first to choose the easy path.

Simon—Living in the barn with all the horses pleases this opossum, who also likes Harry, as much as he can like humans. She gives him treats.

Flatface—Sharing the loft with Simon, the great horned owl looks down on earthbound creatures, figuratively and literally. However, in a pinch, Flatface can be counted on.

Matilda—She's a big blacksnake and the third roommate in the barn loft. Her sense of humor borders on the black, too.

Owen—Tee Tucker's brother belongs to Susan Tucker, who bred the litter. He doesn't know how his sister can tolerate the cats. When in feline company, he behaves, but he thinks the cats are snobs.

Brinkley—This smart yellow Lab loves and adores Tazio.

Since Mrs. Murphy, Tucker, and Pewter live on a farm, various creatures cross their paths, from bears to foxes to one nasty blue jay. They love all the horses, which can't be said for some of the other creatures, but then, the horses are domesticated. Pewter declares she is not domesticated, merely resting in a house with regular meals.

The Purrfect Murder

1

Morning light, which looked like thin spun gold, reminded Harry Haristeen why she loved September so much. The light softened, the nights grew crisp, while the days remained warm. This Thursday, September 18, there was only a vague tinge of yellow at the tops of the willow trees, which would become a cascade of color by mid-October.

The old 1978 Ford F-150 rumbled along the macadam road. The big engine's sound thrilled Harry. If it had a motor in it, she liked it.

Her two cats, Mrs. Murphy, a tiger, and Pewter, a gray cat, along with her corgi, Tee Tucker, also enjoyed the rumble, which often put them to sleep. Today, all sitting on the bench seat, they were wide awake. A trip to town meant treats and visiting other

animals, plus one never knew what would happen.

Harry had just turned forty on August 7, and she declared it didn't faze her. Maybe. Maybe not. Fair, her adored husband, threw a big surprise birthday party and she reveled in being the center of attention, even though it was for entering her Middle Ages. She wore the gorgeous horseshoe ring her husband had bought her at the Shelbyville Horse Show. She wasn't much for display or girly things, but every time she looked down at the glitter, she grinned.

"All right, kids, you behave. You hear me? I don't want you jumping on Tazio's blueprints. No knocking erasers on the floor. No chewing the rubber ends of pencils. Tucker." Harry's voice kept the command tone. "Don't you dare steal Brinkley's bones. I mean it."

The three animals cast their eyes at her, those eyes brimming with love and the promise of obedience.

Tazio Chappars, a young architect in Crozet, won large commissions for public buildings, but she also accepted a healthy string of commissions for beautiful, expensive homes, most paid for by non-Virginians. The houses were too flashy for a blue-blooded Virginian. However, Tazio, like all of us in this world, needed to make a living, so if the client wanted a marble-clad bathroom as big as most people's garages, so be it.

As Harry parked, she noticed a brand-new Range Rover in the small lot. It had been painted a burnt orange. She walked over to admire it.

"Good wheels," she muttered to herself.

Good indeed, but the closest dealer was ninety miles away in Richmond, which somewhat dimmed the appeal. If that didn't do it, the price did.

Before she reached the door, a stream of invective assaulted her ears. When she opened the door, the blast hit her.

"Wormwood! I don't care what it costs and I don't care if termites get in it. I want wormwood!" An extremely well cared for woman in her mid-forties shook colored plans in Tazio's face.

"Mrs. Paulson, I understand. But it's going to slow down the library because it takes months to secure it."

"I don't care. You'll do what I tell you."

Tazio, face darkening, said nothing.

Mrs. Paulson spun around on her bright

aqua three-hundred-dollar shoes to glare at Harry. Harry's white T-shirt revealed an ample chest, and her jeans hugged a trim body with a healthy tan. Mrs. Paulson paused for a minute because, even though not of Virginia, she had divined that often the richest people or the ones with the oldest blood wore what to her were migrant-labor fashions. Carla Paulson wouldn't be caught dead in a white T-shirt and Wranglers. She couldn't fathom why Harry would appear in public looking like a farmhand.

She knew Harry in passing, so she switched into "lunch lady" mode.

Tazio stepped around her drafting table. "Mrs. Paulson, you remember Harry Haristeen; her mother was a Hepworth. Her father, a Minor." Tazio knew perfectly well that Mrs. Paulson didn't know the bloodlines, but the simple fact that Tazio recited them meant "important person."

Not that Harry gave a damn.

Extending her hand, radiating a smile, the well-groomed woman purred, "Of course I remember."

Harry politely took her hand, using the exact amount of pressure all those battleaxes at cotillion drilled into her year after year. "I can see you've hired the most talented architect in the state." She paused. "Love your new wheels."

"Isn't the interior beautiful? Just bought it last week." Carla Paulson brightened. She checked her diamond-encrusted Rolex. "Well, I'll call later for another appointment. Oh, before I forget, Michael McElvoy said he'd be out at the site tomorrow at eleven."

Tazio wanted to say she had an appointment then, which she did, but if one of the county building inspectors was going to be at the construction site, then she'd better be there, too. Michael lived to find fault.

"Fine. I'll be there." Tazio smiled and walked Mrs. Paulson to the door, while Mrs. Murphy and Pewter jumped on the high chair and onto the drafting table. Those pink erasers thrilled the cats. Tazio even had special white square ones that squeaked when bitten.

Brinkley, a young yellow lab rescued by Tazio during a snowstorm at a half-completed building site, chewed his bone. Tucker lay down in front of the wonderful creature and put her head on her paws to stare longingly at the bone.

Once Carla Paulson exited, Tazio exhaled loudly.

"Murphy, Pewter, what did I tell you?" Harry warned.

Murphy batted a square white eraser off the table. Both cats sailed after it.

"Don't worry about it. I have a carton full of them back in the supply closet. In fact, I'll give you one." She took another breath. "That woman is plucking my last nerve. I thought Folly Steinhauser was high-maintenance and Penny Lattimore a diva, but Carla is in a class by herself."

"I can see that."

Tazio slyly smiled. "The diamond Rolex watch is so over the top."

"Better to wear plain platinum. Worth more and not showy. In fact, most people think it's steel." Harry leaned on the drafting table. "But if Carla owned a platinum Rolex, she'd have to tell everyone it wasn't steel and ruin it, of course."

"Harry," Tazio laughed, "you're so Virginia."

"Oh, look who's talking."

"I'm from St. Louis, remember."

"Doesn't matter. You mentioned that gaudy watch. I didn't."

Tazio was half Italian, half African-American, and all gorgeous. Her family, prominent in St. Louis, had provided her with the best education as well as a great deal of social poise, since her mother was on every committee imaginable. From the time she was small, her mother had marched her to different parties, balls, fund-raisers.

"I'm worn out, because she keeps changing her mind. Well, I'll grant, she's been consistent about the wormwood, but every time she changes something the cost spirals upward. It's not my money, but you move a window an inch and either Orrie"—she named the head of construction by his nickname—"or I have to call the building inspector. Michael McElvoy, as you heard."

Harry started to giggle. "Lucky you."

"Oh, well, everyone has their problems. You came to pick up the numbers on the different heating systems for St. Luke's. Got 'em." She walked back to her large, polished mahogany desk, about ten feet from the drafting table. Picking up a folder, she said, "Here. Digest it, then let's go over it before the next vestry meeting."

Harry flipped open the folder. "Jeez."

"Lots of choices, and each one has pluses and minuses."

"Herb have a copy?" Harry mentioned the pastor of St. Luke's, Rev. Herb Jones.

"I thought we should put our heads together first. Anyway, he's on overload because of the St. Luke's reunion next month."

The reunion would be Saturday, October 25. Each October, St. Luke's held a gathering of all its members. Many who had moved away from central Virginia returned, so the numbers ran to about three hundred.

"Okay. I'll get right on this. Be nice to have this installed before the reunion, just in case the weather does turn cold."

"With luck the old boiler ought to hold out for another month or two. First frost usually hits us mid-October. We'll make it, I hope. You know, that old furnace is cast iron. A welder will need to dismantle it to get it out of there. That will take days. They don't build things like they used to," Tazio said with a big grin.

Harry finally noticed Tucker. "What did I tell you?"

Tazio walked back to the supply room, returning with a dog treat called a Greenies.

She handed it to a grateful Tucker. "Made in Missouri."

"Well, then it has to be good." Harry laughed. "Come on, kids."

"I want the eraser." Mrs. Murphy carried the item in her mouth.

Harry had reached down to pluck it from those jaws when Tazio said, "Keep it. Really. I have a carton."

"Thanks. You spoil my buddies."

"You don't?" An eyebrow arched over one green eye.

"Well . . ."

"If you spoiled Fair like you spoil these three, he'd be fat as a tick." Tazio mentioned Harry's husband, who was six five, all muscle.

"You know, I don't think Fair will ever get fat. For one thing, if he doesn't work it off, he'll worry it off."

"He doesn't strike me as a worrier."

"Maybe not in the traditional sense, but he's always thinking about the future, investigating new technology and medications. His mind never stops."

"Neither does yours. That's why you were made for each other."

"Guess so. All right, madam. I'll get back

to you." She paused. "Speaking of made for each other, you and Paul seem to be."

Tazio shrugged and blushed.

Harry opened the door and the three happy friends scooted out ahead of her. She got in the Ford, ran a few errands, then turned west toward the farm. Once down the long driveway, she could see her field of sunflowers, heads straight up to the sun, her quarter acre of Petit Manseng grapes ripening. How perfect.

2

One acre of sunflowers towered over another acre of Italian sunflowers, their beautiful heads turned toward the sun. The centers, heavy with seeds, barely moved in the light breeze, which lifted the leaves on the wide, hollow stalks.

Harry pulled the truck alongside the barn, cut the motor, and hopped out. Before returning to her chores, she stood, hands on hips, admiring the rich yellows of the big sunflowers and the subtle greenish white of the Italian variety. A twelve-foot grass swath ran between the sunflower acres and the grapes, pendulous beauties drooping on the vine. Since this was their first year, the grapes would not be picked but allowed to winter on the vine. This would thrill the foxes and birds.

"Come on."

Mrs. Murphy and Tucker followed.

"I need a nap." Pewter hesitated.

"I'm sure you do," Mrs. Murphy agreed.

The tiger's ready reply made Pewter suspicious. Mrs. Murphy and Tucker must be hiding something.

Harry walked along, Tucker alongside her, Mrs. Murphy behind, and Pewter bringing up the rear.

"Thought you wanted a nap," Tucker called over her shoulder.

"Decided I needed the exercise." Pewter's dark-gray fur shone, a sign of her overall health.

As they walked through the sunflower rows, insects buzzing, Harry paused, ran her fingers over a large head, then moved on. "Time for some rain."

A huge fake owl on a stake had thwarted some birds, but the blue jay paid no mind. Consequently, he'd eaten so much over the last month that his speed suffered. A red oak in the pasture next to the sunflower acres provided him with a refuge. He unfurled his topknot once the cats came into view. Lifting off, he circled the party once.

"Pissants."

Pewter glanced up. *"Butt ugly."*

The jay swooped low, just missing Pewter as he emitted what he'd eaten earlier. Satisfied, he returned to the red oak.

"One day," Pewter grumbled.

"Least it wasn't a direct hit." Tucker tried to look on the bright side. The dog swiveled her large ears, then barked, *"Susan."*

The cats stopped, turning their heads to listen for the Audi station wagon. It was a quarter mile from the house, but they, too, could hear the motor. Few humans can distinguish the unique sounds each set of tires produce, but for the dog and cats this was as easy as identifying someone wearing squeaky shoes.

As the wagon approached the house, Harry finally heard it and turned to behold an arching plume of dust. "Damn, we really do need rain."

They walked briskly toward the house.

Susan met them halfway. "Hey, sugar."

Sweeping her arm wide, Harry beamed. "Can you believe it?"

Susan stopped, putting her hands on her hips. "Promiscuous in fertility and abundance."

"Worried about rain."

"Me, me, me." Susan bent down to scratch Tucker's ears.

"More."

"Me, too." Pewter rubbed against Susan's leg, so she petted the gray cannonball.

Harry slipped her arm through Susan's as they stood there for a moment admiring the yield. "Agriculture is still the basis of all wealth. Can't have industry or high tech if people can't eat."

Susan nodded. "Course, most people have forgotten that."

Harry smiled as they walked back to the house, the blue jay squawking after them.

As they passed the barn, Simon, the opossum, stuck his head out of the open loft doors. *"Save me some cookies."*

Harry and Susan looked up at him, for he was semitame.

"If I don't eat them first." Pewter giggled.

"You need a diet, girl." Mrs. Murphy arched an eyebrow.

"Shut up." Pewter shot in front of everyone to push open the screen, then squeezed through the animal door into the kitchen.

Once in the kitchen, Harry poured sweet tea and put out some fruit and cheese.

Susan approached the reason for her visit to her best friend. "You're not going to believe this."

"What?" Harry leaned forward.

"Folly Steinhauser pledged to pay for the entire St. Luke's reunion on October twenty-fifth."

"What!"

"She did."

"But she's only attended St. Luke's for two years. I mean, she's only lived here for two years and," Harry thought a moment, "been on the vestry board for one."

"Herb was politically shrewd to call her to the board."

"Well, Susan, if she's going to cough up what will amount to thirty thousand dollars, give or take, I don't wonder."

"He didn't know that originally." Susan closed her eyes in appreciation as she sipped the tea, a sprig of fresh mint from the house garden enlivening the taste. "He was smart because she's a come-here and she knows how to talk to the other come-heres."

"I wasn't aware that one talked to them. I thought, dumb rednecks that we are, we simply listened to their cascade of wisdom."

"Don't be snide."

"All right, then. How about I'm tired of them telling me how they do it up North."

"Harry, they aren't all from the North."

"Oh?"

"Some are from the Midwest."

"That's just as damned bad." Harry burst out laughing.

"You are so prejudiced. Now, shut up and do listen."

"Yes, ma'am." She sighed. "Maybe turning forty has allowed me to enter the realm of crankiness." She raised an eyebrow. "But I will listen to *you.*"

"Folly's on the board of Planned Parenthood, and she's gotten the other new girls—Carla Paulson, Penny Lattimore, and Elise Brennan—to all pitch in with stuff for the silent auction. She's even gotten some of the doctors who work at Planned Parenthood to give a free consultation."

"Do we have to get pregnant first?"

"They aren't all OB/GYNs, smart-ass. Come on, now, give Folly some credit. This is wonderful and takes so much pressure off Herb. Every year he had to scramble to get the money for the reunion."

"That's a sore point with me. I've said for years, charge enough to cover the food."

"He won't do that. Herb says everyone should come home to St. Luke's without feeling they have to write a check." Susan reminded Harry of what she already knew.

"Fishes and loaves."

"Boy, there have been some years when we've had to pray for a miracle, but this year it's delivered."

"Well," Harry cupped her chin in her hand, her elbow on the table, which would have infuriated her long-departed mother, "it is, it is, but it irritates me that these people want to buy their way in."

"To St. Luke's?"

"Susan, you're a political creature. You know as well as I do that the Episcopal church and the Lutheran church are the two most socially prominent churches. Worship is one thing. Mixing with people who can help business or make you feel like you're with the A group is another."

"Where does that put us?" Susan sliced a thin wedge of Brie, positioning it on a large Carr's cracker.

"We were born to it. I don't feel socially prominent. I don't care about that stuff. I think it hurts people's feelings."

"It does, but people need their little groups. It comforts them."

"You've been reading Edmund Burke's *Reflections on the Revolution in France* again." Harry smiled, as both she and Susan read voraciously, and not fluff.

"Mmm, no, but I remember it well enough. Back to your point. Yes, it can hurt feelings. Being excluded from a group is painful."

Harry shrugged. "Find another group."

"Stop being thick. We need to thank Folly at the next board meeting, and I suppose whatever she wants to do in the future we'd better go along on at least one project." Susan stopped. "Do you hear me?"

"Yes," Harry said. "That reminds me. Stay put." She rose and hurried out the door, the screen door flapping behind her, Tucker running along. She came back and placed Tazio's papers in front of Susan. "Haven't even looked at them."

"She's written a cover letter for you."

Harry leaned over Susan's shoulder as they read the letter together. "She's right."

In the letter, Tazio proposed that in the long run it would save money to also replace the furnace in the offices and at Herb's house when they replaced the furnace in the church. "The cost of materials and labor would rise over the years as surely as the sun rises in the east. Do it now" were her polite but forceful last sentences.

"She is. Once the workmen are there, just do it all and then every dwelling or business will be on the same system. But, oh, the expense."

"Well, if Folly's given us thirty thousand dollars, why can't we work really hard to keep the reunion costs down and throw the excess toward the heating overhaul?" Harry suggested.

"Makes perfect sense, but Folly would have to agree to it. After all, she earmarked the money for the reunion, and she won't want to cut corners on a social do." Susan quickly perused the different systems that Tazio included in the folder. "Willikers, I need a course in engineering."

"I know." Harry poured more tea from the large pitcher. "Jesus had it easy. All He had to do was walk around Judea in His sandals. No buildings to maintain. No cars."

"Harry." Susan shook her head.

"Of course, you're deeply shocked."

"No. I think Christ had it easier than we

do because He was born before the credit card."

Harry choked on the tea she'd just swallowed. Tears filled her eyes. Susan leapt up to slap her on the back.

Once recovered, Harry wiped her eyes and murmured, because she still had difficulty speaking, "Kill me. You'll kill me."

They both laughed.

Susan then said, "As you know, Planned Parenthood is mostly Democrats, so Ned has close ties. I wouldn't be surprised if at some point Folly will want something for them."

Ned, Susan's husband, was serving his first term as a representative to the state legislature.

"I hope not. Religion and politics don't mix."

"James Madison showed us the way on that, but, Harry, you know as well as I do that religion is currently being used to divert us from the true political issues. Not that Planned Parenthood is religious, but it is a target of right-wing Christians."

"America's falling apart." Harry leaned back in her chair, swallowing again to ease the ache in her throat. "It's such an old trick and it amazes me that people fall for it. Get them lathered over something superficial but emotional so they won't notice that our interstates need repair, we're so in debt it's horrifying, and we're in a mess in the Middle East that will now last generations. And you know what? I intend to grow my grapes and sunflowers. I want to harvest the timber we share. I'm done worrying about the world. It will get on just fine without me."

"It's a vain hope to be left to private concerns." Susan, like Harry, wearied of the manufactured crises as well as the genuine articles. "Back to my point: be good to Folly."

"I'm always good to Folly."

"You don't like her."

"I'm nice to her."

"Harry."

Harry's voice rose. "I *am* nice to her."

"I've known you since cradle days. You can't stand the woman."

"She doesn't know that." Harry sighed.

"Of course she doesn't. She doesn't know how we do things in these parts. So keep being nice to her."

"I will. Speaking of not liking someone, Carla Paulson was cussing out Tazio. She shut up when I walked into the office. There's a piece of work."

"Is, isn't she?" Susan hid her smile behind her hand, even though it was just the two of them.

"A three-dollar bill."

"She has enough of them. You know, Harry, this is a case of what your mother would say: 'Praise a fool that you might make her useful.' "

Harry sighed. "Mother was so much better at those things than I am."

"It's not too late to learn." Susan sliced more Brie, handing one cracker to Harry. "You're not rude. It's just that sometimes you say what you think too directly."

"I know."

"You can say the exact same thing with more flourish."

"I know. Fair tells me the same thing."

"So at the next board meeting, shine on Folly."

Another car pulled up in the driveway, a county squad car, and Tucker barreled outside to say hello to their next-door neighbor, two miles away as the crow flies.

Officer Cynthia Cooper stepped in; she'd

been driving home after work. "Heard there was a tea party."

"We're plotting revolution." Susan got up before Harry could and fetched a glass, plate, and utensils.

"What's up?" Harry liked Coop.

"Two wrecks at Barracks Road Shopping Center. One robbery at the bank up on Rio Road, and you'll love this." She leaned toward them. "He pulled out a gun and dropped his driver's license on the floor. How dumb is that?"

"Not as dumb as the guy who rammed the stand-alone kiosks at Wachovia." Harry laughed, naming a large interstate banking chain.

"He did get money, but it sure was easy to trace the car." Coop laughed, too.

The three enjoyed one another's company.

Susan told Coop about Folly's generosity. Coop asked if she could pile up a truckload of manure for her garden.

Her cell phone played "Leader of the Pack."

"Thought you were off duty," Harry said.

"Am." Coop flipped the small phone open. Hearing the sheriff's voice, she simply said, “Chief.” Then she was ominously silent, getting up from the table with the phone still to her ear.

Harry and Susan stood up, too, as Coop hurried for the door.

They ran out with her as she flipped the phone closed.

“Can we help?” Harry asked.

“No. Will Wylde has been shot.”

Dr. Will Wylde, OB/GYN, was on the board for Planned Parenthood.

The two best friends watched Coop peel out of the drive. Thoughtfully, she didn’t hit the siren until she reached the paved road.

“Antiabortion nut,” Susan uttered through taut lips.

“So it would seem,” Harry replied.

Susan turned to Harry. “Why would anyone else want to shoot Will Wylde?”

“I don’t know, Susan, I really don’t know, but I have learned that the obvious answer isn’t always the correct answer.”

3

The Madison office complex, a pair of inoffensive brick two-story buildings with basement offices as well, was tucked in between Route 29, Route 250, and the back way into Farmington Country Club.

Dr. Wylde's office was there, making it convenient for his patients, most of whom lived in the western part of the large county. He lived in a lovely home on the country-club grounds, golf being his passion, as well as that of his wife, Benita. Convenient for him, too.

Coop stood on the roof of the building catty-cornered to Wylde's office. Sheriff Rick Shaw stood with her, the heat seeping up through the thick soles of their shoes.

"No shells?" Coop asked.

"No. Too smart for that." Rick paused.

"Kind of like a rapist using a condom." He paused again and, knowing Coop as he did, knew she wouldn't take that the wrong way.

She knelt down so her eye would be level with the top of the roof. "The trajectory of the wound will no doubt confirm your thoughts. And it makes sense, because if he shot from an office window, he'd need to move through the office. Can't do that and go undetected. All these offices are full up."

"He'd have to walk down the hall with a rifle or get inside the office and assemble it quickly, if the weapon was one that can be broken down. I expect it was." Rick watched the emergency squad finally place the body in the ambulance; they'd had to wait for Rick's officers to thoroughly inspect everything. "So he came up here—easy enough, since few people use the stairs—waited, fired, walked down, and drove away."

"Car parked on the side of the building near the stair door?"

"Yep. Macadam. No print."

"And no one saw anyone drive away?"

"Coop, that's just it. Cars pull in and out of here all the time. No one saw any vehicle leave in a hurry, and no one knew Wylde was shot until probably five minutes after he was hit, which makes me think the perp may have used a silencer. No one came out of either building. So whoever drove out, it just looked like business as usual, or so it seems. The only people identified so far who drove off the lot close to this time are Dr. Harvey Tillach and Kylie Kraft, one of the girls in the office. She came right back with four frosties for everyone."

"They're a mess in Will's office, but that's understandable."

"What if the killer had help on the inside?" Rick kept trying to put the pieces together.

"Ah." Coop once again appreciated her boss's mind.

"The antiabortion extremists have become more sophisticated and patient. I say extremist because I don't think most antiabortionists are willing to kill doctors to prove their point; it does the reverse."

"Can't say you revere life, then take it away." Coop nodded. "Well, boss, this one's going to bring the press down like vultures, as well as every local and state politician on both sides of the issue. And in the process, people will forget that Will was a talented OB/GYN, who also performed terminations."

He turned toward the door leading out

onto the roof. "I know." He opened the door for Coop and they both descended the stairwell, their steps reverberating.

Before going outside, Coop stopped a moment and knelt down. Rick knelt beside her and reached in his deep breast pocket for a small plastic Ziploc.

"Could be nothing."

"One smoked Virginia Slims cigarette is still worth bagging." He used the tweezers she handed him, plucked it up, and dropped it in the bag, sealing it.

"Not my brand."

"Mine, either." He paused. "I didn't know you had a brand. I thought you just bummed fags off me."

"That's a low blow." She stood up, her left knee creaking even though she was in her thirties. "I'll bet five bucks this didn't belong to Wylde's killer."

"Why?"

"Men don't smoke Virginia Slims, number one. Number two, I know of no case where a woman has killed a doctor who performs abortions. It's always men."

"This could be a first." Rick pushed open the door into the bright light.

"Take the bet?"

"Sure, what's five bucks?" They crossed the parking lot and entered the building. Then turned right to Will's office.

Margaret Westlake, the office manager, who was in her early forties, stood to greet them. Her eyes, puffy and bloodshot, testified to her tears.

Sophie Denham, the senior nurse, in her early fifties, had a paper cup in her hand as she stood over Kylie Kraft, a young nurse verging on hysterics.

Sophie glanced at the sheriff and deputy. "Thank God you're here."

"I want to go home," Kylie wailed.

"Gave her a Valium," Sophie, hands shaking slightly, informed them.

Having seen their fair share of hysterics, Rick replied, "Terrible shock. I know Officer Sharpton took your statements. Deputy Cooper and I will carefully go over them. On the outside chance that something occurred to you since he was here, I thought I'd come in."

The three looked mutely at one another, but both Margaret and Sophie were sophisticated enough to recognize that Rick came by to scope them as well as the territory.

Anyone with contact to Will Wylde was potentially a suspect.

"Did Dr. Wylde gamble?" Cooper asked.

Margaret, surprised, answered, "No. Why?"

"If a person falls behind on the debts, this can be the payback," Cooper quietly informed them.

Sophie blinked. "As far as I know he didn't gamble."

Reaching for Cooper's slender hand, Kylie moaned, "Can't I go home?"

"Not just yet," Cooper said as Kylie dropped her hand, disappointed and beginning to get a little fuzzy from the sedative.

"Women?" Rick questioned.

"No." Margaret shook her head.

"There was that rumor about the first Mrs. Tillach," Sophie added, then instantly felt disloyal to the deceased doctor.

"There was a creature given to fantasy." Margaret's lip curled upward slightly. "Typical Charlottesville rumor. Everyone smacks their lips but no one actually ferrets out the facts. The entire episode was repellent." She calmed herself, then added, "Sheriff, given that this appears planned—I mean, no one broke in here waving a gun and screaming—I have to think it's political."

"Could be political if someone did come in screaming. Dr. Wylde was on the hot seat." Cooper said this in a kind fashion.

"That he was." Sophie's eyes teared up.

"Ever mention names of people he thought were violent?" Rick asked.

Margaret, folding her arms across her chest, said, "If only it were that simple, Sheriff. The short answer is no. The anti-abortionists who incline toward destructiveness are never your neighbors, because you can hold them accountable. What these antiorganizations do is bus people in for demonstrations, throw packets of blood at the doctors—"

Kylie interrupted with a wail, "And us."

Margaret ignored her, feeling that one dealt with pain and suffered by holding it together and never, ever, by blubbering or seeking pity. "I'm not saying local people didn't join in barricading our office, but you can pretty well bet the killer is not a local. At least that's one woman's opinion."

"And one I certainly respect." Rick nodded to her. "Ladies, this is a vicious blow. I am so sorry for you all, for Will's family. I promise you we will get to the bottom of this." He paused. "In the future, either Deputy Cooper or myself may call upon you again. I apologize in advance for the inconvenience."

"We'll be glad to help in any way," Margaret replied.

"Indeed." Sophie wiped her eyes again.

Rick opened the door into the corridor. Cooper followed, but as they reached the front door, she turned and hurried back to Will's office. She rapped on the door.

Margaret unlocked it. "Come in."

"Channel Twenty-nine just pulled up with the mobile unit. You might want to lock this door again and go somewhere in the office where they can't see you."

Kylie started to rock back and forth and cry again.

Margaret turned to Sophie. "Let's get her back in the supply room and cut the lights."

"I expect they'll be out of here in an hour. They'll want to talk to people in other offices and then they'll probably go shoot footage of his house or the hospital. But if you want to avoid their questions, sit tight for at least an hour."

"Thank you, Deputy Cooper." Margaret closed the door and cut the lights.

Rick turned as Cooper joined him on the raised outside steps. “And?”

“Going to lock up and hide in the supply room.”

He nodded. “That will give them a little time. Until tomorrow, at least.” He watched the small crew quickly set up. “Come on, we’ve got to get to Benita before someone else does and certainly before this breaks. You know once they’ve got the video shot, they’ll interrupt any show going.”

“Damn.”

“That’s a nicer word than ‘shit.’ I’ve got to watch my language.” He took a deep breath, lifted his chin, and strode toward the television crew. He made the time-out sign before the camera rolled. “Dinny, I’ll give you a statement, I’ll keep you in the pipeline, but I have got to get to Benita Wylde before she hears of this. All right?”

Dinny Suga, who was pretty and petite, knew enough about the community to know she had to respect this or she’d never get another good story out of Shaw again. Even though she’d worked for Channel 29 for only a year, she was becoming part of the community, one she was learning to love—if for nothing else than the fact that no one would dream of calling her Asian-American. She was just Dinny Suga.

"I understand." She looked to her camerawoman, nodded, and the light blinked over the top of the minicam.

Sheriff Shaw gave a terse statement that the murder had occurred at around two-thirty P.M. No suspect had been apprehended, and, yes, Dr. Wylde had been targeted in the past for harassment.

"Thank you, Sheriff."

"Dinny, give me an hour. If she's not home, she's on the golf course, most likely."

"Okay."

Within twenty minutes, Rick and Coop were zipping toward the back nine in a golf cart. When members started to wave at them as they roared through their games, they quickly discerned this was the sheriff and his number-one deputy; something had to be really wrong.

Benita, back on 13, had just hit a gorgeous approach shot, which her three bosom buddies admired. When she heard the cart, saw who was in it, she dropped her club. There'd been enough threats on Will's life these last ten years. She just knew. So did the others.

She said nothing as Rick stopped and climbed out.

"Benita, I am so sorry to tell you this."

"He's gone, isn't he?"

Rick nodded. "Yes, yes he is."

Coop, now also out, walked up alongside Rick.

"How?" Benita remained calm, although she was as white as paste.

"Sniper. One shot clean through the heart. At least he didn't suffer."

She fought her tears. The rest of the foursome—Folly Steinhauser, Alicia Palmer, and BoomBoom Craycroft—quietly came up to Benita's side.

Alicia put her arm around Benita's waist and said, "Let me drive you home, honey."

"Yes." Benita's voice faded.

"The reporters." Folly's mind worked quickly. "Girls, we need to be there to get rid of them."

"We can take turns." BoomBoom, who was tall, commanding, and beautiful, knew how to handle most situations, as did Alicia, a former movie star in the seventies and eighties.

"You're right," Folly agreed.

"Before anyone leaves, Benita, if you can

stand it, it would be very helpful if you could answer a few questions."

"Yes." A tear splashed on her lemon-colored golf shirt.

"Have there been threats recently?"

"No. In fact, we were just talking about that last night. We thought that maybe those nutcases finally realized violence is counterproductive."

"Any problems apart from the abortion extremists? A disgruntled employee or unbalanced patient, debts?"

"No."

"Any old enemies from the past that you can recall?"

She thought as she knelt down to pick up her club. "Harvey Tillach. Harvey hated him, but they avoided each other."

No reason to inquire about why Harvey hated Will Wylde, since everyone knew that Harvey, also a doctor, had accused Will of seducing his then wife. An accusation that Will hotly denied, but the damage had been done, because rumors take on a life of their own.

Although, in truth, sexual peccadilloes rarely elicited the tongue-clicking found in the Puritan states. The people upset were the people directly involved. Most Southerners assume nature is taking its course and best to stay out of it.

Alicia, firmly but with respect, said, "Sheriff, let me take her home. This is a staggering blow."

He nodded, then added, "Benita, I'll need to question you again. I truly am sorry."

"I know, Rick, I know you are. Everybody loved Will."

BoomBoom said to Rick and Coop, "Let us know if there's anything we can do, including strangle the killer."

Coop had grown fond of BoomBoom. "You'll have to get a ticket and stand in line for that. But if we need you, I'll call. Right now, do anything you can for Benita. It's going to be tough. A media circus."

Folly shook her head silently, fearing the onslaught, as Alicia gently led Benita to one of the golf carts.

As the two carts drove off, Rick turned to Coop. "She's a good woman. She deserves better."

The sheriff and his deputy knew the wife is often a prime suspect in the husband's murder. But these two didn't think Benita Wylde had killed her husband. For one thing, she was on the golf course at the time of the murder. For another thing, it was a happy marriage. Whoever did kill the doctor knew the layout of the office buildings, his schedule, and could drive away without calling attention to himself.

They climbed back into the squat golf cart. Rick drove, the noisy little engine competing with the usual sounds of a late afternoon on a prestigious golf course.

Coop flipped open her notebook. "Want to give me names to question?"

"In a minute. The first thing we've got to do is pull in as many people as we can on this case. Right now it's a local murder. If the FBI agent for our territory decides this is a civil-rights violation, then we have to deal with the agency."

Coop grimaced, since the feds often treated local law-enforcement people like water bugs. "Been there. Done that. Remember the fuss five years ago when the pro-life people barricaded Will's clinic? Boom! Civil-rights violations, because he couldn't operate his business. Let's hope this is just murder."

"Yep, sure as shooting." He realized what he'd said but grinned despite himself. "Sorry."

4

Death and destruction didn't seem to shake up country people quite as much as it did their city cousins. The cycle of the seasons, the thrilling rebirth of spring and the rich harvests of fall, allowed people to know that death and life weave together each day. Not that anyone celebrated the untimely death of Dr. Will Wylde, but the people it sent off into the deep end were only those hovering on the precipice anyway. His family and friends, overwhelmed by deep grief, remained calm. It had always been in the back of their minds that this could happen, but nothing really prepares one for the dolorous reality.

Carla Paulson was all but suffering grand mal seizures because of the shooting. Weeping, she called Tazio Chappars, informing her that she wouldn't be at the construction site today, Friday, but she advised—which meant ordered—Tazio to go.

The house, which was situated on a three-hundred-foot-high knoll, commanded 270-degree views. The 90-degree area behind the house was filled with large rock outcroppings, which blocked the view in that direction. Carla, who was determined to improve nature, had worked on drawings with a San Francisco landscape company to stick wondrous plants in crevices. Eventually, the outcroppings would underline Carla's vibrant creativity. That was the plan. Surely, a spread in *Garden Design* would follow.

Interior work goes more slowly than the initial framing up and roofing, and this house proved no exception.

Tazio and Mike McElvoy stood in the cavernous living room while the marble, green-veined and hideously expensive, was being placed around the fireplace. The Italian workmen had a gift for the task.

With arms folded across his chest, Mike watched Butch Olivera supervise. One tiny crack meant another slab would be cut, which would mean more delay, more expense. Carla would spend money, but she possessed little tolerance for other people's mistakes. Then, too, she harbored the not entirely unfounded suspicion that she might be charged more than the "old families"—or "tired blood," as she dubbed those Virginians only too ready to recite their pedigree. Her pedigree was her bank balance; it was also a crowbar to open doors and windows.

"Lattimores used the same marble when they built Raven's Roost." Mike enjoyed passing on these tidbits. "She's already adding a wing. Penny can't stop building."

Tazio had been a guest of the Lattimores from time to time, so she already knew this. She simply smiled. Why take away Mike's little moment? "Penny and Marvin are a bit more understated than the Paulsons."

"Christ." Mike shook his head. "Waste. That's what I see but, hey, gives me a job."

"Me too." Tazio smiled, hoping this meeting wouldn't be lengthy, for Mike liked to hear himself talk.

The more he talked, the smarter he thought he was—not that he was stupid, but he needed attention.

"Let's go to the kitchen."

They walked through the living room,

which was being painted then sponged to create a dappled effect. They passed from there through the "transition room," as Carla called it. It was really a discreet bar. Then they moved into a truly magnificent country kitchen.

The appliances weren't in yet, of course, but the cabinetry was up. Carla's ideas for the kitchen proved she could get it right if she just thought things through. She did spend money here, but it wasn't quite so gaudy. The cabinets, glass fronted, had six panes of beveled glass. The wood, a lovely warm simple pine, had been lightly stained. The floors, beautiful blue slate with radiant heat underneath, set off the whole room, which was full of light.

"Every time Carla drops one piece of glass, poof." Mike spread his fingers wide to indicate the flying bits.

"Yes, but it does look fabulous."

"Does. Didn't use Buckingham slate, did she?"

"No. For some odd reason, she thinks anything local can't be that good. She wants wormwood for the library. Good old cherry, walnut, or mahogany won't do. Well, mahogany isn't local, but you know what I mean."

"Do." He stopped in front of the space where the six-burner stainless-steel Vulcan stove with grill would be placed. "Before I get into this, what do you think about Wylde's murder?"

"Terrible."

"Think the antiabortionists did it?"

"Well, I don't know, but it certainly seems most likely. What do you think?" she asked, knowing what he really wanted to do was expound.

"Loony. Smart loony though. Cased the buildings. I mean, you have to do something like that exactly right or you're toast yourself. You know, the way things are today, I'd never go into women's medicine if I were in medical school."

"You mean OB/GYN?"

He nodded. "All it takes is one mistake and everyone's down your throat. Can you imagine the cost of insurance?"

"You're right, but an OB/GYN usually has happy customers. There aren't that many problems in pregnancy. I'd hate to be in oncology."

"Got a point there." He paused, put one

hand on his hip. "What do you think of abortion?"

"That it's a woman's decision."

"You don't think it's taking a life?"

"No." She held up her hand. "Mike, I can't imagine anyone dancing in the street saying, 'Hooray, I just terminated a pregnancy,' but isn't it better than just outright killing girl babies like they do in India and China?"

"That is pretty terrible."

"I read in the *Manchester Guardian* from March 2007—I saved the issue because it was so upsetting—that the rough guess is that in the last ten years, God knows how many million girls have been destroyed either in the womb or at birth."

His eyes popped. "God."

"In some places in China the ratio of males to females is one hundred twenty-eight to one hundred. That spells disaster. It also points to mass violence, because most crimes are committed by males between the ages of fifteen and twenty-nine. Didn't the governments of those countries think of that? And how will they find enough jobs for all those men? It's a sure bet they won't want to work in day care. They're planting the seeds for their own overthrow, especially China."

"You've made quite a study of it."

"Oh, well, I was forced into it by Folly Steinhauser. When I designed her house last year, she peppered me with Planned Parenthood information plus everything else she could find." Tazio shrugged. "At first I resented it, I'll be honest, but then I actually became interested. Global warming is caused as much by overpopulation as by cars. I mean, who drives the cars? Who uses electricity, furnaces? If you have six billion people, you have more emissions. If you have 7.2 or 9 billion by the end of this century, what do you think will happen? And what about the water table?" She threw up her hands.

"Never really thought of it that way." Mike reached into his back pants pocket for his small notebook. "Funny, all those people breeding so easily, and Noddy and I never could. We're still in the game," he smiled, "but you know we don't have but so much longer." He flipped open his notebook. "All right . . ."

A car drove up outside, and Carla emerged from her burnt-orange Range

Rover. "Hello," she called as she walked through the front door.

"In the kitchen," Tazio called back, then under her breath said to Mike, "She said she was too upset to come."

Wearing lime-green driving loafers with tiny rubber pebbles on the soles, Carla silently walked into the kitchen. Her eyes were swollen. "There you are." She turned to Mike. "What do you think?"

"Coming along. We have a problem here. You need a larger outtake for the stove you're putting in."

"Why?" Carla walked into the alcove where the stove would be located, looking up at the four-inch opening.

"Six inches."

"Why?"

"That's the code for this type of stove. You could change the stove, of course." He knew perfectly well she wouldn't.

"Why didn't you know this?" Carla turned on Tazio.

"I thought I did."

"She did." Mike came to her defense. "This has been under discussion for the last two months."

"Is it code yet?"

"Yes and no." He hesitated. "Let me put it this way: it will be in writing by the time your stove gets here, and then the kitchen will be finished and you'll have to tear things up, make a mess, wash all this glass. Just do it now."

Face reddening, Carla took it out on Tazio. "I expect this done in the next week, and if you can't get Arnie back"—she named the fellow responsible for ductwork—"I expect you to do it yourself!"

"Now, Carla, it's not her fault." Mike winked at Tazio, which Carla saw.

"I don't give a damn! I want it done and I want it done now, and if there's anything else, Mike McElvoy, find it now, because I'm not backtracking."

He stiffened. "I'm doing my job."

"Sure. That's what everyone says, but I know you can do it better for some people than for others."

"That's not true."

She turned silently on her heel and walked out.

Mike called after her, "Carla, I resent that."

She stopped, wheeled to look at him. "You know, Mike McElvoy, you're not as smart as you think you are, and I'm on to you."

As Carla left, Tazio noticed Mike's hands shaking as he slapped shut his Moleskine notebook. "I hate that bitch."

"Join the club." She did wonder why he'd misinformed Carla, though. The building code didn't change that quickly. This house was under way. The county couldn't make the code retroactive. There was nothing wrong with her four-inch outtake duct.

He took a deep breath. "Can't let it get under my skin. You know how these people are. I thought Penny Lattimore was a pain in the ass. Hell, she's an angel compared to this one."

Tazio, no fan of Mike's, did appreciate his task. "Call her tonight. Spread a little oil on the waters."

"I can make her life more miserable than she can make mine."

"That you can, but how often do you want to attend special hearings or, worse, testify in court if she brings suit against the county? She's the type, you know."

Jamming his notebook back in his pocket, he grumbled, "Right." He paused. "You know, I'm against abortion. But I tell you, Carla Paulson makes a strong case for free abortion on demand. If only she'd been flushed out of the womb."

Shocked at Mike's harsh statement, Tazio wondered what was happening in his life to make him so crude.

5

Rain poured at long last. At times Rev. Herb Jones's cats, Elocution, Cazenovia, and Lucy Fur, could barely see out the window. Dutiful, the three felines attended every vestry-board meeting. Sometimes, Harry's cats and dog also attended, but not this morning, Saturday, September 20.

Harry, Susan, Folly, BoomBoom, and Herb eked out a quorum. Nolan Carter, the local oil supplier, was in Tulsa on business. Marvin Lattimore, Penny's husband, was also out of town on business. He bought used airplanes, from Piper Cubs to 747s, refurbished them, and sold them to rich individuals and to corporate clients. For the heck of it, five years back, he'd started a small charter airline, and business had boomed.

"We should table this until Marvin can study the figures," Folly insisted.

"We can't put this off indefinitely." Tazio didn't think Marvin knew all that much about heating systems, but Folly was dazzled by him. This fact was not lost on Penny Lattimore, although Ron, Folly's usually jealous husband, didn't seem to notice. Twenty years older than Folly, Ron Steinhauser—brash, controlling, opinionated—had begun to slump into a slower gear. At seventy-five, he'd pushed himself hard, drunk too much at times, and finally his body was rebelling.

"When does Marvin come back from Moscow?" Harry asked the obvious question of Herb.

"Next week. I'll be sure he gets the study, and I will also be sure he knows we are operating under some time constraint. The last thing we want is for the furnace to be torn up when a cold snap hits us."

Folly listened to Herb, then replied with a lilt of humor in her well-modulated voice, "Doesn't seem likely."

BoomBoom said, "One October—first week, I think—we had a freak snowstorm, and the weight of the snow with the leaves still on the trees brought down branches all over Virginia. You could hear the creaking and breaking." She paused a moment. "Actually, we don't have to wait until next week. We can e-mail this to Marvin."

"Good idea." Susan nodded.

Folly, not an obstructionist, had never lived in a structure built shortly after the Revolutionary War. She had little sense of how cold it could get even with a half-decent heating system. "Well, do be sure that he doesn't feel pressured. We want Marvin on board." She smiled at her little pun.

"We do." Harry smiled at Folly, trying to do as Susan asked.

"All right, then." Herb turned to BoomBoom. "You do it."

"Happily," BoomBoom agreed.

It was not lost on the group that Herb asked BoomBoom instead of Folly to communicate with Marvin. Obviously, he'd heard the gossip, too.

Shortly thereafter, the business part of the meeting frittered away and the group focused on what they really wanted to talk about: Dr. Will Wylde.

Herb glanced at his agenda, noted the request for smokeless tapers, and figured it could wait. He was amazed that he'd kept the lid on it this long.

A gust of wind splashed so much rain on the handblown windowpanes that it sent the cats jumping off the ledge. They joined the group.

"Usually, these political killings, well, someone wants to take credit. The newspaper or TV station receives an acknowledgment. Hasn't happened." Folly plucked an orange out of a large bowl.

"Maybe they're waiting, or maybe they want people to think this was the work of a single crazy." BoomBoom got up and left the room, calling over her shoulder, "Tea or coffee?"

"Both." Susan rose to help her. "Anyone for iced tea?"

Folly raised her hand.

Harry said, "I hope this doesn't kick off a wave of violence across the country—doctors being targeted, clinics blown up."

"I do, too." Herb leaned back in the old club chair, Lucy Fur now on his lap. "Benita . . ." He shook his head, tears welling up. "Remarkable."

"She is." Folly also teared up. There was no need to recount that Folly, BoomBoom, and Alicia were with Benita when Rick told her what had happened. Everyone knew.

Susan and BoomBoom reappeared with two trays of drinks.

"What does Ned say?" Folly asked Susan as she poured tea.

Without taking her eyes off the cup, Susan said, "It was funny in a way. They happened to be in session, and when the news crept into the chamber, thanks to a zealous page, the men who came in on the coattails of the far right, vociferously antiabortion, couldn't distance themselves fast enough. Ned said as much as he mourned Will Wylde; it was all he could do not to laugh out loud at these opportunistic buffoons."

"Ned's pretty conservative." Folly did not yet have the feel for Virginia politics. In her mind, Democrat equaled liberal.

"About financial issues, he certainly is. He's live and let live on everything else."

Herb smiled at Folly and said, "Ned's what you might call an old-time Southern Democrat. Well, let me amend that: he's a new-time Southern Democrat. He's not racist and he's not pushing women back in the kitchen, but he's part of the old-time religion."

"Which is . . ." Folly arched an eyebrow.

BoomBoom, smiling, handed a plate of cookies over to Folly, who passed it on. "When you go into the voting booth you ask one question, 'Is it good for Dixie?' "

Folly, thinking this was a joke, laughed. "Oh, BoomBoom, you don't mean it."

The others in the room realized it was best to shut up.

Tazio returned to the murder. "Yesterday I was at the Paulsons' house, meeting with our fave, Mike McElvoy, and I was surprised to learn he's antiabortion. But he seemed genuinely upset about Will."

"He's a perfect ass," Folly said venomously.

"That insults mules." Harry was surprised at Folly's emotion. "He's a dumb human."

"Ego," BoomBoom simply said.

"Give a little man a little power and he abuses it every time." Tazio had Mike's measure.

"Carla's on the floor about Will. She'd gotten to know him socially. He was her doctor, too. She's a mess." Folly shrugged. "But you know Carla, she's not one to let slip the opportunity to call attention to herself."

Herb laughed despite himself. "We can pray that Carla . . . um . . . Let me think about this."

That lightened the mood.

"Carla's like Teddy Roosevelt. She wants to be the bride at every wedding and the corpse at every funeral." Susan used the famous quote.

Herb looked at BoomBoom, then Folly. "Girls, thank you for being with Benita. Boom, give my thoughts to Alicia, too."

"I will. The kids fly in today, and that will be a big help."

"Will Junior is the spitting image of his father." Harry liked the whole Wylde family.

"Funeral date?" Folly wondered.

"Can't do anything until the coroner releases the body." Susan knew a bit about this procedure, since Ned was a lawyer. "In the case of any suspicious death it takes longer, but I expect the funeral will be next weekend, if all goes as it should."

"Oh, no, that's the fund-raising ball for Poplar Forest, in Bedford County, September twenty-seventh. Everyone has to be there." Folly's face registered disappointment.

Poplar Forest was Thomas Jefferson's

summer home, which was in the process of a painstaking restoration.

"Even if it is, the funeral will be in the morning and the fund-raiser's at night," Tazio logically reminded her.

"But people will be . . . you know," Folly countered.

"Let's not worry about it until we know. And if the funeral is in the morning, we can all remind people that Will would want us to have a good time and to raise as much money as we can that evening. After all, he was a strong supporter of the restoration and sponsored a table."

Susan frowned. "In a way, I still can't believe it."

Folly, head of the ball committee, added, "Benita won't be there, but she's encouraged the office staff to go and to fill out the table. An empty table at a fund-raiser looks forlorn, and as you said, Will would want the project supported."

"One good thing that's come out of this dreadful event is that every priest, pastor, and preacher is meeting tonight at the Greek Orthodox Church out on Route 250. Even though we don't agree about abortion, we all agree that a killing such as this is the work of man, not the will of God," Herb interjected.

"Gods may come and go, but greed and the lust for power remain." Harry listened to the rain.

"That's hardly a Christian statement." Susan knew Harry hadn't meant to be disrespectful.

"Well, I meant that the Egyptians worshipped a slew of gods, as did the Greeks, Romans, and Norsemen throughout history. Whenever they'd want to justify something, they'd declare it was to serve Ra or Thor. Whoever shot Will is pretty much part of the common herd. You twist religion to serve your own ends."

"Harry, that's so cynical." Folly neatly piled up her orange rind.

"Realistic." Susan shrugged.

"Doesn't mean we can't strive to rise above it." Herb reached for a large chocolate chip cookie. "I have never wanted riches or power, but I certainly weaken when it comes to cookies."

The people laughed, but Lucy Fur patted at Herb's hand. *"Poppy, what about your diet?"*

Sheepishly, Herb broke a bit off the cookie

to give to Lucy but regretted it, since Elocution and Cazenovia zipped right over; they liked chewy dough.

"All right," Herb sighed, sharing his cookie.

After the meeting Susan drove Harry back to the farm.

Harry found the rhythm of the windshield wipers hypnotic. "Funny crack about Carla wanting to be the bride at every wedding, the corpse at every funeral."

6

"This is the second time in two days that you've questioned me," Harvey Tillach, beefy-faced but not unattractive, grumbled.

"I appreciate your continued cooperation, especially over the weekend," Rick simply replied.

"Didn't know you worked Saturdays."

"Sometimes." The genial sheriff nodded, then leaned forward slightly. "The acoustics are incredible. Can't hear the guns. Can't hear the downpour outside, either."

"Still coming down in buckets?" Harvey's light eyebrows raised.

"A day for accidents." Rick sighed, hoping none of them would be fatal.

As Harvey snorted agreement, the manager of this exclusive gun club ducked his head in the office. "You two need anything—a drink, hot or cold?"

"I'm fine, thanks, Nicky." Harvey smiled.

"Me, too."

"All right, then. Holler if you need me." He shut the door.

Central Virginia Gun Club was snugged right up to the base of the Blue Ridge Mountains. Boasting clays, skeet, a fabulous indoor range, and organized pheasant hunts, as well, the waiting list was years long. The owner pushed women's names up the list, since if the Second Amendment was to be saved it would only be with the help of women. A few of the men moaned, but most of them realized how imperiled their constitutional rights had become.

Two former Olympians were on the staff, one wildlife conservationist, and a variety of groundsmen and gamekeepers. Classes were quite popular; the place hummed.

"You've been a member of CVG a long time?" Rick asked.

"Twenty-three years. Last year we all traveled out to Reno for a clay competition and, you know, the air is different. Had to swing that gun up a little faster," he recalled. "Do you mind getting to the point?"

"Sure. You ever shoot handguns?"

"Rarely. I'm a clays guy. Don't think I'll be out today, but I can still work on my hand–eye down at the range."

"How long have you competed?"

"Since med school. I was at New York University. Not much outdoor sports. I stumbled on an indoor firing range, so you can say I started out with a handgun. Got completely hooked. Also started playing squash then. It's easier playing squash in Manhattan than tennis. Better workout, too."

"That's what I hear. And you met Will Wylde when you moved here?"

"We both started at Martha Jefferson at the same time." He named one of the area's hospitals.

"Did he enjoy shooting?"

"No, although he did admire my Purdy." Purdy was an exquisite brand of shotgun. "I'll bequeath it to my daughter. Thirteen and she's club champion for clays. Men or women. No wasted motion." He meant her technique.

"It's something you can do together."

Harvey laughed. "Well, she beats the pants off her old man, but we have a lot of fun together. She'll even go duck hunting with me. I'm very, very blessed."

"You and your first wife had no children?"

"No." His voice shifted, became more clipped.

"Ever see her?"

"No. She moved to Savannah."

"Remarried?"

"One of the richest men in Georgia. That woman can smell a bank account a mile off."

"Remind me: you own shotguns but no rifle?"

"I own a few rifles. Jody and I are going to Idaho this winter, going to pack in the mountains and hunt elk. A first for both of us, so, yes, I own rifles."

"Can you repair your own equipment?"

This surprised Harvey. "I could. I used to have my own repair workshop, but as my practice increased I just didn't have the time."

"What'd you do with all your tools?"

"Sold them to Mike McElvoy. He's good, too."

"I didn't know Mike was an enthusiast, if that's the right term."

"He's not. He likes the money and the

quiet, I suppose. At least, that's what I liked, but I'm glad I sold my equipment. I wanted to spend more time with Babs and Jody."

Babs was his second wife.

"Could you get a silencer if you wanted one?"

A pause followed this question. "I believe I could."

"Illegal."

"So's dope, and you can buy that on the streets, at the barber's, in restaurants. Supply and demand."

"Don't I know it." Rick slouched back for a moment in the chair. "Will Wylde was killed by a rifle with a silencer."

"Makes sense. Don't expect me to utter the formulaic phrases concerning his death. I'm not that big a hypocrite."

"Yes." Rick had gotten a blast from Harvey during their first questioning session, the evening of the murder. "Remind me again of the circumstances of your rupture."

"I already told you." Irritation flashed across Harvey's face.

"Tell me again," Rick coolly commanded.

"Like I said"—Harvey's tone registered his continued irritation—"we started out at Martha Jefferson together. A whole group of us just beginning our careers were there, and we had a pretty lively social group. Of course, we worked like dogs, too, but when we weren't working we partied hard. Will and I were close then; so were our wives. It helped that we weren't in competition. He was OB/GYN and I was in oncology. Back then most of us hadn't started our families, so we had more time to stay up late."

"Anyone other than you interested in guns?"

"Not that I know of. Golf was the big sport. You don't need to be entirely sober to play golf, but you'd better damned well be sober if you have a firearm in your hands."

"Where do you think it all went wrong?"

"Will was attracted to Linda," he named his first wife, "and she returned the compliment. If you've ever seen photographs of Linda, you know she is a knockout. Always will be. Her vanity will ensure that. I was accustomed to men wanting her. I just wasn't accustomed to her wanting them back." He paused a moment and then gallantly referred to his current wife. "Mind you, Babs is no slouch." He folded his hands together. "You want to know the secret of happiness? Marry the right woman."

"I did." Rick smiled.

The two men relaxed for a moment.

"Lucky us." Harvey smiled back.

"How did you find out about them?"

"She told me."

Rick hadn't expected that. "She did?"

Harvey threw up his hands. "Oh, I'd caught her in some lame excuses about staying out late. She fessed up. I'll give her points for honesty."

"Did you confront Will?"

"Damned straight I did. He lied through his teeth. Affected shock, then hurt, then anger. Quite the performance."

"How long did your marriage last after that?"

"About two minutes."

"Given the size of the medical community in this county, the various fund-raisers for disease cures, you must have run into Will and Benita a lot."

"I did. I was polite. I am a Virginian, after all."

"A special breed," Rick sardonically added, since he, too, was one.

"No point in making everyone around you uncomfortable. Babs likes Benita. Well, who doesn't? Obviously, they weren't close."

"How'd you meet Babs?"

"Blind date, would you believe it? At the end of the date—she lived in D.C. then, and I'd drive up to go to the Kennedy Center with her—well, anyway, she looked at me and said, 'You're not the first man to be betrayed by his wife and best friend. If you stay bitter, they win.' I drove all the way back to Charlottesville furious. I mean bullshit mad. I got up the next morning and I was going to call her and tell her just what I thought about that statement. When I heard her voice on the line, I knew she was right. I asked her out. Any woman sensitive to me that way, telling me the truth, I wanted to know her."

"And Will?"

"He knew better than to cast one sidelong glance at her. I swear I would have killed him, and I know I'm under suspicion now."

"Harvey, did it ever occur to you that Linda lied to you?"

"Why?" His eyes grew larger, since it never had once crossed his mind.

"Some women like to hurt men, like power over us. Maybe she was one of them. She wanted to hurt you."

As this sunk in, Harvey breathed deeply, then said, "She richly succeeded, but I'm grateful. I found the right woman, and she gave me a daughter who is truly the joy of my life."

"You never could forgive Will, assuming Linda told you the truth?"

"No. Betrayal is betrayal. Maybe someone else could forgive, but I couldn't." He folded his hands together. "In time the wound healed. Scar faded. It's still there, but I don't much notice it."

"You had motive and the skill to kill him."

"Why do you say that?"

"One clean shot straight through the heart."

"An easy death." Harvey struggled with conflicting emotions. "So be it."

"Did you kill Will?"

"No. Wouldn't it have made sense for me to kill him a long time ago?"

"Revenge is a dish best served cold."

7

The rain continued, slackening at times only to pick up again. Harry, frustrated since she wanted to paint the tack room in the barn, decided to clean out the trunks in the center aisle. She no sooner opened the first one by the tack room than she closed it.

"It's too damp." She looked at Mrs. Murphy, Pewter, Tucker, all looking up at her. "Let's make a run for it."

"Use the umbrella." Pewter didn't like getting wet.

"The one in the tack room?" Tucker asked.

"Yes," Pewter said.

"Has holes in it," Mrs. Murphy answered.

"Then why doesn't she throw it out?" Frustrated, Pewter walked to the end of the barn, knowing she'd be drenched by the time she reached the porch door.

Tucker laughed. *"Pewter, you know Harry never throws out anything."*

"What can anyone do with a Swiss cheese umbrella?" the gray cat wondered.

"She'll convince herself that the silk can be cut up and used to patch things." Mrs. Murphy jumped back as a gust of wind sent rain inside the large open double doors.

"You might want to wait," Tucker advised Harry, who had jumped back also.

"Know what? Let's sit in the tack room until the worst of this passes."

Before the sentence was completed, all three animals rushed to the tack room.

Once inside the cozy little place—its odor of cleaned leather was pleasing to Harry—she knelt down to turn the dial on the small wall heater.

"Chill in the air." Pewter snuggled on a lambskin saddle pad.

"September can fool you." Harry dropped into the director's chair by the old desk.

The phone, an old wall unit, rang. Harry picked it up, smiling when she heard Miranda Hogendobber's voice. The two had worked together for years at the post office.

"Harry, what are you doing?"

"Waiting out the rain in the tack room."

The older woman's voice was warm. "Going to be a long wait. I called to see how you're doing. Haven't seen you at all this week."

"Busy as cat's hair." Harry smiled as Mrs. Murphy hopped onto her lap. "What about you?"

"Pretty much like you. Not enough hours in the day." She paused. "I liked it better when we saw each other Monday through Friday."

"Me, too."

"Isn't it awful about Will Wylde? I can't believe it."

"It's a shock, but I'm starting to think evil is the norm and good is unusual."

Miranda paused. "Oh, I hope not, but people have changed. They'll say and do things we would never have done way back in my day."

"True enough, but I expect even then there were murderers, cranks. You just didn't have twenty-four-hour media to inundate you. Actually, I think coverage encourages more crime. Just sets nutcases right off. They become antiheroes." Harry noticed a mouse pop out from behind the tack trunk up against the wall, the one containing her special coolers. "I haven't seen the news or read the paper today. Spent the morning at a vestry-board meeting. Anything new?"

"No. Mim's in a tiz." Miranda mentioned her old friend, Big Mim Sanburne, a very wealthy and imperious resident of Crozet.

Although only a size 4, Mim was called Big because her daughter—same name—was called Little.

Many whispered "the Queen of Crozet" behind Big Mim's back.

"About Will?"

"She can't stand things like that. I know there are times when she can pluck my last nerve, but she does have a strong sense of justice. She's been on the phone canvassing everyone since she found out."

"What does she think she'll find that Rick won't?"

"She believes people will tell her things they might not tell the sheriff, especially other women." Miranda summed up Big Mim's thoughts.

"She has a point there," Harry conceded.

"And the other thing is, she's furious at Little Mim, so furious she won't speak to her."

This past summer Little Mim had married

a male model, Blair Bainbridge. Her mother spent a small fortune on her daughter's exquisite wedding, a second marriage at that, and she expected obedience. But then, Mim expected obedience from everyone.

"Now what?" Harry, like everyone else in Crozet, was accustomed to family spats.

"Little Mim won't make a statement declaring a woman has a right to choose and this murder is horrible."

Harry was incredulous. "I can't believe that." She thought a minute. "Well, no one has come forward to say they shot Will because he terminated pregnancies. She may be prudent."

"Prudent! She told Big Mim she's the vice mayor of Crozet, elected as a member of the Republican Party, and her mother knows perfectly well the party plank about overturning *Roe v. Wade.* Now, mind you, I am very uncomfortable with this, and as you know, the Church of the Holy Light is dead set against abortion." Miranda was a member of the small charismatic church. "But I'm not eighteen. I'm far from the danger of an unwanted pregnancy. Well, anyway, you know what I think about all this. It's Little Mim who's the fly in the ointment. Mim says if her daughter doesn't make some kind of statement, she is all but countenancing such a dreadful deed."

"Mim's right. There's no reason that Little Mim can't say she feels deep sympathy for the Wylde family and she finds such an action repugnant. She doesn't have to go on about *Roe v. Wade.*"

"She's dug her pointy toes in. Of course, her father made a statement immediately."

"Saw that."

Jim Sanburne was the mayor of Crozet and a Democrat. It complicated family life as well as the running of the town.

"And Mim says that Little Mim and Blair can't sit at her table for the Poplar Forest fund-raisers. So Little Mim said she wouldn't go, and Big Mim about tore her hair out by the roots. I mean, I never heard such a thing, and the only reason I heard it is I was at Mim's to discuss her zinnias as well as this new kind of chestnut tree she is determined to plant, but that's neither here nor there. I tell you what, sweetie, it was scalding."

"Sorry I missed it."

"My ears are still ringing. Anyway, Big Mim said if her daughter and her son-in-law missed the fund-raiser—one dear to Mim's heart—that she would cut her off without a penny."

"Big Mim said that?"

"Did. Indeed she did, and I tell you what, we've been friends for all of our seventy-some years and I have never, ever heard Mimsy threaten her child like that. It's beyond comprehension. I mean, over this?"

But it wasn't beyond comprehension. Harry, Little Mim's contemporary, knew that Little Mim had had an abortion in her sophomore year at college. No one knew except Susan and Harry, not even Miranda.

"This is pretty upsetting."

"Yes it is, because for one thing, how can Little Mim sit at anyone else's table? Whoever invites her will be in her mother's bad books, and no one is that foolish."

"What a mess." Harry sighed. "It's a week until the ball. Maybe it will work out."

"I hope so, because it will cast a pall over the whole evening. As if what's just happened isn't bad enough."

"Can't you talk to Mim?"

"I can and I will. Will you talk to Little Mim?"

Harry gulped. She hated to get in the

middle of things. "Yes. I'm not very persuasive, but I'll try."

"It's so important. For everyone. This is a time when we all must stick together."

After hanging up the phone, Harry regretted her promise. A promise made must be a promise kept. The rain accentuated her unease.

"I can't just sit here. Come on. To the truck. Make a run for it, kids."

They dashed out, splattering as they ran. Harry opened the driver's door and lifted up Tucker as the two cats hopped in. She sat where wet paws had marked the seat, but so what.

Within twenty minutes she had pulled into the crowded parking lot of Keller & George on Millmont Avenue. Other people must have decided to use a rainy day to shop.

Harry had left off her father's old rectangular Bulova watch for repair. It was the only watch she wore.

As she breezed through the doors, she saw Marilyn Nash from Waynesboro, talking with Kylie Kraft. Both women did rescue work for their county's respective animal shelters.

"Harry." Marilyn waved.

"What made you come over the mountain in the rain?" Harry smiled.

"Present for Lauren."

Lauren was Marilyn's teenage daughter.

Kylie kept admiring the watch on her wrist, as Bill Leibenrod, the manager, folded his hands behind his back.

"I just love it," Kylie gushed.

Marilyn, who had been admiring the gold Rolex with the heavy gold link band, said, "Fits you."

"I have to have it."

Harry, knowing full well that watch cost at least nineteen thousand dollars, couldn't restrain her shock. "Kylie, do you know how much that costs?"

"I do. My boyfriend told me to buy whatever I wanted, and he gave me a blank check. Can you believe it?"

"Best to keep that boyfriend," Marilyn noted wryly, a slight Texas twang to her speech.

She wasn't raised in Richardson, Texas, for nothing. But there a Rolex was called a Texas Timex.

As Kylie squealed and hugged herself, red curls bobbing, Bill winked at Harry and

Marilyn, moved from behind the counter, and motioned for Kylie to follow. He headed for the cash register.

"Jesus H. Christ on a raft," Harry said under her breath. "I could build a big new hay shed for that."

"You could. Most people couldn't." Marilyn laughed, because she knew how practical and tight with money Harry could be.

Harry smiled. "Marilyn, not three days ago she was flattened with grief because Will had been shot, and here she is all giddy and silly over a watch."

"It is a very nice watch. Common enough but nice, and they do last."

"I'll never know," Harry flatly stated. "I came to pick up my dad's watch. Howard is back there somewhere." She nodded in the direction of the closed door where the "surgeons," as she thought of them, worked.

Both Marilyn and Harry knew Howard because he was a bird aficionado, raising many with the help of his wife. He was also a Vietnam vet and tough despite his mild exterior.

"If anyone can fix your dad's watch, it's Howard." Marilyn took a deep breath. "A terrible thing, what happened to Will Wylde."

She glanced at Kylie leaning over the counter as Bill rang up the sum. "No one has ever accused Kylie of being a deep well."

"I don't know why I'm surprised."

"Well, will I see you at Poplar Forest?"

"You will. Can't wait to see what you're wearing. I know what Urbie will wear." Harry grinned, because the men would be in black tie.

"Men have it so easy."

"They sure do. One good tux, one good dinner jacket, white for summer, one set of tails for white tie, and, if he's really social, a morning suit."

"And if he's not social, all he needs is a pair of jeans. Doesn't even need a shirt."

"Marilyn, we're being abused." Harry affected anger.

"I don't think the men would mind if you just wore jeans."

Harry laughed. "Well, my husband would pitch a fit, but how wonderful it must feel on a hot day to be out there without your shirt, sweating, and a soft breeze comes up. Must be heaven."

The two women caught up, compared notes, then Marilyn walked over to the repair section of the store with Harry. They both waved as Kylie skipped out.

On the way back to Crozet, Harry's mind returned to what she'd promised Miranda. Despite Pewter's begging for Harry to stop at the market and pick up treats, Harry kept her mind on her worry.

Harry's husband had been covering for another vet who was on vacation. When Fair came home, she recounted the conversation. In fact, she was so focused on talking about Little Mim, she forgot to tell him about Kylie buying a gold Rolex. He listened intently.

"Fair?"

"Yes, honey."

"Say something."

"I'm thinking. It's sticky." He sliced a succulent cooked chicken. He'd stopped on the way home and bought supper, along with treats for "the kids."

"I don't want Big Mim mad at me."

"She isn't going to be mad at you. You're trying to bring Little Mim around."

"What if I fail—and I probably will?"

"First of all, baby doll, don't underrate yourself. Tell yourself you're going to succeed. And if, for some reason, you don't,

Big Mim will know you tried your best. Here." He handed her a heaping plate.

While they listened to the conversation, the cats, on the counter, chewed their chicken bits with delight, as did Tucker, who loved chicken almost as much as beef.

Harry, with a small voice, said, "Will you go with me? I know you can't be part of the conversation but I'd feel better if you were close by."

"Of course I will. You talk to Little Mim by yourself, I'll chat with Blair. I was going to drop by, anyway, because Alicia gave me some cigars today and I thought he'd enjoy a good smoke."

"Horses okay?"

"Fine. She dropped by the office. Actually, that damned place was Grand Central today. Only had one call, a client of Dean's." Dean Vargas was the vet who'd taken the weekend off. "But every time I turned around, someone was walking through the door."

Harry exhaled. "I feel much better now. I really didn't want to go over there by myself." She filled her fork with sliced green beans. "These are good. Why do you think people were coming by the office on a Saturday?"

"Oh, hunt season's started, so some people had questions about this and that, some wanted to pick up vitamin supplements, and all of them wanted to talk. The murder has upset everyone. Will was a much-loved man, and he delivered half the people we know."

"Do you think there's a chance his murder has nothing at all to do with abortion?"

"It's possible." He nodded. "Back to your conversation with Miranda: she's right. If Little Mim won't come around, it will make the ball difficult socially. Who would dare cross Mim and host Little Mim after this?"

"Someone who wants to challenge the queen," Mrs. Murphy sagely noted.

8

Rose Hill, harking back to 1810, was nestled under a low ridge, this ridge being the last line before the Blue Ridge Mountains rose up in their ancient glory. Eons ago these were the highest mountains in the world.

The drive to the lovely peach-painted clapboard house, four miles from Harry's farm as the crow flies, took a little longer on the two-lane state road.

The pink, red, yellow, and white climbing roses on the stone fences enlivened the winding drive. The rain had ended at four this Sunday morning, September 21, leaving a sheen on everything. Fair drove slowly, and Harry could see tiny raindrops tucked into the folds of the rose blooms.

She'd called Little Mim last night after

supper, and Little Mim said she'd be happy to see her. Harry felt that her friend needed to give her side of the story to someone sympathetic, which Harry was, although she truly believed the vice mayor needed to make a forceful public statement.

Aunt Tally, silver-headed cane in hand, greeted them at the door. In her nineties, Big Mim's mother's sister had deeded her wonderful farm to Little Mim and Blair, with the proviso that she had life estate. The newlyweds lived in a stone two-story cottage one hundred yards from the main house, with a glorious formal garden between the structures. Aunt Tally's high spirits bubbled over even more ebulliently, because she loved having them near.

Old as she was, she evidenced not a jot of slowing down, apart from the cane, which she needed thanks to years of riding and a bit of hip damage. Nor did she pop pills. Long ago, in her forties, she discovered the medicinal benefits of doping her coffee. Each morning she poured in a dollop of Bombay Sapphire gin, another hit at noon, and one true cocktail when the sun passed over the yardarm. Worked a treat.

"Aren't you the best," Aunt Tally enthused

as Harry handed her a bottle of Bombay Sapphire adorned with a huge blue bow. "Come on in." As she led them toward the sunroom, she asked, "What did you think of Herb's sermon this morning?"

Fair answered, "Provocative."

"But dead on." She swung out her cane, then planted it on the hard maple floors.

Old maple trees still dotted the landscape of the original land grant.

"What he said about the sanctity of life was eloquent. That voice of his, you know—well, you believe everything that comes out of his mouth. Voice like Orson Welles. Maybe better." Aunt Tally nodded as she sat down in a large, comfortable "summer" chair, which meant intricately woven willow, graced with wonderfully comfortable pillows.

"Doodles." Harry greeted the year-old Gordon setter.

"You know, when my old buddy died I just went to pieces. Swore I'd never have another dog. Then every time I'd visit Alicia I noticed how lovely her Gordon setter was. When she gave me a puppy I was half thrilled. Now I'm all thrilled." She smiled. "I think I'll always have a Gordon setter." She paused. "Where are your three hooligans?"

"In the truck." Harry leaned back in the seductive chair. She could have fallen asleep.

"Well, for goodness sake, bring them in."

"Their paws will be wet," Fair said.

"That's what mops are for." Aunt Tally lifted up her cane like a marshal's baton.

"I'll get them, honey." Fair stood up, then left the room.

"Smartest thing you ever did, remarrying that divinely handsome man. He's a good man."

"He is."

Aunt Tally, shockingly white hair in a French twist, leaned forward. "Hell to pay. I'm so glad you've come over to talk to Little Mim. I know you'll try to get her to come 'round, and I quite agree." She shook her head. "Don't think she'll do it. She finally has an issue where she can square off against my niece, the tyrant, and it won't look like a mother–daughter blowup." She inhaled deeply. "Which, of course, it is."

"It's delicate."

Aunt Tally leaned even farther forward. "I know exactly why, which is why I'm glad

Fair went out to the truck. She told me *everything.* Riven with guilt. I understand—I do, you know."

"Yes, Aunt Tally, you would know better than anyone how painful this can be."

Tally had had an affair with Harry's grandfather, a rollicking handsome devil of a man. Tally's father put a stop to the affair and broke his daughter's heart. The pain subsided, the scar remained.

"You and Susan are the only other people who know. Blair knows nothing, and I told her to keep it that way."

"Right."

"We're here!" In raced Tucker, Mrs. Murphy, and Pewter, although the gray cat, in sight of the humans, slowed down to affect a nonchalant entrance.

"I have a fuzzy toy! Wanna see?" The glistening Gordon setter immediately picked up a well-worn green froggie, which Tucker grasped for tug-of-war.

"I wouldn't dirty my mouth with that thing," Pewter sniffed.

"Me, neither." Mrs. Murphy found a wet, chewed toy unappealing. *"Wouldn't mind a ham biscuit."*

"Think she has some?" Pewter showed some excitement.

"Aunt Tally always has ham biscuits and cheese straws," Mrs. Murphy replied.

"She can keep the cheese straws." Pewter hated those things almost as much as a slobbery toy.

Fair didn't sit down, but he said, "I'll go over to Blair." He patted his sport-coat pocket, where the cigars were. He couldn't wait to try the H. Upmann Corona Junior. He also had a Romeo y Julieta Short Churchill for Blair.

Just as he left, Little Mim came in and kissed Aunt Tally as well as Harry on the cheek.

The two younger women, quite different in temperament and not good friends as children, had grown closer over the years. Both were remarried months apart, so discussing their upcoming weddings had brought out the happy side of each woman.

"Precious, there's a tray in the fridge. Would you bring it in? And the lemonade and tea, too?"

"Of course."

Tally's maid—really a majordomo—had Sundays off.

When Little Mim returned, Aunt Tally gracefully excused herself under the pretext of catching up on her correspondence. Well, she did go to the den and sit at her desk, but not before she swept past the bar and poured a shot of gin in her iced tea. Sounds awful, but tasted divine to Aunt Tally. On Sundays she allowed herself some extra liquid cheer.

"I'm glad you came. Mother's being a beast, as only she can be, but this time it's the worst. The worst!" Little Mim launched right in.

"She does have a habit of living all our lives for us. Must get exhausting." Harry lifted her iced tea in tribute. "In her defense, she's often right. Look how she bore down on me for years to remarry Fair."

"She was right about that," Little Mim ruefully conceded. "But not about this."

"Are you worried that it will look as though you're breaking from the party?"

"Yes and no. We all know that right now the party looks like the Party of Hatefulness and Repression." She flopped back in the chair, but didn't spill a drop of her drink. "Going to take us a long, long time to overcome the legacy of Karl Rove and Company."

"The problem was, he was effective in getting people elected. The radical Christian right is about five million people out of almost three hundred million, but they are organized and well funded. Rove gave them a political focus. The ends justify the means."

"Do you believe that?" Little Mim raised her eyebrow, looking very much like her good-looking, perfectly coiffed mother.

"No, but millions of Republicans do. They aren't right wing, but they'd rather have a Republican in office no matter what they have to do to get him or her there."

"It's going to cost us power, for a long time. Two election terms, at least. I need to walk a fine line. I didn't come in on right-wing coattails, but I soft-pedaled. Well, you know that. You remonstrated with me."

"We did have a good fight about that, didn't we?"

"Ned Tucker's always good for a fuss, too, but since he's a Democrat that's to be expected. He's doing a good job down there in Richmond, and Aunt Tally counsels me not to buck him and not to run against him, so we have to divide up who will run for what and when. I fully intend to become the first woman governor of this state."

"You will." Harry relaxed a little.

"Give me your pitch, Harry." Little Mim smiled slightly.

"Oh, you know." Harry shrugged. "This terrible shooting of Will Wylde is a Pandora's box. It's let out fear, recrimination, wild rumor. We need to pray retribution doesn't follow, especially since there's no perp in sight."

"That scares me. Although, you know, Harvey Tillach was there around the time of the shooting."

"Well, Sheriff Shaw hasn't arrested him. We have to assume the killer is loose."

"Or killers. This could be the work of a group," Little Mim said.

"Because there's so much rumor and fear, you should speak to the press. You don't have to come out in favor of abortion. You only need to decry violence."

"Any statement I make, I'm going to be grilled. I'll be forced into a discussion about abortion." Little Mim reached for a thin lemon wedge to drop in her tea glass, which she refilled. "More?"

"No, I'm fine." Harry felt a heavy kitty run right across her foot.

Pewter had found a little ball that emitted a glow when rolled. Mrs. Murphy ran alongside her, but Pewter, good at kitty soccer, maintained possession with fancy dribbling.

"Harry, you understand."

"I do. I do, but it seems to me you'll be grilled anyway, sooner or later. It's one of those hot-button issues used to divert us from the real issues, the ones no one has the guts to solve."

Little Mim smiled appreciatively. "I'm not afraid of them. But I'd like to sidestep or downplay all the fluff stuff."

"Yep." Harry leaned back and stretched out her feet. "If people want to get farted up about abortion, homosexual marriage, whatever, let them settle it in church. Doesn't belong in politics." She crossed her feet at the ankles just as Pewter, reversing field, leapt over them, as did Mrs. Murphy. "Do you really want to go to war with your mother?"

"Oh," Little Mim waved her hand dismissively, "it's always something with Mother."

Finally, Harry fired her arrow. "Are you sure your reluctance isn't because of your history?"

Flushing suddenly, Little Mim almost barked, "Don't tell me the personal is political. I hear that from Herself all the time. And she knows nothing."

"All I know is this is a deeply personal issue and many women have to face it. It's been made political. You faced it." Harry lowered her voice.

A long pause followed where the only sounds were the cats batting the ball—since Mrs. Murphy had managed to snag it, then Pewter got it back—the dogs joyously tossing the fuzzy, and the pronounced breathing of Little Mim.

"I feel terrible. I was wrong. You heard Herb's sermon today about the sanctity of life, but the issue is when life begins. We all agree it's sacred, or at least Christians do." Her hand flew to her mouth. "Better never say that in public."

"Just think what your Buddhist constituency would say." Harry couldn't resist the dig, although the Sangsters, remarkable souls, were the few Buddhists in Crozet.

Little Mim folded her hands. "If I'm pushed by my constituency, I will say something. But I won't do it because of Mother. I just won't." Her jaw jutted outward.

"Back to feeling guilty: you were a sophomore in college. How could you have cared for a child? You weren't ready."

"Millions of other women do it."

"They do, but you," Harry chose her words carefully, "you are highly educated. You could make choices. Many of those other women really can't, the law notwithstanding. And what comes of it? Poverty. A cycle of poverty that's hard to break, and we all know the men tend to leave."

"Yes, for the most part they do."

"I don't think men have any right to vote on women's reproductive decisions. I feel the same way in reverse. What if vasectomy became a political issue? I don't believe you or I should vote on it. I don't have a right to make decisions about a man's body."

"But we did when we sent them to war through the draft." Little Mim hit the bull's-eye.

"Yes, but those days are gone." Harry considered this. "And being drafted wasn't about their reproductive equipment or their future as fathers."

"Fine line, I think."

"It's absurd, isn't it?"

"What?"

"The times in which we live. Do you think other Americans see the contradictions and the corruption?"

Little Mim took a long sip. "I do, but no one has emerged to focus the anger, to build for the future. Most of what's done is Band-Aids. It's going to take tremendous courage to reform root and branch."

"Think you can do it?"

"Yes."

"You know, you're a lot like your mother."

Little Mim sat bolt upright. "No woman ever wants to hear that!" Then she flopped back. "But I suppose there's some truth to it. I wish I were more extroverted, like Dad. I have to work at this shake-and-howdy stuff."

"You're doing great. Well, I've said what I had to say. Obviously, your mother will hear all about it."

"She sent you?"

"No. She wouldn't do that. Miranda asked me to talk to you, because she's worried that this will cause social rifts, and she's worried about the fund-raiser for Poplar Forest. She told me your mother said you couldn't sit at her table."

"Mother is being very petty. She also

threatened to cut me out of her will. Go ahead, Mother. Just go ahead." Little Mim waved her hand. "Aunt Tally named me as her heir, and that's half the family fortune. It would kill Mother for me to be completely independent."

"Little Mim, none of us is ever completely independent of our mother. Even Hitler couldn't shake his love and grief over his mother's early death."

"I can try," she uttered defiantly. "Come on, let's go to the cottage. Blair and I are building an addition. You haven't seen the plan." As they left the main house, Little Mim called out, "Aunt Tally, we're going to the cottage."

"All right, dear. Good to see you, Harry."

"Good to see you, Aunt Tally."

The formal gardens, with their boxwood clipped and crisp, overflowed with fall flowers. Aunt Tally kept up the old spring gardens, summer gardens, and fall gardens laid out with such thoughtfulness back in 1834. Her additions to the original plan were to have climbing roses on every fence line and over the old stone outbuildings and to nurture shiny dark-green ivy to embrace the gorgeous stone stables.

Those stables finally housed four horses. Like all horsewomen, the first thing Little Mim did when she moved into the cottage was to refurbish the stables, fallow since 1982. Blair attacked the cottage, realizing, thanks to Harry, that horse people are in the grip of an obsession not addressed by logic.

Doodles—the fuzzy in his mouth—Tucker, Mrs. Murphy, and Pewter scampered throughout the garden path, which was brick laid in a herringbone pattern. Pewter hated to leave the glowing ball behind, but outdoors provided the chance to snag a bug or maybe something bigger.

Then something bigger slithered right across her path: a four-foot blacksnake.

"Snake!" Pewter froze in her tracks.

Mrs. Murphy pounced on the tail, which made the large snake curl up.

"Don't you dare," Harry reprimanded her tiger cat. "Blacksnakes are friends."

"Oh, bother." Mrs. Murphy stepped backward.

The snake, flicking out his pink tongue, murmured, *"I catch more mice than you do."* With that, he disappeared under the periwinkle ground cover.

"What an insult!" Mrs. Murphy puffed out her tail, but Harry paid her no mind.

"We're home." Little Mim threw open the cottage door, painted royal blue, as were the shutters.

"In the back," Blair called out.

The wives came out on the patio to find two happy men, wreathed in smoke, drinks in hand.

"I want to show Harry and Fair what we're doing."

Blair stood up, kissed Harry on the cheek. "Let me get the plans." He disappeared inside, then reappeared, unrolling the plans on the wrought-iron-and-glass table.

"It's a two-pronged attack." Little Mim pointed to the south side of the cottage, where one bedroom now existed. "We can use the existing door so we don't have to tear out stone, and we'll create a master suite on that end, which will be warmer in winter than building on the north side." She moved her finger to the west, to the patio on which they now stood. "Here we'll build a great room and a new patio. No point in missing all those gorgeous sunsets over the Blue Ridge. I mean, I just love Aunt Tally's view, so this will be our smaller view."

"What will you do when Aunt Tally finally goes to her reward? This place will be wonderful," Harry wondered aloud.

"We'll move into Rose Hill, of course, and then we have to decide whether to make this part of a farm manager's package or to rent it. Always nice to produce a little income." Little Mim, though rich, respected profit and thought squandering resources sinful.

This view was shared by her mother except in practice. If Big Mim wanted something, she bought it. Her daughter would search relentlessly for the best bargain and, if she couldn't find it, would do without.

"This farm isn't what it used to be." Blair slipped his arm around Little Mim's small waist. "Given her age, Aunt Tally has done yeoman's labor, but we want fields of corn, better grades of hay, cattle, and you know, Harry, you've inspired us to try a small vineyard."

"I have?"

"You certainly have." Little Mim smiled. "I remember when I was a girl how this place hummed. Tractors running, fences being painted, stone fences being repaired. Fabulous Thoroughbreds playing in the pastures. Aunt Tally bred great horses. Remember?"

"I do." Harry nodded, as did Fair. "And Aunt Tally always gave us a Dr Pepper or Co-Cola."

"You taught me a lot when I was your neighbor." Blair smiled warmly at Harry. "Now that Mim and I are married, I don't want to be on the road anymore. I want to be right here with my beautiful bride. I think with a little luck and a lot of hard work, we can make a bit of money. Neither of us believes in hobby farming."

"Good for you." Fair slapped him on the back. "Besides, with Little Mim's whole political career in front of her, having you here will help. You see things differently than we do, because you weren't raised here."

"He's so smart." Little Mim was besotted with her gorgeous husband.

"When do you start?"

"Tomorrow morning. Mark Greenfield's company has the project. He doesn't waste money."

"No. That's a wise choice." Harry liked Greenfield ICF Services. "The trick is to get Tony Long as your county inspector, not Mike McElvoy."

Blair exhaled. "That's a roll of the dice. You should hear Carla Paulson, Folly Steinhauser, Penny Lattimore, or even Elise Brennan on the subject of Mike. Elise, whom I've never seen show temper, blew like Mt. Vesuvius on the subject." Blair shook his head. "Well, we'll just deal with it when we deal with it. My concern right now is that the stonework matches the original."

"That will be tough," Fair said.

It would, too, but stonework would be the least of their problems.

9

"Amazing how heavy your boots get when they're caked with mud." Harry lifted up a foot, displaying the red clay embedded in the sole.

Fair lifted up his right foot, his work boot covered with wet red clay, too. "Could be worse."

"Like what?"

"Oil sludge. Then we'd slip across the field." He pushed his baseball cap down over his eyes, for the sun was fierce. "Your black-seed sunflowers are about ready."

"Grey Stripe, too." Harry, hands on hips, surveyed the seven-foot giants, their massive golden heads pointed straight up to the sun. "You know," she grabbed his hand, "I love this. I wish I'd quit work at the post office years ago." She paused. "Course, I don't know if I'm going to make a dime, but I truly love it."

"Well, you know you won't make any money on the grapes. You have to let the fruit hang until it falls off this first year."

"I know. Seems so wasteful, but if Patricia Kluge tells me what to do with my Petit Manseng, I'd better do it. The foxes will be happy."

"Yes, they will. They'll start eating the grapes even before they fall."

"The one that makes me laugh is Simon." Harry mentioned the opossum who lived in the hayloft along with Matilda, the blacksnake, and Flatface, the owl. "He's got a sweet tooth."

Matilda—no sweet tooth there—was actually on her hunting range. The large circle that she made around the barn and the house took up spring and summer. She'd return to her place in the hayloft in another three weeks. Right now she was hanging from a limb in the huge walnut tree in front of the house. It pleased her to frighten the humans and the animals when they finally caught sight of her. Nor was she above dropping onto someone's shoulders, which always provoked a big scream. Then she'd shoot off.

Harry and Fair walked over to the pendulous, glistening grapes. Although the vines would produce better with each year, Harry was delighted with what her first year had brought.

Fair draped his arm around his wife's shoulders. "Abundance."

"Lifts the heart. I was worried that yesterday's hard rain would just pepper these guys right off the vine."

"Tougher than you thought."

They turned for the barn. The four mares and foals lazed in their pasture. The three hunt horses and Shortro, a gray three-year-old saddlebred, munched away, pointedly ignoring the youngsters born in March. Every now and then, a little head would reach over the fence to stare at one of the "big boys."

Tomahawk, the most senior of the hunters, looked back at the bright chestnut filly begging him to play with her along the fence line.

"Worm," he said, returning to the serious business of eating.

"Momma, do you know what he called

me?" The little girl romped back to her mother, a patient soul.

"Oh, he gets all grand and airy. Pay him no mind." She touched noses with her child.

Mrs. Murphy, Pewter, and Tucker, who were walking ahead of the humans, heard the exchange.

Pewter called out, *"He's a meanie."*

"Shut up, fatso." Tomahawk raised his head.

"When's the last time you got on the scale?" Pewter noticed a big belly.

"Pewter, leave him alone," Mrs. Murphy counseled. *"If you irritate him he'll start picking the locks on the gates. That's the only horse I've ever known who can actually open a kiwi lock."*

A kiwi lock, shaped like a comma, slipped into a round ring secured on the post. A smaller ring then flipped up on the comma to securely hold it in place and to prevent horses from opening the lock, something for which the species evidenced a marked talent. Tomahawk would work the kiwi with his lips. Granted, it took him at least an hour—his determination remarkable—but he would finally release the little ring, then pluck the kiwi out of the big ring and push the gate open with his nose. Off he'd go, tail straight out, to rush around the pastures. After doing this enough times to become both tired and bored, he'd walk into the barn, go to his stall, flop down on his side, and sleep, complete with musical snoring.

It infuriated the other horses that they couldn't pick the locks.

Just as Harry and Fair reached the barn, Coop drove up in an old beat-up pickup truck she'd bought so she could haul stuff. A deputy's slender salary prevented her from purchasing a new truck, much as she lusted after one.

"Hey," Harry greeted her.

"Didn't get you on the phone, so I thought I'd come over."

"Need a hand with anything?" Fair asked.

"No. I wanted to tell you we've heard from Will Wylde's killer." She paused, while the other two held their breath for a moment without realizing they were doing so. "No name. No anything except he—I assume it's a he—says he has the list of all Will's patients over the years and he is going to do to them what they did to the unborn."

"What?"

"Dropped off an envelope sealed with Scotch tape—obviously he's smart enough not to lick the envelope. Dropped it in Rick's mailbox at his house. Smart there, too. Too big a risk to leave it at the station, even in the middle of the night."

"Good God." Fair was aghast.

"He could be bluffing."

"Harry, he could, but I keep coming back to someone on the inside. It's not that hard for a nurse or office manager to steal files. Everything is on a disc. How hard is it to copy it and give it to our killer?"

"True." Fair was more computer literate than Harry, but she was pretty good at doing agricultural research on her computer.

"Thank heaven," Harry whispered, "I've never had an abortion."

"Me, either. But there are so many women who have and no one knows. Apart from the danger if he does make good on his threat, what about the mess in their personal lives?"

"Are you going to make this public?"

"Well, that's not my decision, but I don't see how Rick can keep it quiet. It's important to the case, and people must take precautions."

"This could destroy marriages, careers." Harry wiped the sweat pouring down her brow. "There are an awful lot of women in this county keeping a secret."

"Exactly." Coop leaned against the truck's grille. "We've got to catch this guy."

"If he starts killing women, you will, but let's pray he trips up before that." Fair felt sick about the threat.

"Why now?" Harry asked.

"What do you mean?" Coop respected Harry's mind.

"Why kill now? Will Wylde has been practicing medicine in our county for three decades. What's set off this person?"

"Could be he's found out his wife or girlfriend had an abortion and didn't tell him," Fair stated logically.

"Or it could be his mind is deteriorating in some fashion," Harry thought out loud.

"Like drugs?" Coop had seen plenty of what booze and drugs can do to the human brain.

"That, but sometimes the mind goes when it's diseased and the person doesn't know. He thinks his thoughts and actions are normal. That's the truly frightening thing about being crazy: so often the person doesn't know. And sometimes a head injury can change a person's personality," Fair informed them.

Harry turned to Coop. "You might want to check the experts on this. I guess psychiatrists would be a good place to start."

"I will. Either way, if this guy is a raving lunatic or a political fanatic, we've got major problems."

"Coop, come on in. It's sweltering out here." Harry touched Fair's hand.

As they walked into the house, Matilda, eyes glittering, swayed gently on her limb. Mrs. Murphy glanced up at her but said nothing.

They were grateful to come into the kitchen, the large overhead fan cooling the room. Harry refused to put in air-conditioning, because she thought going from cool air to the hot outside all the time made you sick. Fair knew in time he could wear her down. As it was, the fans in the house helped, but sometimes all they did was push around humid air.

"The statement?" Coop gratefully took a beer offered her by Fair as she queried Harry.

"We drove over this morning after church. Harry tried." He shrugged.

"It's the talk of the town: the murder and

the face-off between Big Mim and Little Mim." She swallowed straight from the bottle. "Perfect."

"A cold beer on a hot day, one of life's little pleasures." Fair sipped his, too.

After Cooper left, Harry called Little Mim and gave her the news so she could be calm when she heard it from the sheriff.

"Mother is probably being briefed by Rick as we speak," Little Mim replied, trying to push down the rising terror.

Rick had learned the hard way to keep Big Mim informed. Part of it was because she felt she ran the town along with the western part of the county; part of it was because she knew a great deal that a sheriff might not know and could be helpful. In this case, she was blissfully ignorant of her daughter's dilemma.

"She'll come out both guns blazing."

"She will." Little Mim reached down to touch Doodle's glossy head. Touching the dog reassured her, calmed her. "Harry, I can't thank you enough."

"Don't mention it, but, Little Mim, please, please be careful, and whatever you do, don't lose your temper with your mother."

Easier said than done.

10

Yesterday's rains had scrubbed the sky, and the cleanness of the air intoxicated Mrs. Murphy as she sat on a paddock fence post, gazing at the twilight. Pewter perched on another fence post, and Tucker sat on the ground.

Around the time of the autumnal equinox, the light began to change slightly, the winds from the west began to hum low over the mountains, and summer's thick haze melted as if on command. Even the humans noticed.

The nights grew cooler, the days shorter. Animals stepped lively, the vital business of securing food for the winter taking precedence for squirrels and other hoarders. The foxes, who usually found fresh supplies, created bigger caches just in case.

This Sunday evening, the fiery sunset splashed red gold across the western horizon. It was all the more dramatic as the Blue Ridge Mountains deepened from blue to cobalt in front of Apollo's show. Now streaks of pink and lavender enlivened the deepening velvet of oncoming night.

"I love this time," Mrs. Murphy purred.

"Me, too. The big moths come out," Pewter said.

"You've never caught a moth, not even a rosy maple, and they sit still on boxwoods for a long time," Tucker taunted Pewter.

"I didn't say I wanted to catch one. I like to look at them and smell them." The gray cat lifted her chin. *"Since when have you caught anything, bubble butt?"*

"I don't hunt, I herd." Tucker's large brown eyes were merry. *"If you'd jump down, I'd herd you."*

"You and what army? One swipe from my razor-sharp claws and your nose will look like a plowed field." Pewter lifted the fur on her back for effect.

"Shut up," Mrs. Murphy snapped. She was intently looking way across all the fields toward the creek that separated Harry's farm, which had always been in her paternal

family, from the farm that Cooper rented, which originally belonged to Herb Jones's ancestors.

Pewter widened her pupils. She then saw the shuffling movement about a half mile away. The bear that lived up in the hardwoods behind the farm was moving toward the high ridges. They knew this bear; she'd had two cubs, which would be full grown and on hunting missions of their own by now. Sometimes the families would stay close, but usually they established their own hunting territories. Fortunately, this year game was plentiful.

"Think she'd remember us?" Pewter whispered.

"Sure. Bears are smart." Mrs. Murphy respected the large, usually gentle bear.

Then again, she was grateful that grizzlies lived in the west and not Virginia. The native bears usually kept to themselves and were no bother, although they might rip out the side of a clapboard house if a bees' nest was behind it.

"I can't see," Tucker complained.

"Runt." Pewter giggled.

"You can be hateful, you know that?"

Tucker sat down, resting her head on the lowest plank of the three-board fence.

A slight rustle picked all their heads up. Talons extended, Flatface, the great horned owl, flew not one inch over Pewter's head. It scared the cat so badly, she soared off the fence post, rolling in the fragrant white clover.

"Hoo hoo." The huge bird laughed, tipped a wing in greeting, and continued on her way.

Tonight would be perfect for hunting.

"That was mean!" Pewter scrambled to her feet, tiny bits of grass stuck in her claws.

"You know how she is." Tucker marveled at how silently the winged predator could fly.

"Makes me think of Matilda and Simon. Those three live in the loft and everyone gets along," Pewter said. *"How they can get along with her, I don't know."*

"They get along because Flatface rules the roost, forgive the obvious statement," Mrs. Murphy replied. *"And Simon really is a generous fellow. He'll share treats with Flat-face. Matilda doesn't like the sweets, but the owl will eat them. Course, Matilda usu-ally goes into a semihibernation state. Have*

you noticed she's been on that tree limb for two days?"

"She's waiting for a victim." Tucker smiled.

"Oh," Pewter said airily, *"she doesn't scare me. You can hear the leaves when she drops. I always know it's her."*

Neither Mrs. Murphy nor Tucker responded. Each was praying Matilda would drop on the fat cat and they'd be there to witness the explosion.

The sky turned from deep blue to Prussian blue and finally to black. The stars glittered brightly, and the three friends picked out blue ones, pink ones, yellow ones, and stark white ones. They hadn't seen the stars this bright for the last three months, since the summer's haze dropped its veil over the sky, even at night.

"Whenever a human is murdered, the apple cart is upset. Ever notice?" Tucker mused.

"Like dominoes set on end. Push one and they all fall down," Mrs. Murphy commented. *"But if a dog was shot, we'd be upset. We'd want to find out who did it and make them pay."*

"That's just it, isn't it?" Pewter, back up on the fence post, picked the tiny grass bits from her claws. *"Even if a human gets*

caught, they get off most of the time, if they're rich. If they aren't rich, they sit in jail, get three squares a day. All that manpower wasted." She spat out a green tidbit. *"I say, shoot their sorry asses. Harry was reading the paper out loud and said it costs about $100,000 per year per prisoner. Think of the catnip that would buy."*

Mrs. Murphy laughed. *"That's why eighty percent of them are in there, selling human catnip."*

"I don't understand it," Tucker confessed.

"Neither do the humans. They want to feel good about themselves and waste money. Doesn't solve squat." Pewter, crabby since Flatface scared her, enjoyed moaning about this.

"Well, that's the nature of the beast. We aren't going to change it," Mrs. Murphy wisely noted. *"They never really address an issue until it's a full-blown crisis. Kind of like the War between the States. They knew at the Constitutional Convention they had to resolve slavery as well as some major economic differences between the North and the South. Eighty years pass. Nothing. And then hundreds of thousands die, to say nothing of the million and a half horses and*

mules. It's not any different now, whether it's crime or global warming."

"Are you reading over Harry's shoulder again?" Tucker asked.

"Yep." Mrs. Murphy watched a shooting star. *"So here's my question: where's the crisis? Will Wylde is shot dead. That doesn't mean that's the crisis. See?"*

"No, I don't see." Pewter turned to look at her friend.

"Murder is common, let's face it." The tiger cat watched some rabbits at the far edge of the pasture. *"For all we know, this is a garden-variety murder dressed up in politics. Everyone jumps to conclusions. My hunch is . . . well, it's like the equinox: the earth tips on its axis. Something is tipping but we don't know what. And if it doesn't involve our humans, I don't care."*

"Tipping like a power shift?" Tucker asked shrewdly.

"Could be," Mrs. Murphy said.

"You know as well as I do, Murph, that Harry will stick her nose in it. She can't help herself. Curiosity didn't kill the cat, it killed the human who made up the statement." Pewter had always hated that axiom about curiosity.

"Let's not talk about killing. It's such a beautiful night, I want to enjoy it," Tucker pleaded.

They inhaled the night's sweet fragrance, enjoying one another's company for five minutes.

Flatface returned to the barn with a squirming mouse in her talons, which finally ruined the mood. Mrs. Murphy hoped it wasn't a portent, but it was.

11

"Why didn't you tell me the other day!" Carla, hands on hips, spoke crossly to Mike McElvoy.

"Because I didn't check it out. Tazio and I focused on the kitchen."

"So now you're telling me, let me get this right, egress—"

He interrupted her, further infuriating her. "Forget the terminology; you need a door in the guest bedroom to the outside."

"Why? I've been in hundreds of houses, and there are no exterior doors from guest bedrooms."

"And I'll guarantee you those houses were built before 2000. The county changed the code." Mike, sleeves rolled up on his plaid shirt, shrugged.

"What's the point? To make more money

for the construction crew? You aren't getting any of it. The county's not getting any of it."

"The point is in case of fire, whoever is in that room can get outside in a heartbeat. It's not the flames that kill you, it's smoke inhalation." He paused dramatically. "What's extra expense compared to a human life?"

"Don't try that on me." Carla, lips glimmered with iridescent pink lipstick, stared at the wall of the guest bedroom. "Tazio should have known. I'll skin her alive."

"That's between you and Tazio, but if you want to come out to the truck, I can show you the code book. It's formidable, and every time there's a change, architects and construction bosses have to memorize it plus how it affects other things. I know you think I'm thick, Carla; you treat me like a redneck." His directness surprised her. "But I'm not. I have every item in that book memorized, and furthermore, you're not the only kid on the block. Every one of these jobs has to be cleared, and every single person, like yourself, is in a God-awful hurry."

"How dare you call me by my first name. I never gave you permission." This said by someone who knew her etiquette even when she chose not to practice.

"I'll call you whatever I want."

"I'm going to report you to the county commissioners."

"Go right ahead. And when you do, remember that I will put your job last on the list. You won't finish this house until next year."

"Are you threatening me?"

"No, I'm promising you that I'll drag this out forever." He stretched the syllables in "forever."

"I'll get you fired, you arrogant ass."

"No, you won't. You'll get yourself an ulcer."

"I don't have to put up with this." She started to brush by him.

Mike held out his arm like a barrier, then handed her a sheet of paper. "You might want to read this at your leisure. Just a few little things I've noticed that will need changes for you to get your certification."

"What would you do if I moved in before that?"

"Throw the book at you."

Carla, entertaining a high opinion of her

own intelligence, actually began to use it. "How much?"

"How much what?"

"Money. What do you want in order to check these things off the punch list?"

"Are you trying to bribe a public official?" He pretended mock horror.

"I'm trying to figure out why you're being so difficult. If it isn't money, do you want a suite of teak outdoor furniture?" Carla's husband, Jurgen, owned a large outdoor-furniture manufacturing plant over in Waynesboro.

"No, I don't. Wouldn't have the time to use it, anyway."

"What do you want?"

"For you to study that list." He walked past her to the hallway. "And you might reconsider how you treat this public official."

In the living room, the painting crew was putting the finishing touches on the woodwork. Not knowing whether they'd heard the conversation back in the guest room, Mike winked as he passed them.

Orrie Eberhard, on a ladder, smiled. He didn't like Mike, but he didn't get in his way, either. Mike could hurt his business through rumor and innuendo. Orrie kept on the good side of him.

Carla, puce-faced, came into the living room just as Mike pulled out in his county truck. "How long have you known Mike McElvoy?"

Orrie carefully put his brush crossways on the open paint can. "Most of his life. We went through school together."

"Did he cheat?"

"Ma'am?"

"Did he cheat on tests and stuff like that?"

"No, not that I know of."

"Do you think he's honest?"

Orrie ignored that question, since he didn't want the reply to come back to him. "The thing you have to understand about Mike is, his father shamed the whole family. I mean, they were lower than earthworms. Mike has some power and he likes that. He's kind of aggressive about it."

"What did his father do?"

"Drank himself to death. Found him dead as a doornail on the swings at the elementary school."

"Therefore I shall assume that Mike doesn't touch a drop."

"No, ma'am, he doesn't."

"Any vices?"

"Now, Mrs. Paulson, I haven't made Mike a life's study. I mean, we get along okay, but he goes his way and I go mine. Plus, I don't want him criticizing my work, even though it has nothing to do with the building code."

"If it has lead paint in it, it does."

"Yes, ma'am, that's true." Orrie began to appreciate how quick she was.

"Is his marriage strong?"

"I don't know."

She lifted an eyebrow, still looking up at him. "Everyone has an Achilles' heel, Orrie, everyone."

"Well, Mrs. Paulson, for what it's worth, I didn't much like Mike in school and I don't much like him now, but I get along to go along. Life's a whole lot easier that way."

Carla gave him a tight smile and left. She had never learned to get along to go along, and she always felt there was something vaguely immoral about it or, if not immoral, weak-willed.

Mike McElvoy wanted something. She was sure of that. Most people, if you hand them a fat envelope of cash, will take it. The question was how much. If he didn't want cash, what did he want?

She couldn't bear more delays on this house or the expense they would entail. Jurgen would fuss.

Carla had a sense, like many people, that there was a clear division of labor assigned by gender. Jurgen made the money. She spent it. She had to cajole him into it, but she used her arsenal of tricks to good effect.

12

"I wish I'd never said I'd do this." Tazio slumped down in the passenger seat of Susan's Audi station wagon.

"You really didn't have a choice," Susan consoled her.

"Mim's going to think I'm disloyal. And I don't want to put pressure on Paul," Tazio moaned.

Paul de Silva, Tazio's boyfriend, managed Big Mim's stables. Tazio found him charming and irresistible. Fortunately, the feeling was mutual.

Harry was half dozing in the backseat since the ride was so smooth, plus she was surrounded by the warmth of Mrs. Murphy, Pewter, Tucker, Owen—Tucker's brother—and Brinkley, Tazio's yellow lab.

She opened one eye. "It was Big Mim's idea."

"I know." Tazio nodded. "But the way things are breaking, she might forget and take it out on me."

"She's not like that. She can be despotic, but she's fair." Susan had known Mim all her life.

"Besides, she's taking it out on Junior." Marilyn Sanburne, Jr., was Little Mim's correct name. "Junior" was a term loathed by Little Mim.

"Got that right." Susan checked her speedometer and slowed, for she was doing eighty on Route 29.

"You don't know how fast you're going in this car." Tazio liked the wagon. "Good thing you slowed. Look up on the curve."

There sat a cop car waiting to feast on speeders. It was quota time, although the local police, sheriff's department, and state police would never, ever, admit they met a monthly quota. The state laws had been changed. Going fifteen miles an hour over the limit netted a Virginian a one-thousand-dollar fine. Out-of-state drivers could go as fast as they wanted but only pay the old lower fees determined by a judge. The results, predictably, were that troopers and cops went after the Virginians. If anything, the new law, in effect July 1, 2007, made the roads more dangerous.

"Mmm, on the one hand, I'm glad they're out here. On the other hand, I'm not," Susan commented. "Given the way cars are built today, the speed limits are outdated and the new laws are beyond absurd. I'm waiting for the citizen revolt."

"Wait until you drive the autobahn." Tazio had piloted a BMW M5 two years ago when visiting Germany.

"That will be the day." Harry sat up straight now. "Back to this Poplar Forest do. Big Mim suggested you to head the decorating committee—"

Tazio interrupted. "Sure, so I could build the scaffolding. You know this fund-raiser is about as elaborate as a Louis the Fourteenth fete. Little did I know."

"At least the committee has gotten the materials donated. Can you imagine the cost otherwise?" Susan checked her rearview mirror.

"Thirty-five thousand dollars." Tazio's voice was clipped.

"What!" Harry grabbed the back of Tazio's seat.

"Thirty-five thousand dollars."

"Oh, my God." Harry flopped back. "The fund-raiser won't make that. Good thing the stuff is donated."

"Are you kidding? With Folly Steinhauser heading the committee, they've already received fifty thousand dollars in tables. She's nabbed corporate sponsors for those. By the time individual contributions roll in—the silent auction plus the two live-auction items—this thing could very well clear two hundred thousand dollars."

"That's big money for central Virginia fund-raising." Susan was astounded. "You know we aren't unfeeling, but Southerners are taught to take care of our own. What's left over goes to people you don't know. That's why charities can't raise as much here as they do in the Northeast."

"No one told Folly. I'd like to know how she vacuumed this cash out of pockets." Tazio smiled. "Big Mim had no idea what she'd unleashed when she handed over this charity to Folly."

"She is overcommitted," Harry replied.

"Big Mim could run the country." Susan

laughed. "She thought she was adding new troops by allowing Folly the glory of spear-heading the Poplar Forest fund-raiser and ball. Little did she know she gave her rival a plum."

"But she didn't know Folly's ambitions at the time." Harry appreciated how intelligent Big Mim was, how subtle and political, too.

"And there we have to give the nod to Folly. She shrewdly kept her ambitions under wraps. Even now she's not saying anything. Her deeds speak for her. She's become a power, one that isn't going to bow before Her Highness," Susan said.

"Majesty," Harry corrected.

"For Great Britain," Tazio replied. "Later wasn't it 'Your Imperial Majesty'?" She paused. "Let's not get off on that. Here's my problem. Every person that Folly placed on the steering committee is a new person and someone for whom I have designed a house."

"That's why you had to take the decorating committee. Everyone knows that, Taz, especially Big Mim." Harry petted Tucker, sound asleep, as was Pewter.

"But Folly has invited Little Mim and Blair to join her at her table," Tazio told them.

"What!" Harry sat bolt upright again, which disturbed the two sleepers.

"Bother." Pewter dropped her head back on Tucker's flank.

"I wanted to see if I could hold my tongue until we were halfway to Poplar Forest." Tazio smiled.

"You succeeded," Harry dryly commented.

"Little Mim and Blair at Folly's table"—Susan counted couples—"along with the Paulsons, the Steinhausers, obviously, the Lattimores, and who else?"

"Elise Brennan," Tazio added.

"Who's her date?"

"Major Chris Huzcko." Tazio cited a very attractive blond marine, who would dazzle in his "ball" uniform.

"Are they an item?" Susan was curious.

"I don't know. At any rate, they'll need a marine at the table if Big Mim launches artillery fire." Tazio smiled.

"Chris can handle it," Harry said confidently. "And you know that Tracy Raz can handle it, too."

Tracy Raz, in his seventies, had seen combat in Korea. After his army career, he served in the CIA, and when he finally retired, he came home to Crozet and wooed his high-school sweetheart, Miranda Hogendobber. Both had married others and had lost their spouses. When Tracy returned from living in Hawaii, the embers reignited. For a man in his seventies, he was in better shape than many a forty-year-old, plus he was bull-strong.

"I assume Miranda and Tracy will be near Big Mim and Jim's table?" Harry said.

"Yes, so we'll have one tough army guy at one table and one rugged marine at another. Maybe the two men can keep the peace." Tazio sighed. "Meanwhile, I've got Folly on one hand and Big Mim on the other. Of course, my loyalty is to Big Mim. After all, she gave me the commission to design her steeplechasers' stable, and that was my ticket in, truly. I feel I owe her a great deal."

"In our own way, we all do. For all her ordering us about, she does a lot of good." Susan slowed again as she noticed everyone else doing the same. "And if you're really worried, go talk to her, Taz. She really will understand. She knows these people have been clients, are clients. She knows you have to make a living. Go talk to her before the ball. Don't wait until something ugly happens, and remember that she didn't know this challenge was coming." Susan made a sensible suggestion.

"I will."

"What about Little Mim's statement this morning?" Harry had heard on the six o'clock morning news that the vice mayor of Crozet stated she would do everything she could to help the authorities find and prosecute Dr. Will Wylde's killer. She said nothing about abortion, which meant her mother would not be satisfied.

"Slight progress." Susan noticed another cop car ahead.

She didn't mind cars slowing to the speed limit, but it irritated her when they crawled below the limit as though that made them a better driver in the cop's eyes.

"Wonder if they have made any progress." Harry worried, as did they all. "Coop has worked day and night. She can't tell me much, but I do know Rick had the presence of mind to demand patient records from Margaret Westlake. Margaret was worried, but Rick assured her the names of those who had abortions would be confidential. Kylie Kraft pitched a fit and fell in it."

Susan lifted her hand dismissively. "Kylie Kraft is an airhead. She goes through boyfriends like potato chips. She must be good as a nurse, though, or Will wouldn't have hired her."

"She's young and sympathetic. Most women having abortions are young. I can see why she'd be a valuable member of the team. Sophie Denham is a good nurse, but she's in her fifties now."

They rode along in a brief silence.

Tazio said, "I appreciate you two coming down here with me."

"A break in the routine, plus I'm dying to know what you've planned," Susan said.

"You'll see." Tazio smiled.

"Are you all building the platform and scaffolding at home, then transporting it?"

"No," Tazio replied to Harry. "There's a local construction company that is donating their labor. Good thing, because it makes it easier on everyone. They'll get business out of this."

"Good." Harry thought if someone pitched in for a charity, those attending the function should employ their services if they liked what they saw.

Once off 29, the long road from Lynchburg down to Poplar Forest was crammed with subdivisions.

"I can't believe this," Susan cried.

"When was the last time you drove down here?" Tazio inquired.

"Must be two years ago," Susan answered.

"At least the developers have taken some pains with landscaping." Harry peered out the window. "For some of them, anyway."

When they at last pulled into Poplar Forest, they let the animals out to go to the bathroom. Harry carried water and treats.

"You all go ahead. I'll attend to these guys and then I'll join you."

"We'll be outside in the back," Tazio told her.

"I want to go in the house." Mrs. Murphy liked prowling in old houses.

"We have to stay outside," Tucker, usually obedient, replied.

"Mom might need help with her plans," Brinkley, even more obedient than Tucker, said.

Pewter, drinking, couldn't care less one way or the other. What she wanted were the dried fish and chicken treats she knew reposed in a Ziploc bag in Harry's food tote.

"Harry, Harry!" Susan ran toward them, a big smile on her face. "They got him!"

"Who?"

Susan, chest rising and falling, reached her friend. "The man who shot Will Wylde. Robert Taney just told us. Was on the radio." She caught her breath. "He confessed and made a big statement. Walked right in to the station and turned himself in."

Robert Taney was the director of Poplar Forest.

"I can't stand that we let people run their mouths when they've killed someone. We make celebrities out of them." Harry's eyes narrowed.

"That's so, but we can all rest easy now." Susan put her hand on her chest.

"I wouldn't." Mrs. Murphy flicked water droplets from her whiskers.

"Why not?" Brinkley asked.

"Too easy," the tiger replied.

13

The south lawn at Poplar Forest afforded views of both the house and the Blue Ridge Mountains, the perfect outdoor setting for the fund-raiser.

Tazio, mindful of the staff's time pressures, spoke to Robert Taney for fifteen minutes, then returned to Harry and Susan.

Mrs. Murphy and Pewter prowled the grounds. The house, filled with people, would be difficult to get into without being detected.

"We'll get in. Maybe not today but someday," Mrs. Murphy grumbled.

"We may not be back," Pewter reasonably replied.

"Mother's curiosity will be lit. She'll come back when she has time to really go through the building and the outbuildings. But for

now we might as well enjoy the grounds. Lots of goldfinches to harass." For once Pewter looked on the bright side.

The mercury climbed to the mid-seventies this September 22. The dogs rested in the shade.

"So the platform isn't just for speeches. I should have asked you that in the first place." Harry noted the dimensions that Tazio told her: twenty feet by fifteen. "You know, this is going to be big."

"Building it in sections. We won't drive one stake in the lawn." Tazio, hands on hips, stood where she planned for the center to be. "Well, of course, there will be speeches after dinner. There always are. We're even hiding a Porta-John behind the platform, in case someone up here has to go. Given the length of speeches, that seems inevitable."

"I'd give more money if there weren't speeches." Susan smiled.

"Wouldn't we all," Tazio agreed. "However, the organizers need to be thanked, the chair always has to blab, and the politician of the moment really blabs on. And, of course, the director of restoration must speak. That I'll enjoy. The rest of it is pure torture."

"Aren't you going to speak?" Susan asked.

Tazio's hand flew to her bosom. "Me? God, no. I hate speaking in public."

"Ned can give you lessons. He's become one of those politicians, you know." Susan loved her husband but had noted a certain amount of garrulousness creeping into his conversation.

"Bet he can," Tazio wryly replied.

Harry, ever eager to keep on track—except when she veered off—said, "This is a big platform."

"There will be a lattice behind it with fake ivy and wide ribbons woven through. That will be backlit. I've got to keep the generators somewhat quiet. With the restoration there's a lot we can't do, but the house isn't wired for this kind of draw, anyway, hence the generators."

"When you figure out how to silence a generator, let me know." Harry appreciated the problem.

"I'm building domed ventilated housing. You'll hear a hum but it will be muted, and the roof of the small little hives will be soundproofed."

"That is so clever." Susan admired Tazio's

creativity as an architect and practicality as a woman.

"Taz, what are you going to do on the platform?" Harry was impatient.

"It's supposed to be a surprise, but I can tell you a few things. Okay, when people park, they will be led back to the lawn by servants in livery. And all the manner of the early nineteenth century will be in force. So each person will be addressed with their honorific, which was terribly important then, as was a graceful bow."

"Great. I can be introduced as Farmer Haristeen."

"You all will be Doctor and Lady Haristeen. Ned and Susan will be the Honorable and Lady Tucker, and so forth. Anyway, trays of drinks will be circulated, plus there will be a discreet bar under the arcade right over there." She pointed to the arcade under the southern portico. "Then trays of hors d'oeuvres from the periods. Okay. So far so good. Nothing unusual. Then it's time to sit and eat what would have been a feast in 1819. A feast now, too. I'm not giving away the menu. Folly would shoot me. But there will be a presentation, a tableau, and music while people eat."

"A play?" Harry didn't like the idea.

"No, Harry, a tableau. People will be in scenes, then the scenes will change. We aren't doing a play, because you can't really eat and watch a play. Dinner theater never works."

"A pretty thing but no major distraction." Susan figured it out.

"Right. Plus, it's set on the southern side here, and people can watch the sun set over the Blue Ridge Mountains, as well, since the views are good to the west. It should be fantastic unless it rains."

"Long-range predictions?" Harry watched the Weather Channel the way some people watched porn. "Clear. Cross your fingers."

Tazio exhaled. "Okay, then come the speeches, and I will do everything in my power to keep them short, but you know how that goes."

"Then what?" Harry was becoming intrigued.

"Then a little surprise."

"On the platform?" Harry prodded more.

"Umm, some on the platform. You'll see. It really will be so lovely, and this place deserves it. Everyone knows about Monticello and the University of Virginia as expressions of Jefferson's creativity in architecture. Some even know about the state house in Richmond, but so few know about Poplar Forest, even in Virginia, which surprises me."

"Oh, we learned about it in fifth grade, but it went in one ear and out the other." Susan recalled their venerable fifth-grade teacher at Crozet Elementary. "You were in St. Louis, so you missed Mrs. Rogers's breathless reenactments of Virginia history."

"The moans while she died of tuberculosis were particularly compelling." Harry grinned.

"Don't forget her yellow-fever death," Susan said.

"Or being shot by a minnie ball."

Tazio stopped this romp down Memory Lane. "Was her husband an undertaker? One death after another."

"Mr. Rogers ran the Esso station. Exxon now. She was a frustrated actress and figured out that death scenes carried more impact than pretending to be on a bateau rolling down the James River."

"She did that, too," Harry reminded Susan.

"Actually, she did."

"See what I missed growing up in St.

Louis," Tazio replied. "Well, I've done my due diligence here. Let's go back. I'll have to make a few calls from the car, and I apologize."

"Noticed your cell didn't ring." Harry never turned hers on unless she had to make a call.

"I needed a break. If Folly isn't bugging me, it's Carla. My other clients are okay. Oh, that reminds me, I need to get updated quotes on those furnace systems. Did a little more work on that. Haven't had time to send it over to Herb, but it can wait until tomorrow. And, of course, thanks to Folly, I have to present all this to Marvin Lattimore."

"Think Folly's sleeping with him?" Susan could say this among friends.

Given Folly's dazzlement by Marvin at vestry-board meetings, the possibility had become obvious to all.

"I don't know. Penny won't much like it." Harry had wondered the same thing.

"She can't be naive." Tazio stooped to pick up her plans from the deep-green lawn. "He runs a charter airline. People who travel a lot, especially in those circumstances, have ample opportunity to indulge in affairs."

"Marvin doesn't strike me as the affair type," Susan said.

"One-night stands." Harry winked.

"Well . . ." Susan's voice trailed off.

"All right, kids," Harry called, and Tucker, Owen, and Brinkley scrambled to their feet.

Mrs. Murphy and Pewter followed at a more leisurely pace.

At the parking lot, Susan lifted up the hatch on the station wagon and the animals jumped in. They'd stay in the back for a while. Sometimes the dogs fell asleep back there, but the cats always leapt into the backseat to keep the humans company.

No sooner did Susan pull out of the lot than Tazio's cell rang.

"On course?" was all Folly Steinhauser uttered in Tazio's ear.

"Yes," came the equally terse reply.

"Good. Talk to you tomorrow. Have to meet again with the caterer."

"Tazio, can you make calls if the radio is on low?" Harry asked.

"Sure."

"Susan, see if you can get the news. I want to know about who shot Will."

Susan clicked on the radio.

"Just press 103.5," Harry said.

"NPR." Susan knew the numbers. "That's not going to work south of Lynchburg."

"Damn."

"You've got ants in your pants today."

"Well, I want to know. Don't you?"

"I do," Susan agreed, while Tazio nodded as she punched in the number of the company building the platform.

As Tazio talked, Susan finally got a news station. First they endured the national news. The international was already over. Finally, local news came on, but it started with Richmond and the governor's latest push for new road construction.

"I don't care about northern Virginia." Harry cupped her chin in her palm.

"Don't be ugly." Susan smiled. "If Ned ever runs for governor, they'll vote for him up there."

"I suppose." Harry remained unconvinced.

"Today in Charlottesville, the sheriff apprehended Jonathan Bechtal, who confessed to the murder of Dr. Will Wylde. Bechtal stated that 'Death must be met with death.' " The announcer continued on, then switched to baseball.

"The Orioles today—"

"Turn it off," Harry groaned. "I can't stand the bad news."

"Cards." Tazio cupped her hand over the mouthpiece of her mobile, a big smile on her face.

"Every dog has his day," Susan, another Orioles fan, promised.

Tucker lifted her head but decided a comment would be useless. The humans wouldn't understand, anyway.

"What a relief, they've got the killer."

"Saves Little Mim's behind," Harry succinctly put it.

"Maybe," Susan slowly drawled, for she was processing the road, her speed, the news, "but he said he had Wylde's records. Who's to say he won't find a way to make them public? After all, he's now the center of attention."

"Bluffing." Harry paused. "I hope."

Tazio ended her call and another came in. "Yes." Long silence. "I did." More silence. "Give me the punch list. I'll go over everything and I'll measure everything, too. He's blowing smoke up your fanny." An even longer silence. "Good-bye." This was said quite crisply. "I hate her!"

"What?" Harry leaned forward.

"Carla is having a cow because Mike McElvoy handed her a punch list of things that are supposedly not up to code at the house. It's bullshit. I know the code. Unfortunately, she offered him money."

"Oh, good God." Susan rolled her eyes.

"A box of rocks." Harry tapped her forehead.

"Much as I can't stand her, Carla's not stupid. I think she underestimated Mike. And I don't know what his game is. I had some trouble with him on Penny Lattimore's house and on Folly's job, but nothing like this. I mean, Carla is raving mad, raving. She called me 'incompetent,' 'high-handed'—it goes on."

"Bet she's sorry that the committee invited Mike and Tony Long." Harry named the other building inspector going to the fund-raiser.

"That was the committee's decision. There's some sense to it. Mike and Tony get to see restoration in process, which can only help as more people try to be historically accurate. That's the thinking, anyway."

Harry offered an explanation. "Tazio, maybe she drinks. I mean, to explode like that or do something stupid like try to obviously bribe Mike. We all know palms get greased every day, but for God's sake, she could have been subtle."

"Now I have to deal with Mike pretending to be outraged. I loathe him, and she really was stupid," Tazio complained.

Susan commiserated. "You've got your hands full."

Tazio's phone rang again. Carla, with more expletives.

Harry smiled when Susan glanced briefly in the rearview mirror. "Glad I'm not building anything."

Tazio pressed the off button. "I am going to kill that bitch!"

14

Each day contains twenty-four hours, except Monday, the longest day of the week. It contains thirty. That's how Harry felt when she opened the back door, dropped her gear bag on the bench outside the kitchen door, and walked inside.

The phone rang just as she closed the door behind her.

"Hello."

"Honey, I won't get home until late," Fair apologized. "I'm behind on the billing."

"How about if I leave a casserole in the oven? You can heat it up when you get home."

"Thanks, but I'll order something."

"Crozet Pizza," she teased him.

"I love Crozet Pizza." The little pizza joint was his favorite.

"You know how you're always at me to streamline, become more efficient? Why don't you hire a true office manager? Someone who can bill, answer the phones, and code."

A veterinarian's files, like a physician's, have colored stripes called codes on their edges.

The process is so complicated that people take courses to understand it. If the bill doesn't go out on time, the vet doesn't get paid. If insurance companies are involved—and increasingly they were for horses—the cycle slowed even more.

"I can't make up my mind. It's not just the salary, it's the payroll taxes, their insurance. Remember, I'm a small business, and there aren't insurance packages that won't blast the budget. We get by with workers' compensation, another government cook-up. By the time I'm done paying out, that's fifty or sixty thousand a year."

"Be so much better if you could just hand the money to your employee."

"What? Just think what would happen to all those sticky fingers along the way. No money would be on them. The whole thing is a giant con, and for the life of me, I can't figure out why people just go along."

"Me, neither." Harry's impulse was to fight.

It seemed to Harry that most other people's impulse was to allow themselves to be used, robbed, herded, so long as they could buy what they wanted. They told themselves, "You can't fight city hall." Funny, Harry thought, our ancestors did.

"How'd today go?"

"Poplar Forest—you won't believe how much they've done. We stayed outside. I can't wait to get inside, but the foundations for the old outside offices are uncovered. It's just amazing."

"I'll soon see. How about Will's murderer getting caught? That's a blessing."

"Sure is." She paused. "But I'm suspicious. I don't think it's the whole story."

"You wouldn't be you if you weren't, but, Harry, stay out of it," Fair warned. "Let me go back to the salt mines. Love you."

"Love you, too."

After hanging up the phone, Harry fed the kids. The Fancy Feast smelled so good that she realized she was hungry.

"I hope you know, your food costs as much as mine." She washed out the two tiny tins of cat food.

"We're worth it," Pewter replied saucily.

Harry then opened a small can of dog food, which she mixed into kibble for Tucker. Tucker could put on weight quickly, so she monitored the corgi's diet.

"Here you go, Wonderdog."

"Thank you."

Harry checked the time on the old railroad wall clock. Six-thirty. She walked outside; the sun was setting behind the mountains. Whatever time was listed for sunset in the papers, it was earlier on her farm because of the mountains. Once the equinox approached, a chill seemed to descend upon the earth along with the sun. Along lower ridges, long golden slanting rays still pierced through. No one day looked like any other, and that pleased her.

She walked back inside and dialed Cooper. "You on your way home?"

"Yep."

"I made a tuna casserole and need help eating it."

"Glad to be of service." Cooper laughed.

Figuring she had about twenty-five minutes before the deputy showed up, Harry popped the casserole in the oven on low. She'd made it last night. Although not much for cooking, occasionally she could be roused to culinary labors—simple labors, nothing fancy.

She used the time to check the mares and foals, now six and seven months old. Time to wean. The hunters greeted her. She brought them in the barn in the mornings to eat a bit of grain and to have some alone time, then back out in the pastures they'd go. In winter's bitter cold she'd usually bring them in at sunset, turning them out again in the morning. But the late-September nights, though carrying a chill, would stay in the high forties, low fifties. Pleasant enough, especially for horses, as these were their optimum temperatures, in contrast to those of humans.

No sooner had she come back in and set the table than Tucker announced Cooper's arrival.

"I hate Mondays." Cooper, in uniform, strode through the door.

"What would you like to drink?"

"A beer."

With Fair back in the house, there was always good beer in the refrigerator. He limited himself to one a day, but he really wanted that one.

Out came the beer, the beer glass placed before Cooper. Harry, hotpads to the ready, pulled out the casserole, the aroma filling the kitchen.

"Do you want a salad?"

"Let's eat the casserole. If I have room left, I'll make it myself." Cooper was delighted to have supper with her neighbor and friend. "Where's Fair?"

"At the office doing the billing."

"He needs help."

"You tell him." Harry put the casserole on a trivet, a large spoon alongside it, and sat down herself. "Dig in."

Cooper did just that when Harry filled her plate. They ate in silence for a few minutes.

"Can you believe they're not running their mouths?" Pewter thought it amusing.

"They will," Tucker predicted.

Halfway through her first helping, Cooper started the conversation. "What a day. If I have to talk to one more person, I will just blow up."

"Person or media?"

"Both. Reporters are already digging up reasons why Jonathan Bechtal is a killer."

Cooper's worldview was black and white. If you as an individual broke the law, you went to the slammer. Her job was to find you and arrest you. The rest was up to judge and jury, and usually her work was undone in the courtroom. You do wrong, wham. That was Cooper's attitude. Gender, race, a bad mother had nothing to do with it. Thousands upon thousands of people endured similar circumstances and they didn't rob, maim, or kill. But someone would make out Bechtal to be a victim.

Harry, on the other hand, did think about mitigating factors.

Coop fired up again. "And this creep, Bechtal—full beard like an Old Testament prophet—is screaming about how God talks to him. How he is an instrument of the Lord. Damn!"

"Well, honeybun, it must have been quite a day."

"It was. This was one of the most irritating days of my whole life. I'm glad the perp turned himself in, but I don't want to listen to him. The media is making a celebrity out of him."

"Take another drink." Harry, not usually one to push alcohol, thought this a wise course tonight.

Calming a little, Cooper leaned back in

the chair. "This is really good. If you don't watch it, you can get fat as a tick being a cop." She laughed. "I go to the gym three times a week, and now that I have that place to take care of, I work outside a lot. That helps. Helps to just be away from people."

"Decompression."

She ate some more hot food. "I feel better." She sighed. "I need a wife."

"Doesn't every woman?" Harry smiled. "Although I give Fair credit: he really does his share, and he's a good cook. He's better than I am, but, of course, he has to cook on the grill. I think this passion for the grill occurs when they start to shave."

"Does taste good, though, and the different wood adds flavor."

"Have you seen my husband's different wood piles? He puts them in small garbage cans—clean, I mean. He has mesquite, charred oak, regular charcoal, even dried sassafras roots. He has special sauces. He won't give the recipe. That'd be like asking for the Coca-Cola formula."

Coop returned to the topic of the killer after listening to Harry.

"Once you weed out the philosophy, the

justification, the sheer insanity of Bechtal, you're left with details, most of which correspond to the shooting."

"Most?" Harry's interest spiked.

"He puts the elevator bay on the west side of the lobby. It's on the east."

"Is that so important?"

"Harry, I don't know, but I'm," she paused, "unconvinced."

"That he's the killer?"

Mrs. Murphy's ears pricked up. She walked over to the table. Pewter, face in food bowl, figured she'd get the information later from Mrs. Murphy, in case she missed anything while chewing lustily.

"When Rick and I first arrived on the scene, we secured the area, investigated the body. Fortunately, backup came in less than five minutes. We walked over to the other building, because you could see immediately from his wound that he wasn't shot face-to-face. We went inside. He couldn't have been shot from an office window, because people were there. Nor could the killer have taken the elevator. We went to the roof. That's where he had to have been, and forensics will confirm it. Oh, he confessed to using a silencer, too. When we came down the stairwell, there was a crushed Virginia Slims butt on the floor. I bagged it. Neither Rick nor I thought it came from our killer. Men don't usually smoke Virginia Slims, not butch enough." She smiled. "But maybe he did. A nicotine fit is a nicotine fit."

"What'd Rick make of it?"

"Nothing." She smiled again. "He owes me five dollars, though. I bet the killer was a man. Always is in a case like this. He said he'd be wild and bet it was a woman."

"People are supposed to go outside to smoke, but," Harry shrugged, "probably someone in that building who wanted to stay in the air-conditioning."

"Could be."

"Have you mentioned the elevator-bay location to Rick?"

"No. I will, but he's distracted. All the chaos, plus he's working up a budget request for the county commissioners. It's always a fight. There are a couple of people on the commission who question him as though he were the enemy, not a public servant trying to protect life and property."

"Don't you think Bechtal's surrender might put them in a better mood?"

"We can hope." She paused. "I'll bring this up to Rick in a couple of days."

"Want to hear about my day?" Harry smiled.

"I'm sorry." Cooper drained her beer.

"Want another?"

"No. But if you have green tea, I'll take a cup."

"Do. Fair's buying green tea, white tea, orange tea, and Sleepytime tea to drink at night. He reads everything about this stuff. I try it and if it works, fine. If not, I learned my lesson."

She rose, put the kettle on, and sat back down. "Not much for dessert, but I have cookies."

"No. I made a pig of myself." Cooper patted her stomach. "I am sorry. Tell me about your day."

Harry related the events, laughing about Carla's harassing Tazio.

"She is a piece of work."

"Tazio swears she'll kill her." Harry's peals of laughter filled the kitchen.

"Well, if she does, I'm off duty and in my ball gown. Someone else can take care of it."

They both laughed.

15

Big Mim might be despotic, but she kept the large goal of a harmonious, well-knit community in mind. Although Mim passionately pursued politics, she gave democracy lip service. The most effective forms of organization were run by a strong individual with a clear purpose.

Although much of what she pursued tended to duty, she possessed a kind heart, and her visits to those in distress, be it emotional or financial, buoyed her as well as the recipient.

On Tuesday afternoon, September 23, she sat across from Benita Wylde, the humorous needlepoint pillow behind Benita's back underscoring her loss. It read, "He's my husband, my lover, my friend, but he's not my responsibility."

It had been a strong marriage, enlivened by vibrant humor and a few good fights now and again.

The deep buttery gold of late-afternoon sun filled the room, decorated by Benita herself and a source of pride. Although too modern for Mim's taste—she ran to Colefax and Fowler or Parish-Hadley—she recognized that Benita had an eye for proportion, color, and quality. Nonetheless, the stark lines never felt homey.

"You've been so good to visit me every day. I keep thinking this will lift, but it doesn't." Her light-brown eyes registered confusion and pain.

"The first year is dreadful. The second is numbness." Big Mim smiled as Benita's oldest daughter, home from Portland, Oregon, placed a tea tray on the sleek, lacquered coffee table.

"Thank you, dear."

"Georgina, if you want to ride, let me know. Sometimes a nice trail ride helps."

"Thank you, Mrs. Sanburne. I'd love to, but there's so much to do, and I have to return to Oregon Sunday."

Georgina left them.

"She's turned into a beautiful young woman," Big Mim noted.

"Loves her job. I keep hoping she'll come home, but she says the only way she can come home is if she gets a job in Richmond or Washington. Those markets are so competitive, but I think she'll land in a big market eventually."

"Did you think she'd wind up in television?"

"Well, I knew she always was fascinated by the weather, but both Will and I were surprised when she chose meteorology as her career and then double-majored in broadcasting—journalism, really."

"She is in a perfect spot, with all those storms sweeping in off the Pacific."

"That's what she says." Benita poured them both tea. "In a way, the impact didn't fully hit me until the kids came home. They've been wonderful," she paused, "although my son says he's going to kill Bechtal if he can figure out how to get into the jail."

"Normal."

Benita nodded. "Would it solve anything? One more death?"

"I know I'm supposed to say no, but the

years have taught me that killing the right person at the right time can make all the difference. Think what would have happened in the world if the plot against Hitler had succeeded. There would have been a struggle between those dwindling few who wanted to pursue the war and the rest, who knew Germany was lost. We would have had an earlier peace. So many lives would have been saved." She held her cup with all the grace of one who had manners drilled into her upon leaving the womb. "The older I get, Benita, the less convinced I am that turning the other cheek is the answer. You can imagine how Miranda and I go 'round on this."

"She's visited regularly, too." Benita smiled slightly. "Reads germane passages from the Bible, but she's not as bad as she used to be. We read the Twenty-third Psalm together and it was comforting."

"Beautiful voice, Miranda has, speaking or singing."

"She brought me some cuttings from the garden, and, would you believe it, Alicia Palmer, down on her knees, put them in. I can tell my grandchildren, if ever they get born, that a movie star planted my pachysandra and variegated ivy. Miranda brought some American Beauty roses, too."

Big Mim, ever competitive on the garden scene, simply said, "Miranda displays a great gift."

"Her only vanity, I think." Benita's eyes filled with tears as she looked out the huge windows. "Will's maple. It was four feet high when he planted it. Look at it now."

Big Mim guessed the maple to be twenty-five feet high. "Just blushing orange at the top."

"Should be a spectacular fall."

"You never know. The conditions can be perfect and a big windstorm comes up. Poof." She waved her hand, the spectacular diamond on her ring throwing tiny rainbows of light. "Is there anything I can do to help with the funeral?"

"No. Because of the publicity, we decided to cremate him and to have only family here. I think we'll commission a celebration of his life on the first anniversary of his death." Benita looked back at the older, quite attractive woman. "I can't bear the people, the questions. A year from now, only those of us who loved him will honor him."

"Wise."

Benita's rich-brown hair evidenced a few red highlights. Apart from being ten pounds heavier than when in college, she looked marvelous for a woman in middle age. The suffering told on her face, but that was to be expected. And the ten pounds added to the womanliness of her figure.

"Mim, I don't know how I can live," she said without fanfare, a flat statement.

"You will. You must." A gust of fierceness invaded the older woman's voice.

"For the children, I know, but inside," she touched her heart, "I feel dead."

"That's natural, Benita. It passes, but slowly. You can't give up or give in."

Benita's lustrous eyes registered the challenge. "I know."

"It's not what the world throws at us, it's how we handle it. Even inflicted pain, something as terrible as this, can be borne because one must. The duty of life is to live and to give."

"We do let others control our emotions. If I collapse, then this hideous person wins. I see that." She stopped, placed her cup and saucer on the table. "How dare anyone play God! Even Will, a physician, did not, and when anyone used that phrase about doctors he corrected them. He used to say, 'I'm a skilled mechanic. I deal in the human body, not cars.' He was right."

"Did he ever question abortion?"

Benita shook her head. "Never. Not once. He believed the fetus contained the possibility of life but was not life. He always said, when he slapped the bottom and heard that first cry, that was life. And you know," she leaned forward, "his mission was intelligent planning. When all this hoopla started about global warming, Will would throw down the paper or talk back to the TV: 'What do you expect when people breed with no sense of responsibility to the environment?' Oh, he could get worked up."

"He's right. Was right." A slight breeze lifted the top leaves of Will's maple. "Benita, nature makes sense. People don't."

"I tend to agree." She was quiet for a few moments. "You know who else has been reading the Bible to me? Alicia. Another voice like liquid gold. She surprises me. We play golf when we can, but I . . . well, she feels for people. She reaches out, where others keep their distance. And when she and BoomBoom come, they check in with the kids and do whatever needs to be done—which is quite a lot, I'm afraid, because I haven't lifted a finger. I feel like I can't move."

"She and BoomBoom do seem to have brought out the best in each other. We seem to be surrounded by surprises of all manner." Big Mim now placed her cup and saucer on the silver tray. "I'm sure all is secure, but if some unforeseen financial burden should . . . well, you know, don't hesitate to call me, Benita. That's what friends are for, and I hope you won't let pride stand in the way."

A long pause followed as Benita searched for words. "I don't know where I stand, Mim. I hope I would accept assistance if I needed it. I went through some of Will's papers when I went down to the office. Georgina drove me. I don't trust myself to drive, because I burst into tears at the most inopportune moments. Anyway, I went through the business checking account. I asked Kylie Kraft for the outstanding invoices. Actually, Margaret does that. I didn't really know the girls' specific jobs. Everything was in order, although I noticed there wasn't as much money in the account as I anticipated. I asked Margaret—she sends out the bills—why it was a bit low, and she said some of the larger payments were still outstanding."

"Is Margaret good at the details?"

"Yes. Each time a check comes in, she copies it along with the invoice. Everything goes on a disc. The original copy is kept in the back-room files—which are bulging, I might add. When those files overflow, they are transferred to a U-Store-It."

"Why?"

"If there's a fire or flood, no records. Without records, no money. The insurance companies will leave you in the lurch. They make life hard enough, the insurers. Do you know we carry thirteen policies? Thirteen! And only one is for the house, one for the cars. All the others are medical in one way or the other. Mim, it's a nightmare. People have no idea what's happened to medicine."

"I know." Her curiosity aroused, Big Mim inquired, "Who had a key to the storage unit?"

"Will, and there's one in his desk here. Margaret keeps one on her key ring."

"Will was smart on so many levels."

Benita changed the subject. "By the way,

I was grateful when your daughter made a statement."

"Finally." Big Mim's face flushed. "She won't say anything about terminating pregnancy, though. She's toadying to the religious right in her party, which, as you know, I feel is a party of untrammeled greed and corruption."

"Of which I am a member," Benita said lightly.

"I forgot. I'm sorry, but you know I'm a yellow-dog Democrat." Meaning she'd vote for a yellow dog before she'd vote for a Republican.

Benita waved her hand. "Will registered Republican, so I did, too. He always said one party was as bad as the other, but he felt that doctors received slightly more consideration from the Republicans. You know me, Mim, no interest in politics and no stomach for it."

"Saves indigestion," Big Mim joked.

The grandfather clock in the hall, an eighteenth-century one of high value, struck five. While it could have looked out of place in the house, it didn't, which was a testimony to Benita's abilities.

"Soon Daylight Savings will be over and

night will fall so much more quickly." Benita noted the lovely light. "I've never much liked winter."

"Because you can't play golf. Now, if you'd foxhunt, winter would fly by."

"And so would I." Benita laughed for the first time.

They chatted some more; Benita cried a little.

Big Mim actually quoted a passage she herself remembered from the Bible, Philippians, Chapter 4, Verse 13: " 'I can do all things in him who strengthens me.' "

"Miranda has rubbed off on you," Benita remarked.

"She can go on. She must have the entire Bible memorized. I try to have her faith but I'm too logical, I fear."

"I'm discovering mine."

"What I have I found when I was diagnosed with breast cancer those years ago. I looked inward. Something I don't usually do." She inhaled. "Who wants pain? Who desires suffering? I can't imagine anyone in their right mind wanting a dose, but one learns such important lessons that can't be learned any other way. My mother, when I complained, used to tell me that suffering was a gift if you looked it in the eye. I never believed her, but now I do."

"I'm learning."

As Big Mim rose to leave, she stopped for a moment and glanced again at Will's maple, the slanting rays hitting the top perfectly so the blush became more radiant, promising outrageous color soon. "Benita, keep your eyes on those unpaid invoices. With Will's death, some people may drag their heels sending in the check."

Little did she know she'd hit the nail on the head. Almost.

16

"So teach us to number our days, that we may apply our hearts unto wisdom."

The antiphon thus spoken, the Rev. Herb Jones continued with the service for burial, his bass voice making the beautiful service even more memorable.

Benita, Georgina, Will, Jr., and Will's two brothers and his sister with their families stood quietly under the maple tree as Herb, in his vestments, consoled them with *"Domine, refugium"*—the Lord is my refuge.

The long, verdant lawn added to the peacefulness of the moment.

At the close of the service, Will, Jr., placed his father's ashes in a three-foot-square hole dug near the maple. Georgina covered it with dirt, patting it down.

Benita knelt, placing a cascade of pale

yellow roses over the spot. Each family member, in turn, added their flowers.

The office staff, not in attendance because the service was family only, had brought a sumptuous luncheon to the house, to follow the funeral.

The three women cried quietly. Kylie sobbed the most, but she was the youngest. They'd come by at nine in the morning, and when Margaret, who'd driven everyone, dropped Kylie back at her apartment, she breathed a sigh of relief. All the drama was getting on Margaret's nerves.

The family filed back to the flagstone patio, where the luncheon had been set out with the best china and crystal. They stood behind their seats at the two long tables.

"Herb, please take the seat of honor." Benita motioned for him to head her table.

"The girls thought of everything." Will, Jr., opened the first bottle of champagne.

Everyone called the office staff "the girls."

When all the glasses were filled, Benita stood, faced the tree, and held her glass high. "To the memory of a good husband, a man of integrity and exquisite taste. How fortunate we were to have him in our lives. To Will."

"To Will," all repeated in unison.

She sat back down and leaned toward her daughter. "How he would have loved this."

The day passed quickly enough with all the family around. An hour before sunset, under the direction of Will, Jr., they all piled into cars and drove west to watch the sun set over the Blue Ridge.

Not until their return home did Benita give way. When Will, Jr., turned the car down the drive, they saw that it had been lined with sugar maples, one for each year of their marriage.

At Big Mim's behest, Tim Quillan had put everyone he had at Waynesboro Nurseries on the job, and they'd planted those maples, six feet each, in two hours' time and left without a trace.

Will, Jr., stopped the car; the cars behind him stopped, as well. One by one, they all got out of the vehicles.

"Oh," was all Benita could say before her legs gave way.

"Mother." Will, Jr., grabbed her.

She rested her head on his shoulder. "Who did this?"

"We all did. Big Mim arranged everything and paid for the lion's share. But we all pitched in. You know Dad and his maple." He cried; he couldn't help it.

Later that night, when Benita crawled into bed, she cried and cried. She cried for Will. She cried because she was wrapped in the love of her wonderful family. She cried because Big Mim had proven to be such a good friend.

She thought a moment about what Big Mim had said about how people can take advantage of you when you suffer from a ferocious blow. She'd pull herself together and keep on top of the billing and the money. She couldn't play golf twenty-four hours a day, no matter how much she loved it. She needed a focus, a job, and tending to the business part of Will's practice would suffice, for now.

She hadn't discussed business with the children, but she would before they left. The choice would be to close the practice or sell it. If they closed, then the three women in the office would be out of work. Sophie would land a job first, because everyone needed a good nurse and she was the most experienced. Will would want Benita to do all she could for his staff.

But who would buy his practice after this?

The whole medical community had stepped forward to help with those patients in need. Again, she was overwhelmed at how good people were, how ready to work.

She had a little time. She was praying someone would step forward, a young doctor just wrapping up a residency, perhaps.

Then the oddest thought flitted through her head. Jonathan Bechtal looked familiar to her. The FBI had showed her photographs. She didn't recognize him. But now, in her exhausted state, she thought there was something familiar.

She closed her eyes. Big Mim was right about how huge emotional events distort your mind, wear you out. She was going to have to be vigilant.

17

"You have it easy." Harry wiggled in her seat. "All you have to do is shave, comb your hair, and put on your clothes. Okay, maybe tying the bow tie is difficult, but the rest is easy."

"You look beautiful." The line into Poplar Forest, a quarter mile long, demanded patience.

"You like this color on me?"

"Honey, I like every color on you. You can wear anything."

The full-length dress, adjusted to fit perfectly by a seamstress, felt confining to a woman used to jeans, work boots, and a T-shirt or sweatshirt.

Harry's mother used to say, "A woman must suffer for beauty."

Harry's reply was, "Let someone else suffer. I'm happy to look at her."

Her suffering wasn't nearly as bad as she thought it was. She'd never endured plastic surgery, she didn't spend bags of money once a week for facials and manicures. She'd only once enjoyed a massage. She dabbed on mascara, blusher, and lipstick. That was it. However, she had spent a pretty penny on the gown, and it showed.

So exclusive was the fund-raiser that it was white tie, not black. Years ago, Fair had bought a bespoke suit of tails, two tuxedos, and one white dinner jacket with a satin shawl collar. Like Harry's mother, his father had sought to prepare him for many of the social functions one needed to frequent. Nothing looked better than clothes cut for you, and if a man kept his weight steady, he need never buy more.

"I didn't paint my fingernails."

"I didn't paint mine, either." He smiled.

She looked out the window at the sun, forty-five minutes from setting. "I think it's going to cool down."

"You have your mother's fabulous coat."

"I do. I wish I had my mother's fabulous style."

"I like your style: fresh and natural."

She looked at him. "You must want hot sex tonight."

He leaned back. "Harry, whenever I'm with you the thought is uppermost in my mind."

"Do you think men think about sex more than women or do you think it's cultural? You know what I mean." Harry wasn't always the most articulate soul.

"We'll never know what's cultural and what's biological, because science is always in service to power. Even veterinary medicine. What do I personally think after forty-two years of observation? That men think about sex more than women do. However, I don't think women are that far behind. They display it more discreetly, if they display their thoughts at all."

"That's what I think."

"Then why did you ask?"

"Because I'm bored sitting in this line and I'm already crabby about being in this gown. I feel like a drag queen, even if I am a woman."

"A lady. You're an elegant Virginia lady of black-type bloodlines."

"Honey, if you said that to someone who

wasn't a horseman, they'd think you were talking about race."

"Guess they would."

Black type in a Thoroughbred pedigree meant the animal had won Grade I races. Obviously, this was highly desired.

"I admire Tazio's outlook," Harry said. "Being half African-American, half Italian certainly provided her with insight, not just into race but into culture, people's petty prejudices, you name it. You know, I have never heard her once utter a remark about race, pro or con."

"You can bet she heard about it in school."

"Well, her parents sent her to the most expensive girls' prep in St. Louis."

"Doesn't mean she didn't brush up against ugly remarks. If anything, rich kids can be even more snide than poor ones."

"I don't know about that. Small little minds looking for something to hold against someone else bite you sooner or later."

"Luckily for her she is beautiful."

"She really is, and that's another thing I admire about her: she doesn't use it. Some women can use it like a whip against men and women."

"I know." He smiled ruefully. "Lately, though, Tazio has looked drawn."

"Carla and Mike. She's worried about offending Big Mim, too, over this ball."

He cleared his throat, moved forward a bit. "The whole situation with Little Mim is pretty ridiculous. It's not Tazio's fault. And, remember, let us always remember, it was Big Mim who suggested—no, insisted—that Folly chair the fund-raiser."

"I know and you know that, but it's still going to be sticky with Little Mim and Blair at Folly's table." She sighed. "At least Tazio and Paul will be at ours."

"There's a reason I work with horses and not people."

"I hear you." She laughed. "Have I told you how handsome you look?"

"You're trying to soften me up for sex tonight, aren't you?" He paused. "Soften is the wrong word."

"I never worry about you." She smacked his arm. "God, this is taking forever."

"Look at it this way, the ball is already a success."

"Tell that to my bladder."

"Mine, too."

Another fifteen minutes, amid lights flashing on sheriff vehicles, and the Haristeens had parked.

Harry, holding on to Fair's arm as would a proper lady from the early nineteenth century, whispered, "There's got to be Porta-Johns somewhere."

Since Fair was so tall, he looked around. "Over there. A whole row, before we even are escorted to the festivities."

They made a beeline—not easy, since Harry was in low heels. Her long dress covered up that she wasn't tottering in high heels.

Each hurried into adjoining johns.

She heard him laughing.

"What are you laughing at? I can hear you!"

"I'm not telling."

He emerged first, of course, and waited dutifully. Finally, a red-faced Harry came out, the metal and plastic door reverberating behind her.

A line had already formed for the johns, so she kept her voice low as they walked away. "What's so funny?"

"I was imagining you trying to balance yourself, hold up all the voluminous material, pull your panties down, and then go. Whew."

She laughed so hard she had to stop. "At least you appreciate the problem. One of these days, I'll dress you up and you can really learn what we go through to please you brutes."

"You'll never find shoes big enough."

"Oh, yes, I will. There have got to be drag queens as big as you are." She glanced up at him, his face baby-smooth, as if he had used a five-bladed razor. "Ever do drag?"

"Hazing for Phi Delta Theta when I was a pledge." He named his college fraternity. "I actually liked the silk and the colors, and I loved being hairless. You know, I hadn't really seen my chest muscles or my arms so clearly since I hit puberty. I could see every muscle, plus it felt so smooth. Sexy, really, and then the hair started to grow out. Itchy. Awful. Awful." He giggled.

"Were you a pretty girl?"

"Not as pretty as you."

"Right answer."

A gentleman in attire from the second decade of the nineteenth century held out his gloved hand for Harry, and a young lady in pale-salmon silk held out her hand for Fair.

They walked through a promenade of shaped boxwoods in huge glazed pots, which led to the back lawn. The effect was that of walking through a corridor and suddenly coming into the light.

What light it was. The three hundred guests glowed in the long, slanting rays of the sun, its bottom a few degrees above the Blue Ridge.

Servants in livery opened glass lanterns on wrought-iron stands to light the beeswax candles within, using long tapers.

Small hanging lanterns, strung high, surrounded the stage, and occasional fanciful lanterns suspended from trees added to the extraordinary effect.

Harry could only glimpse the tables beyond the first gathering level. She and Fair would be ushered into the seating area later. But she could just see red, gold, white, and deep-purple floral arrangements.

On a broken Corinthian column in the center of the lawn towered a floral arrangement using the same colors again, with trailing ribbons of silver and gold and one baby-blue ribbon.

Thomas Jefferson would have loved it. The symmetry gave structure to everything and echoed the symmetry of the house. The occasional whimsical items, such as the lanterns or another boxwood carved as a rabbit on its haunches, would have amused him. The animal boxwoods were in large glazed vases.

Could Jefferson have seen Tazio Chappars, in a gown with crisscross chiffon straps over her bosoms, a long waist, and flowing skirts to the ground, all in the palest of pinks, he would have fallen head over heels. Those green eyes flashing above the pink added to her potent appeal.

Paul, sleek in his white tie, noticed every man looking at his date. Well, she was more than his date—he was wildly in love with her and didn't mind telling her so.

She appeared cooler, but sooner or later Tazio would have to admit that she loved him, too.

The young couple fielded all the praise from people who knew that Tazio was responsible for the look of the evening.

Folly Steinhauser sported an emerald-and-diamond necklace with matching earrings and bracelet, which cost a hefty six hundred thousand dollars if one penny. Her husband, Ron, was by her side and engaged in an intense discussion with Marvin Lattimore. Ron's gray pallor accentuated his age. He kept a grasp on Folly's right hand with his left, but he couldn't follow her eyes since he was talking business with Marvin. Folly could hardly keep her eyes off Marvin.

As for Penny Lattimore, she'd already ditched her husband to talk to Major Chris Huzcko, much to the annoyance of Elise Brennan, herself swathed in diamonds and sapphires.

The first couple Harry and Fair ran into were Marilyn and Urbie Nash. Marilyn's white gown, pink ribbon wound through the bodice, wider pink ribbon as a sash at the waist, accentuated her good features.

"Stunning," Harry complimented her after everyone's initial greeting.

"We both clean up pretty good, don't we?" Marilyn smiled.

"We're waiting for the dancing so we can watch you and Urbie."

The Nashes had taken up ballroom dancing, finding that it kept them in shape, plus they had such fun doing it.

They chatted for a few minutes more, mostly about Marilyn's animal-rescue work, then moved on to other couples, as is customary in such circumstances.

Big Mim glided up, husband, Jim, in tow. "Harry, you've never looked so radiant."

Fair gently lifted Big Mim's right hand, brushing his lips over it. "Nor you."

"Fair, you flirt."

"Watch it, buddy." Jim Sanburne, a working-class boy made good, glared with mock anger at Fair.

"We all envy you, Mayor."

"Well, you don't envy my job." Jim laughed and slapped Fair on the back.

It had taken years for Big Mim to realize that the exceedingly masculine Jim would remain, fundamentally, a working-class man. She finally reached the point where she rather liked that. She kidded him that they were beauty and the beast. Jim, being Jim, asked who was whom?

Aunt Tally, silver-hound-handled cane in hand, had a date with a much younger man. Adolfo di Maso degli Albizzi was a count, although Italy no longer considered such titles. At eighty he looked dapper, and everyone called him Dolf.

"Children." Aunt Tally waved her cane.

"My esteemed aunt wants your attention." Big Mim smiled tightly as she nodded to Aunt Tally. "She's on her second martini."

"We're safe until the third." Harry kissed Big Mim, then Jim, on the cheek.

The two pushed through the resplendent crowd to the oldest couple there.

"Signóra." Dolf bowed low, then kissed Harry's hand as Fair kissed Aunt Tally's.

For good measure, Fair also kissed Aunt Tally on the cheek.

"A triumph." Aunt Tally beamed.

"You, my sweet, are the triumph." Dolf oozed Continental charm.

"Go on." Tally lifted her cane ever so slightly. "Isn't this extraordinary? I tell you . . . well, I'll tell you two things. One, that Tazio Chappars has a gift, a true gift. It's all there—structure, proportion, color, and texture. As for Folly," she glanced around, eyes glittering, "it would appear her organizing ability is as formidable as that of my beloved niece."

"That's why Big Mim selected her for the job." Harry wondered how often this would come up tonight.

"I suspect she didn't know quite how formidable Folly's talents are." She knocked back the remains of her martini, eyed the glass, then smiled broadly at Dolf.

"Honey, what would you like?" Fair chose to accompany Dolf to the bar under the portico.

This location proved to be the only flaw in the plans, because people could slip into the house. The bartenders had to keep calling them back. The one person whose task was to keep people out of the house was on overload. He couldn't wait for the supper to begin and the bar to close.

Being as tall and powerful as he was, Fair could run interference for the older, frailer gentleman.

"Tonic water with a twist of lime."

"Champagne! Bring your bride champagne," Aunt Tally commanded.

Strolling flute, violin, and lute players walked among the crowd, as did serving girls bearing trays of delicious tidbits.

Aunt Tally reached over as a college student, dressed in period, offered a tray. "Thank you, dear."

Harry shook her head no. She confined herself to regular meals and tried not to snack.

"Are you going to dance the night away?" Harry smiled.

"I was hoping for more, but Dolf would probably have to lash his member to a pencil." The nonagenarian, almost one-hundred, popped the hors d'oeuvre into her lipsticked mouth.

"Aunt Tally, you shock me."

"No, I don't. I was doing it before you were born. Before Mim was born. By now I should be an expert, don't you agree?"

"Well . . . yes." Harry burst out laughing.

"Where is that man with my martini?"

"Fighting the crows. Hold on."

Carla Paulson stopped by for a moment. "Aunt Tally, you remember my husband, Jurgen?"

"So nice to see you, sir." Aunt Tally extended her hand.

He shook it, then repeated the process with Harry.

Carla, with bracelets obscuring her arms, a huge necklace, and enormous earrings of white and black pearls with sprays of diamonds arching over them, presented a contrast to Harry, who appeared restrained. She was wearing her mother's five-carat emerald-cut diamond ring, along with emerald-cut earrings at three carats each and a matching bracelet.

The diamonds were perfect. Harry knew exactly how to wear jewelry even though she wasn't much interested in it. She could never have afforded her mother's diamonds, but once upon a time, before the Great Depression, the Hepworths, Harry's maternal family, had money.

Aunt Tally wore a diamond choker and two-carat drop diamond earrings, quite subtle but the diamonds were perfect.

In Virginia, less is more.

"Darling, you must get a safety-deposit box." Aunt Tally smiled at Carla, who missed the point.

Fortunately, before the old girl could further sharpen her tongue, Dolf and Fair appeared.

Dolf performed the obligatory hand kiss, which made Carla titter.

Mike McElvoy passed by, Noddy on his arm. "Good evening, folks."

"Mike." Fair smiled at him.

Carla curled her lip, but Jurgen had the manners to wish him a good evening.

"Mike, with all your building inspections,

do you ever have time to build for yourself?" Harry asked.

Noddy answered for him. "You should see his shop. Well, he calls it a shed. It's sacred. I don't go in there." She tittered. "It's where he buries the bodies."

Mike gruffly replied with humor, "I am banished to the shed because I'll dirty her house."

As Mike left, Carla hissed, "I truly hope I see him roasted on a spit."

"Now, Carla, don't let that temper get the better of you. Redhead." Jurgen genially explained her temper due to hair color.

As the Paulsons left to distribute themselves among the throng, Aunt Tally said, "Lucille Testicle red."

Harry, tonic water in one hand, champagne in the other, decided the only way to survive this evening was to knock back the champagne immediately.

Fair smiled as she did so, placing her fluted glass on the tray as yet another serving girl passed by.

"Another?"

"No, honey. I really will stick to the tonic water, but I needed help."

"Oh, Harry, loosen up," Aunt Tally ordered. "A little medicinal application of spirits enriches life."

"Mutes the harshness." Dolf sipped his champagne.

A melody of trumpet notes called the assembled to the tables.

As each gentleman seated each lady, then sat down himself, a moment of hush fell over the lawn. The variety of glasses on the table was truly spectacular.

The band of strolling players left the scene, and an orchestra playing period pieces sat near the back of the platform, itself a wonder of ribbons, topiary, and birds. The tableau commenced on stage.

Tazio, next to Fair, flushed from the praise.

He leaned down to tell her, "All deserved."

Harry noted that Little Mim indeed graced Folly Steinhauser's table—the Number 1 table, too. Her eyes cast over the scene. She was amused to see Mike McElvoy and his wife seated at a back table with Tony Long and his wife. Folly, no doubt, was working these two over for some grand building plan she envisioned for the future. Might work with Tony, but who knew about Mike?

Will Wylde's table was filled with his staff

and their dates and husbands. Kylie leaned on her date. She wore the gold Rolex, which, being a sport watch, wasn't proper. However, she wanted the world to view her treasure.

This reminded Harry how generous Benita Wylde was, because "the girls" would not have been able to afford this evening on their own. Benita had told them Will would be horrified if they didn't attend. He wanted people to live, to enjoy life.

Dr. Harvey Tillach's table, on the other side of the lawn, was also filled.

Miranda and Tracy, at Harry's table, which wasn't all that far from Big Mim's table, filled it with laughter. Miranda turned into the lively high-school girl she once was in Tracy's company. Not that she couldn't be lively on her own, but the years and the loss of her husband, George, had subdued her for a long, long time.

A young man quietly poured the first serving of wine. Harry turned her glass upside down. One glass of champagne was all she could handle. She felt its titillating effects already.

Miranda held up her glass. Cooper, seated

beside Tracy, wondered at the nature of Miranda's toast.

Her deep, honeyed alto voice flowed over the table. "This is the day which the Lord has made; let us rejoice and be glad in it. Psalm One Eighteen, Verse Twenty-four."

Everyone joined Miranda's toast.

The first course, served in a coordinated, balletic fashion, added to the conversation.

Cooper, surprisingly feminine in her bottle-green gown, had a blind date, Lorenzo McCracken, a Nicaraguan. Before the twentieth century, an outpouring of Scots had settled in Central America. The crossing of the Scots with the Spaniards had resulted in some progeny taking the best of both. Lorenzo possessed the square, manly features of a Scot, with intense Spanish coloring.

Cooper, who hated blind dates, was thrilled with this one.

Hard to tell how Lorenzo felt, since his manners were not only perfect but infused with charm.

Cooper kept telling herself, "I know I'm a fool for Spanish-speaking men. On guard."

Yes, but for how long?

This was a happy, happy crowd. Even Big

Mim was happy, so long as she didn't look over at Little Mim. And at Table 1. That grated.

Herb Jones did his best to keep her distracted. If the good reverend's genial patter didn't occupy her, her increasing alarm at Aunt Tally's alcohol intake did.

Aunt Tally was becoming the belle of the ball. Not for the first time.

Tazio, not wearing a watch—which was wise for a lady in a ball gown—asked Paul the time. Most of the courses had been served. She was getting a little nervous about her upcoming presentation.

"Seven forty-five."

"What time does the show begin?" Harry asked.

"After dessert, per usual." Tracy laughed. "If you drink enough wine, you can fall asleep during the speeches."

"Now, honey." Miranda winked at him, although he was in scant danger of falling asleep.

"Let me just slip away. I'm going to be on that dais for some time." Tazio headed for the Porta-Johns out of sight of the tables.

Ten minutes passed.

"She's taking a long time." Paul glanced at his watch again.

Cooper said, "Probably a line. She's not the only one trying to get in ahead of intermission."

A moment of silence prevailed on the dais, the lovely bit of Mozart completed. The violinist spoke something to the others, picked up his bow again, tapped his foot. Before he could draw it across his resonant instrument, a bloodcurdling yell scared even the birds settled in their nests for the night.

Harry's eyes opened wide.

Another scream followed.

Cooper rose. "Excuse me."

"Allow me to go with you." Lorenzo knew she was a deputy.

"You swore you weren't going to work tonight." Harry rose, and Fair pulled her down.

"Let's hope I don't have to."

Wrong.

Cooper hurried to the front of the house. There on the lawn, the twilight wrapped around like a shroud, lay Carla Paulson, her throat slashed.

Standing over her, knife in hand, was Tazio Chappars.

18

The head violinist, a puzzled look on his face, held his bow in midair.

Folly Steinhauser remained in her seat, confused.

Big Mim stood up, held up her hands in a conciliatory gesture, and said, “Ladies and gentlemen, enjoy your desserts.” Prudently, she added, “Please stay in your seats until further notice.” Then, nodding to the violinist, she sat down.

Folly may be a good organizer, but she’s not up to a crisis, she thought to herself, then she turned to her husband and whispered, “Where’s Marilyn?”

Little Mim was not in her seat.

“I don’t know, honeybun.” He started to rise.

She put her hand on his forearm. “Wait. If

she's not back in five minutes, then look. More than likely she went to the bathroom."

As the music filtered over the now-murmuring crowd, Little Mim, ashen-faced, walked not to Table 1 but to her mother.

Leaning over, she whispered, "Carla Paulson's lying on the front lawn. Her throat is cut. Coop is there. So is Tazio Chappars—she had the knife in her hand."

Face composed, Big Mim lifted her eyebrows and forced a smile. "Thank you, dear. Sit down and tell no one. That's the best path for now."

As Little Mim returned to Table 1, Aunt Tally said, "Shall I assume that's the end of the feud?"

"I think you may," Big Mim replied to her aunt.

"What's up, Mimsy?"

"I can't tell you, Aunt Tally. But I will at the opportune moment."

Emitting a long, irritated sigh, Aunt Tally returned to her exquisite sherbet nestled next to a sliver of divine chocolate cake, the layers so thin they looked like tissue paper.

Jim, worried, said, "I ought to go out there."

"Honey, Coop is there. If anyone can handle the situation, it's our own good deputy."

And Cooper did handle it. She told Tazio to simply put the knife on the grass and to remain with her.

Kneeling down, Coop carefully examined Carla, her gorgeous dress's bodice, even the voluminous skirts, red with fresh jugular blood. She felt for a pulse. None. She'd figured that, but one could hope.

As far as the deputy knew, if a jugular was slashed, trying to stop the bleeding by pressure was ineffective. The time for even that measure had passed. This one was cut halfway through.

Cool and clinical, Cooper looked around the scene. The only other persons she had seen were Little Mim and Harvey Tillach, whom she told to return to the party.

"Tazio, you don't have a cell on you, do you?"

"No," Tazio, still stricken, replied.

"Did you kill Carla?"

"No."

"What were you doing with the knife in your hand?"

"I—I saw her sprawled there and I ran up. All that blood. All that blood. I've never seen so much blood, and it was still squirting up, like a fountain, a dying fountain."

Cooper waited patiently, saying only, "Go on."

"I don't know, Coop. I saw the knife right by there." She pointed to Carla's left hand. "And I picked it up. I don't know why."

"All right. Listen to me. Listen hard now. In a few moments the law-enforcement people here who helped with parking will come up. They are going to take you with them. I can't stop them. You are the prime suspect."

"I didn't kill her. I loathed her, but I didn't kill her."

"For your sake, Tazio, I truly hope so. You'll need to compose yourself and go quietly. You'll have the opportunity to make one phone call to your lawyer."

"He's here. Ned."

"All right, then, I'll fetch him after they take you to jail. Say nothing, Tazio. I mean it. Say nothing until you can talk to Ned. I hope he can extradite you up to our facility, but I doubt it. You're in for a rough time. You have to be strong."

"God." Tazio swallowed more tears.

Cooper could see an officer walking

toward them. "I wonder if Little Mim alerted them. You know she's never without her cell. It's attached to her like an enema bag."

"You think I killed her, don't you?" Tazio gulped.

"I hope you didn't, but I can't let emotion sway the evidence. You were standing over the body with the knife in your right hand. Her wound indicates she was slashed by a right-hander. Of course, that's about ninety percent of the population. I have to do my job, Tazio."

"I understand." Tazio fought to control her emotions.

"I'm sorry."

"I am, too, but I swear to you by all that's holy, I did not kill Carla Paulson."

A young officer with a buzz cut arrived. Clearly this was the first murder victim he'd seen.

Cooper had to hold her tongue, because she almost said, "Cadet." Instead, she introduced herself, said her rank, and gave a brief rundown.

He quickly called a superior officer.

Cooper sighed for so many reasons, not the least of which was she had so looked forward to this evening.

"Who's he?" The cadet tilted his head in the direction of a man in white tie, standing off to the side out of Cooper's range of vision.

She said, "Lorenzo McCracken."

He stepped toward them and said, "This beautiful lady is my date. I worried when she didn't return to the table, so I came looking for her. When I perceived the situation, I thought it best not to disturb her since she was"—he thought a moment—"working."

Within minutes a gaggle of officers was there, including the sheriff. He'd had the presence of mind not to drive over the lawn or turn on sirens and lights.

Again Cooper recounted what she'd witnessed and how long she thought the victim had been dead.

The sheriff, Eli Grundy, knelt down, felt the side of Carla's neck. "You're right, Deputy, it couldn't have happened more than ten minutes before you found her." He stood back up, grass stains on his knees. He nodded at his deputy, who began reading the Miranda Act to Tazio. "Take her away."

Tazio said nothing but looked at Coop, and Coop smiled slightly.

"Sheriff, we'd better get back there before people leave," the novice said.

"Son, let me handle this," Sheriff Grundy grunted.

Cooper spoke up. "Currently, they know nothing and the speeches are about to begin, followed by dancing. If I might make a suggestion, Sheriff, it could save time."

Although not a fan of women in law enforcement, Eli Grundy had bowed to the inevitable. And this woman had done everything by the book, so he listened. "What?"

"If you and your men stayed unobtrusively in the background, that wouldn't be unusual. After all, you are security. Allow me, if you will, to go to each table and ask them to write on a napkin who was absent from their table during the time of the murder. The organizing committee has all the table names, so we don't need to waste time with that." She took a breath. "While it certainly appears that you have apprehended the murderer, it is possible there's an accomplice or more to it than meets the eye."

He pondered this. "And we can keep anyone from leaving."

"Right. If we go in now, with your people in uniform, and try to get this information, it will upset people. My experience is if they are calm they recall more clearly."

"We have to tell them."

"We do, Sheriff Grundy, but if I could secure this information first, I think you'll have much of what you need, in addition to the prime suspect. As Lorenzo and I are in evening clothes, we aren't going to arouse suspicion."

"Go ahead." He crossed his arms over his chest and for a moment wished he had someone that sharp on his force. He was staring at the novice officer when he thought that, but the kid had to learn sometime.

As Lorenzo walked with Cooper back to the tables, he said, "You're something, you know that?"

She didn't, really. She smiled and replied, "Thank you. You take the first twenty-five, I'll take the last. They can write on napkins."

"Good."

The two quickly went from table to table.

Cooper swept by Harry's table, Number 11, leaned down, and whispered into Ned's ear. "Tazio's being taken to jail. Can you help her?"

Ned's face registered surprise as he said, "Of course."

"You can't leave until the sheriff gives the all-clear. He's over under the south portico. Lorenzo and I will take Susan home."

"Okay." A grim look passed over Ned's face before he could rearrange his features as though this was a social conversation.

Within fifteen minutes Cooper and Lorenzo had scribbled-on napkins from each table.

Lorenzo returned to Table 11, while Cooper delivered the napkins to Sheriff Grundy.

"Thank you."

"Sheriff, the deceased's husband, Jurgen Paulson, is seated at Table One. He knows nothing except that his wife hasn't returned to the table for a half hour."

"I'll take care of it." The sheriff knew who Big Mim was, an Urquhart before her marriage, thanks to Cooper's tip-off. Like most Virginians of many generations, he knew his pedigrees. The Virginian—indeed, the Southern—obsession with blood seems silly, even punitive sometimes, to non-Southerners. However, Harry's grandmother and mother used to intone like a mantra, "Know your people." Knowing bloodlines meant you knew your people. While it could be used in the pettiest forms of snobbery, it could also be extremely useful. Certain traits, as well as certain medical conditions, tended to run in families. Socially, of course, the knowledge was invaluable.

The rich Urquharts had always been forces for progress and justice, even if high-handed in manner.

Given his station in life, Sheriff Grundy had not met Big Mim before. He looked at Cooper and smiled tightly. She'd helped him twice tonight. He'd remember.

Cooper memorized as many of the Albemarle County names as she could. Margaret Westlake, Kylie Kraft, Harvey Tillach, Ron Steinhauser, and Little Mim had left their tables. She made a rhyme out of it, hoping the names from her county wouldn't drop out of memory. The people she had already thought of knew Dr. Wylde. The minute she had a chance, she'd write all this down.

As Jurgen Paulson strode toward the dais, an officer came up and gently led him away.

Folly Steinhauser, who was announcing

the names for thanks, looked down to behold the sheriff walking toward her. She hoped she could finish her thank-yous.

He waited. She concluded and held her hand over the mic and said, “Sheriff.”

“I need to address the folks, ma’am, and I need you to help keep order.”

“Something’s wrong, isn’t it? That scream.”

“I’m afraid it is, ma’am.”

He stepped up to the mic, his very pleasant voice contained in the tone of command. “Ladies and gentlemen, we ask for your forbearance and cooperation tonight. There has been an unfortunate occurrence. We have, we believe, apprehended the perpetrator. It is my duty to inform you that Mrs. Jurgen Paulson has been murdered—” The crowd gasped. He continued, “If anyone feels they have information relevant to this event, please contact one of my men.” He swept his arm and, as if by magic, the uniformed officers stepped forward. “I know this will spoil this very special occasion, and I’m sorry for it. No one will be allowed to leave until I tell you to do so.”

The moment he released the mic, Folly stepped up to it. “Will the organizing committee please raise your hands? Sheriff, if you need any of us to help expedite matters, we are only too willing to serve."

He nodded thanks. The place exploded with talk. Kylie Kraft screamed and then fainted. Sophie fanned her. Margaret said to her husband, "One murder too many for Kylie." He replied, "High-strung."

Sophie rejoined, "Young," as Kylie's eyelids fluttered. Once they sat her up she asked for a cigarette, which made Margaret laugh.

Kylie, smoking from a pack of borrowed Marlboros, lit one with the stub of another.

Thanks to Cooper's securing of names, the brief questioning at each table proceeded with efficiency. Within an hour, the initial questioning was completed, and the gathering was dismissed.

Crestfallen, Folly slumped in her seat, watching people stream out to their cars.

"Cheer up, Folly, you raised a great deal of money," Big Mim said as she stopped by on her way out. "And no one will ever, ever forget the event."

Smiling weakly, Folly replied, "I guess not."

At Table 11, Cooper took Susan in tow as Ned hurried to the Audi wagon.

"I can't believe Tazio killed her," Harry stated flatly.

Cooper, tired by now, replied sharply, "Harry, she was standing over the body with a dripping knife in her hand. People we like, we admire, can do terrible things."

"Not Taz." Harry was going to say more, but Fair squeezed her arm and said to Cooper, "You know how Harry is. If it were you, she'd be on your side. Seems you rarely get a break, Coop. Here it was to be a night of dancing and you wind up working."

Cooper, appreciating Fair's sensitivity, touched his shoulder. "Thanks." As Lorenzo touched her elbow she apologized, "I am so sorry. I've hardly asked you one thing about yourself. Please forgive me."

He smiled gently. "No apology needed, and if you will allow me, I'll give you plenty of time to ask me questions."

Suddenly, Cooper didn't think her evening had been spoiled at all.

19

Most of the country people attended the first service at St. Luke's or whatever church they attended. The town and suburban people usually went to the eleven o'clock service.

Big Mim, Jim, Aunt Tally, Harry, Fair, Little Mim, Blair, Alicia, and BoomBoom gathered in Big Mim's living room at eleven.

The door opened without a knock. "Sorry," Susan apologized. "Folly Steinhauser waylaid me about Ned representing Tazio." Her mouth was running as she came into the light-filled room. "She can talk when she wants to, that woman."

"Where is Ned?" Big Mim inquired.

"On his way back down to Bedford County."

Paul slipped in by the back door. He attended the Catholic church.

Jim threw his arms around the wiry young man. "Paul, we'll get her out of there. Hold on, buddy, hold on."

"You know she didn't kill that woman." The worry made him appear ten years older.

A moment of silence followed this cry from the heart, then Harry concurred. "That's why we're here, Paul."

Aunt Tally, hands on cane as she sat in a satin-striped wing chair, said, "Even if she did, we'll do all we can to reduce the sentence." Noting the horror on Paul's face, she quickly added, "But I don't think she did."

"Never. Never would Tazio kill anything. She won't even kill a spider."

"Where's Brinkley?" Harry thought of the yellow lab.

"With me." Paul took a seat, being guided there by Jim.

Gretchen, the majordomo, brought in a large tray of tidbits. On the Sheraton sideboard, coffee percolated in an enormous silver pot, a handsome teapot beside it. People served themselves.

Once everyone was seated, Big Mim conducted the meeting per usual. She found herself missing Miranda, who had an uncanny sense of people's inner workings. But Miranda at this very moment would be lifting her golden voice in the Church of the Holy Light's choir, since the choir performed at both services. Well, she could be counted on when need be.

"I wish I'd noticed who else was there. There were short lines." Little Mim was mad at herself for not being alert when she had used the bathroom at the ball.

"How could you know? That's the thing about a dreadful event, one has no idea what may be significant." Big Mim was soothing, part of it due to her former intransigence over what she deemed her daughter's political foolishness.

Big Mim could be flexible, could change her mind. Rare it was, but it did happen.

"Cooper collected the names of everyone who had left the tables. I wonder if she looked at them," Fair said.

"Bet she did." Harry leaned back, balancing her teacup and saucer as she did so.

"Carla has been—or had been—provoking Tazio for months," Paul spoke up. "She probably provoked others. It's one of the others who killed her."

"She provoked Mike McElvoy on a daily basis." Harry put in her two cents.

"He deserves it," Susan simply said.

"We're about to find out ourselves," Blair mentioned. "We hoped we'd get Tony Long as our inspector, but, no, we landed Mr."—he was about to utter a profanity and then substituted—"Jerk."

Fair smiled slightly at him for being quick-witted.

Big Mim decried profanity. Profanity delighted Aunt Tally, who would pepper her comments with some just to see the sulfur hiss out of her niece's bejeweled ears.

"Balls." Aunt Tally lived up to her reputation.

"Aunt Tally." Big Mim stared crossly at her.

"I mean Mike McElvoy doesn't have the balls to kill anyone." She sniffed. "Don't trust him, though. He's like a trombone slightly off-key, but I can't identify what's weird, what's off."

For a moment everyone looked at Aunt Tally, for she had expressed something each had felt.

"On the take?" Fair put his hands on his knees. "It would be so easy to do."

"You mean find problems and then shake down the owner, maybe even the construction boss?" Harry, even though not an idealist, was always upset when a public servant proved crooked.

"Lord," Little Mim simply said. "That makes perfect sense."

"How can we find out?" Big Mim asked. "Is it possible that Carla was being . . . ? It's not blackmail, I guess, it's theft, pure and simple. Maybe Tazio found out." She was puzzled. "And, well, I know this sounds crazy, but Carla was such a drama queen when Will Wylde was killed. It kind of makes one wonder if there's a connection."

"I don't see how," Susan replied, then returned to the subject of Mike. "If Carla was getting squeezed, she wouldn't want anyone to know. Pride."

"Goeth before a fall." Aunt Tally tapped her cane once on the floor, then added, "But if Carla had had an abortion, she wouldn't want anyone to know, either. Yet another fall."

"She may not be the only one to fall on both counts." Fair's mind whirred. "If Mike is dishonest, and I'm not saying he is, but for the purposes of discussion—"

Aunt Tally interrupted, “You don’t have to hedge your bets. We’re family here.”

“Thank you for that singular honor.” He inclined his head toward Aunt Tally, who was thrilled at the male attention.

“Mike crawls through a great many extremely expensive new houses built by new people. Because they don’t understand our ways, they’re vulnerable. Their first impulse is to sue. Right?” Everyone nodded in agreement. “It stands to reason that an outright bribe might not be the wisest policy for Mike.”

“What do you mean?” Big Mim was fascinated.

Harry replied. “However he did it, Mike was putting the squeeze on Carla by finding things wrong in the house.” She paused. “He couldn’t come out directly and ask for a payoff or he’d find himself in court.”

“How does this relate to Taz?” Paul’s purpose was single-minded, as befitted a man in love.

“I don’t know.” Fair put his hands together. “I wish I did, but I do know she didn’t kill Carla.”

“Could a woman have slashed Carla’s throat?” Little Mim asked.

"Why not?" Harry shrugged. "You can slice the jugular without hitting the neckbones."

"It's not as easy as you think," Fair said. "It takes force. Muscle is thick, especially living muscle. It's not like cutting into a steak. But a woman could surely do it."

"According to Ned, who asked the Bedford County sheriff, Carla faced her attacker. The blood covered her bosoms, the front of her dress, her left arm. But he said, and this surprised me, her right arm was untouched." Susan paused. "She didn't defend herself. Didn't throw her arm up."

"Maybe Carla didn't have time to defend herself." Big Mim thought of the seconds of terror Carla must have felt.

"Possible." Jim seconded his wife's opinion.

"Or she knew her attacker and discounted him or her," Harry added. "She may not have liked whomever she was talking with but she didn't fear him."

A long silence followed this.

"Question Folly, Penny, and Elise Brennan. They've all built huge houses in the last year or added onto what they have," Aunt Tally suggested.

"Why would they tell the truth?" Boom-Boom spoke at last. She'd been drinking in everything, as had Alicia.

"Why not?" Aunt Tally held a hand palm up.

"No one likes looking the fool," Big Mim countered.

"What if what he asked for wasn't money, wasn't material?" Alicia surprised them.

"Influence peddling?" Jim thought in political terms.

"Sex." Alicia was brisk.

"What?" Fair couldn't believe it, but then again, women had thrown themselves at him ever since puberty. He couldn't fathom men who had trouble with women—well, trouble attracting them.

"Happens all the time in Hollywood. At least, it did when I was there. I escaped because I was protected, first by Mary Pat and then by my first husband."

Mary Pat Reines had been Alicia's first lover, who taught her manners, diction, foxhunting, and quiet grace.

"But these women are—" Susan stopped herself.

"What?" Harry found herself suddenly irritated, angry, really.

"Why would they? They're rich, all quite good looking, looks on which they've spent a small fortune. Why?" Susan finished her thought, glad that Harry had interrupted her, because Big Mim had certainly made use of plastic surgery's advances. She hadn't wanted to insult Big Mim in any way.

"It's not what they have and how they look, it's how they feel." BoomBoom knew women very well. "Doesn't seem to me that any of them are in very happy marriages, and Elise is divorced. No one would be the wiser if they paid Mike off in the oldest way possible."

"You know, that's really, truly disgusting. I'd tear his face off," Harry blurted out.

"You would." Fair smiled.

"Most women lack your self-regard, Harry." BoomBoom looked levelly at her. "I don't mean conceit, I mean regard. And you are very strong, as am I. Most women purposefully keep their upper bodies weak because they think that's attractive to men. Obviously you've never been to a gym where women working out with a trainer fret that their muscles will get too big. Can you imagine a poor farm woman in Nebraska in 1880 worrying about muscles?"

"Or a poor woman in Virginia or a slave woman working in the fields. All our ideas of female beauty are based on privilege. I should know. I'm very privileged." Aunt Tally had often thought such things but had not discussed them, so BoomBoom's remark triggered hers.

"If Mike leaned on them in some fashion, threatened them physically or because he knew, say, Carla was having an affair, he'd get what he wanted," Alicia said, steering them back on track.

"Money would be easier." Jim noticed Gretchen out of the corner of his eye and nodded slightly.

She came in, took the tray, soon replaced it with another.

"I wish Herb were here. He hears things." Little Mim sighed.

"He won't be free until late afternoon. Not on a Sunday. And even though he hears things, he often can't tell us." Big Mim pressed her lips together. "It could be that Mike killed Carla, if this theory holds water." She turned to her aunt. "I know you don't think he has the courage, but if he was frightened of exposure, he could kill. Most people could."

"It's possible," Aunt Tally agreed, although not convinced.

"And Tazio had the bad luck to find Carla right afterward," Paul half-moaned.

"There's something so wrong, so bizarre, and I can't even imagine what it is." Harry was dumbfounded.

"We've got to get Tazio out of jail," Paul pleaded.

With some tenderness, Big Mim counseled, "Paul, we all understand your distress. For someone of Tazio's breeding and sensibility to be in such an environment is outrageous, but," she waited for a dramatic moment, "she may be safer in there for now. If Mike really did kill Carla, Tazio could get in his way. You know she's sitting in that cell trying to put the puzzle together, and she may not come up with all the jigsaw pieces we have, but she'll come up with a few. We have to root this out first. We don't need two murders."

"We already have two." Aunt Tally gleefully took the martini that Blair had made for her.

His mother-in-law's eyes had watched him as he rose and walked to the bar, but

Blair had learned by living close to Aunt Tally that it was better to keep her happy.

"How can we find out if Mike took bribes or forced women into sex?" Susan was ready to go to work.

"I think Rick can look into his bank account without arousing opposition. Mike doesn't have to know. It's not kosher, but, well . . ." Jim's voice trailed off.

"What about a safety-deposit box?" Alicia asked.

"That might be more difficult. His accounts can be called up on a computer," Blair told them. "And there is the problem of the second key for a safety-deposit box."

"They have skeleton keys," Aunt Tally posited.

"No doubt, but one step at a time. He's not accused of a crime, and if he's tipped off, we'll never get to the bottom of it, at least where he's concerned." Fair comprehended the delicacy of the situation.

"You think after what happened, if it is Mike, that Folly, Penny, and Elise aren't nervous? They might be ready to talk." Harry was hopeful.

"If so, I'd hope they'd go to Rick," Big Mim said.

"That's just it. If they go to Rick, they let their cat out of the bag, don't they?" Harry began to feel that odd tingle when she'd get hooked on a problem. "Susan, let's go back to Poplar Forest tomorrow and look in the daylight."

"We'll go with you," BoomBoom volunteered.

Monday was one of Fair's operating days, so he wouldn't be making the trip.

"Ears open. Come back to me with what you learn," Big Mim requested. "Susan, have they set bail yet?"

"Tomorrow."

Big Mim turned to Paul. "The bail will be very stiff. A couple of hundred thousand, I think. I agree that we need to get her out of there but, as I said before, not right away. It will take time to raise the bail, and then we have to secure her safety. This could get a lot worse before it gets better." She then addressed her aunt, who was visibly improving from the effects of her martini, the little olive resting comfortably at the bottom of the glass. "You're right, there have been two murders, but Will's killer is in jail and he'll never see daylight as a free man again."

"Still, it's very strange, two murders so

close together." The old woman considered it.

"Happens all the time in big cities. It's a jolt for us. But at least one murder is solved. Now we've got to solve this one." Jim, who'd bulked up over the years, loomed over the room, a large presence but a genial one.

"I don't like it." Aunt Tally closed the matter.

As they broke up to chat before leaving, Harry asked Aunt Tally, "Where's your date?"

"Home in bed. I wore him out." She plucked the olive out of her martini, popping it into her mouth.

20

Poplar Forest reflected Jefferson's love of the octagon. The main entrance welcomed the visitor with seven wide steps. Four Tuscan columns, severe in their simplicity, supported a simple pediment with a fanlight in the center and, above that, a balustrade. A simple door with two twelve-paned windows on either side completed the entrance.

Poplar Forest had not been built to inspire awe. This was no Sans Souci nor even a Trianon. The structure reflected the cleansing Palladian ideal. For Jefferson, this strict elegance was to be the externalization of the American political philosophy: a people's nation, not one in thrall to the hereditary principle.

He succeeded.

Harry and Susan wound up coming alone

because, at the last minute, Alicia's housekeeper suffered a wicked angina attack and Alicia had rushed her to the hospital. BoomBoom drove over to Alicia's to finish feeding the foals. Although Alicia could and did hire good people, she liked to manage the mares and foals herself. She'd learned so much from Mary Pat those thirty years ago. Mostly, Alicia learned she couldn't live without horses. The longer she stayed in Hollywood, the more films she made, the more acclaim she received, the lonelier she ultimately felt. She came home to the warm estate willed to her by Mary Pat Reines. Alicia, in her mid-fifties, had shed two husbands over the years, so returning to the place of her greatest happiness was easy. When she landed in Crozet, she felt light as a feather.

Harry wished she had Alicia with her today, because the gorgeous star had an original manner of seeing things, things Harry missed.

Formidable as Harry's powers of logic could be, she missed emotional nuance more often than not. The broad strokes, she saw, but the tiny feathered strokes on the emotional canvas, she missed. Alicia missed nothing; Fair missed very little, too.

They'd arrived at seven in the morning, being indulged by the director, Robert Taney, who had known Harry's mother in his youth. Mrs. Minor's great love of history—of telling the stories of the past through the lives of people instead of dates and battles—had inspired him to study history, specializing in architectural history. Thus began the journey that was to culminate in his directorship at Poplar Forest.

Harry and Susan had known it would be best if they got there before the doors opened to the public.

The two women had risen at four-thirty and hit the road at five-fifteen. They were slowed by dense fog in the swales as well as over the Upper James River, but they made it on the button.

Their footfalls echoed in the foyer.

"It's been trying," Robert admitted.

"Shocking." Susan glanced at the smooth walls. "Why commit such a heinous act at the fund-raiser? Surely Carla could have been dispatched on another day. Not that I'm countenancing murder."

Robert, glad that he'd worn a good cotton sweater because of a chill that still permeated the air, nodded. "I know what you mean. It's almost as though she wanted us to fail. After all her work."

"Tazio didn't kill Carla Paulson." Harry clasped her hands behind her back. "I know it looks like she did, but she didn't. I think in her shock and confusion, she picked up the knife. But no matter, she didn't kill Carla, and I don't care how it looks. That's why we're here, as you know. If we could look around." Harry spied a striped shape blurring past her. "How'd you get out?"

Robert saw a gray shape behind him.

Tucker walked in and sat down. *"Hello."*

"I'm sorry. I'll fetch them." Harry sighed.

"Don't worry about it. We still have the pack rats living here. Maybe those two cats will give them a scare."

"Pack rats are big. Might be the other way around." Tucker giggled.

They left the central room and entered the east bedroom.

Mrs. Murphy and Pewter, rapt and standing on their hind legs, sniffed at the exposed pack-rat living quarters.

"How'd you all get out?" Harry demanded, for Susan had parked under a tree, leaving the windows open only a crack.

Pewter, without taking her eyes off the pack-rat home, replied, *"We have our ways."*

Mrs. Murphy had learned to open doors by practicing in the old 1978 Ford truck. She'd press down on the indoor latch but not push the door all the way open, lest Harry discover the secret. She also stood on her hind legs on the aftermarket running board and yanked the door handle down. The door would then swing open and Mrs. Murphy would run away. When Harry would return to her truck or walk by, she worried that her memory was failing her, since she was sure she hadn't opened the door.

"We? You don't do a thing. I'm the one who can open the car door," the tiger said with slight disgust.

Robert walked over to where the cats stood. "Even the rats are architects here. It's almost like a pink-chambered nautilus, isn't it?" He pointed to successive chambers, each holding treasures. "When we started the restoration in this room, we found all these items. Generations after generations of rats lived here. We left their wealth." He smiled.

In each chamber, the forage of that generation of rats reposed—in some cases, glittered. An amethyst earring in one chamber dated to about 1821. Bits of paper, orange rind, a few apple seeds, all in neat piles, testified to the expert taste and thievery of the rats. They didn't consider this thievery. If the humans were going to leave things lying around and those items might be useful or pretty, then a rat had every right to liberate it.

"How pretty." Harry pointed to a pearl stud.

"1890 or thereabouts. Same family." Robert looked closer. "The human ownership changed, but these fellows are descended from, dare I say, Jefferson's rats."

"I can kill a rat with one big bite," Pewter bragged.

"You can't even catch the blue jay." Mrs. Murphy dropped back on all fours.

"Who can? Birds fly. Rats run, and I can run faster than any rat." Pewter also dropped to all fours.

A tittering from afar alerted the cats and dog that wild creatures still made Poplar Forest home. They sped off to locate the sound.

"Were the doors locked?" Susan asked.

"No." Robert walked back to the central

room and then into the western bedroom. "We had Melvin here. Melvin Rankin is on our staff. In retrospect, I should have placed two people here for each floor."

"There's no way you could have known," Susan said consolingly.

"No, I know that, but still . . ." He paused. "The staff has worked so very hard. I didn't want to take the night away from them. We had security. I just never imagined . . ." His voice strengthened again. "But I felt that one of us should be in the house, not a member of the sheriff's department."

"Why Melvin?" Harry inquired.

"He's a shy fellow. I don't know why—he's a good-looking man, mid-twenties, just out of William and Mary. Anyway, Melvin wasn't up to such a huge party, but he was happy to be in the house, to watch and listen to the music."

"Did he see anything?" Harry pushed on.

"He thought he heard the front door close. He walked to the door but didn't see anything. Not in the house. He looked out the window and saw Carla walking toward the center of the lawn."

"Melvin might not have seen anyone because, if the killer stood right up against the front door, well, you wouldn't see him, would you?" To prove her point, Harry opened the front door, stepped outside, closed the door behind her, and flattened herself against it.

Susan looked out one window, Robert the other. They could just see the tip of her boots as she stood inside the recessed doorway. But they knew she was there. Otherwise, they'd have missed her.

She came back in. "Possible."

"Yes." Robert nodded.

"Did the sheriff think of this?" Susan wondered.

"Well, no, but he questioned Melvin. The killer could have been in the house. If we go outside and check where both lines of Porta-Johns were, you'll get a better idea."

Once outside, Robert walked to the east, where the mist was lifting. "We put a line here, out of the way but easy for the company renting them to pick them up." He strode across the lawn and toward the parking lot. "Another line here, and then we had one single unit behind the platform, for the musicians and if anyone got nervous before their speech."

"Nervous?" Harry didn't put two and two together.

Susan laughed. "Some people have to wee. You know, they get scared, and, well . . ."

"Ah, well, I don't give public addresses."

"You took public speaking in high school. I was there. You were pretty good." Susan counted the depressions on the grass where the toilets had been. "How many altogether?"

"Twenty-five. I thought that was overkill, but Tazio and Folly declared it wasn't and nothing was worse than waiting in line. They were right: we could have done with thirty. Well, excuse me, twenty-six counting the one behind the platform."

"Did anyone see Tazio come from the Porta-John?" Harry inquired.

"I don't know. The sheriff hasn't made me privy, excuse the pun, to his information." Robert sighed.

"Little Mim did," Susan stated. "Ned asked Tazio if anyone saw her. Remember, she left the table early because she knew the timetable and wanted to be clear of everyone and to be ready for the speeches. Ned checked with Little Mim, who said she did see Tazio as she was entering one green box, Harvey Tillach another. But Harvey came out before Tazio did, since men can, well, go a lot faster than women."

The Porta-Johns were green.

"She could have waited behind a tree afterward. I suppose she could have gone into the house." Robert believed Tazio had done the deed.

"We can't dismiss a committee member." Harry didn't censor herself. "Or even a staff member from the possibility of committing the murder."

"There's no reason whatsoever for one of my people to do such a terrible thing." Robert was tetchy.

"Forgive her. She gets like this when she's seized by a notion or a mystery."

"Huh? I do. I'm sorry, Robert. I can't think of any reason why someone who is part of this incredible project would want to do anything like this, but then, that's the key to solving a crime, isn't it?"

"What?" the attractive, well-turned-out man asked.

"Motive, opportunity, will to kill. If you figure that out, you can almost always find who did it. Motive. Tazio did have a motive, in that she hated Carla—well, hate is a strong word. Carla got on her nerves."

"It's rather an extreme way to soothe the nerves," Robert slyly said.

"She had the opportunity," Susan added.

"Did she have the will to kill?" Harry put her hand on her hip. "No. Emphatically no. She's at the top of her game, she's well respected, she's making very good money, and she's in love with a great-looking, terrific guy who loves her back. She'd have to be certifiably insane to muck that up."

"Is she impulsive?"

Susan shook her head no as the words came out of Robert's mouth. "If anything she's too controlled. Too cool. It's completely out of character."

"People do fool you," Robert replied simply.

"They do, but if Tazio had cut Carla's jugular, given the force of the first pulsations, wouldn't her dress have blood on it?" Harry, ever logical, asked.

"Not if she jumped out of the way fast enough," Robert came back, although chances were the killer couldn't have gotten out of the way fast enough.

"But she'd have to have some knowledge

of how the jugular shoots. I mean, it really shoots, and I know that because my husband is a vet, but he has had to work on people in extreme situations."

"Harry, most people know if you cut an artery it spurts. They may not know how much and how far the jugular can spurt, but it's not a secret. Whoever killed her faced her, then jumped away." Susan bought the idea.

"Do they know she wasn't surprised from behind?" Robert rubbed his chin.

"Sheriff Grundy believes she was killed face to face. And she didn't defend herself." Harry told him what they'd all discussed prior. "She wasn't scared."

"Not until the knife flashed." Robert shuddered. "It's too awful."

"It is, but if you knew Carla you would understand how she could provoke it." Susan was beginning to wonder where the pets were.

"Isn't the spouse a suspect? I mean, it's usually people we know well who kill us." Robert was right.

"Jurgen? He was at the table." Susan had gathered some of the table information from Ned, who, wisely, had called each table head; he knew he wouldn't be getting the napkins with names on them.

"Ah." Robert seemed disappointed.

"He's rich. He could have paid someone." Harry couldn't explain why, but she was feeling better, feeling she could clear Tazio with a bit of luck and a lot of hard work.

"And this was a good place. Activity, enough alcohol to raise the spirits and maybe dull the senses. The moon was about full, but in the front of the house the trees provided some cover and there were no artificial lights. It was a good place for someone bold with a plan." Harry looked around one more time. "Robert, I know we've disrupted you and your routine. Thank you for helping us."

"Not at all. I want to get to the bottom of this, too. Anything that touches Poplar Forest is critical to me. I love this place. You know," a wistful note crept into his voice, "I imagine I can hear Jefferson sometimes, the slaves, the horses. Oh, it's silly, but when I'm here alone, I feel them."

Susan remarked, "At least you said slaves and not servants."

"Our ancestors put a good face on it."

Robert thought about slavery quite a lot, since he could see so much evidence of those long-ago lives. It hadn't been plowed under or paved over.

"The hard-nosed could always use the Bible to justify it." Susan knew her history, as did the other two.

"Yeah, but I think most people felt something . . . oh, I don't have the word, but something. Virginia would have had to end it." Harry was convinced of that, perhaps rightly. "The Mid-Atlantic states would have done it probably before the turn of the century, but the Delta, probably not."

"Hopefully, folks would have put a stop to it before 1900." Susan thought Harry's time frame too long.

"I don't know. It's like a nuclear reaction, isn't it? You reach a critical mass. Then boom! I hope you're right and it would have ended earlier." She stopped herself from musing further. "Robert, you're a Virginian, as are we. You may have noticed that Tazio is part African-American."

"I noticed she was beautiful and, yes, African-American—to what percent, I don't know."

"Do you think she'll encounter trouble in

jail or in court if we can't spring her before a trial?" Harry was worried.

"God, Harry, I hope we're past that in Bedford County."

"They're racist in Boston." Susan, anger in her voice, started back toward the house. "But the South takes the rap for it; we're the scapegoat. Do you know they still had slaves in Delaware after the war's end?"

"Lose a war and all sins are heaped on your head. That's just the way it is." Harry accepted that.

"Makes you wonder if we'll ever know the truth about Japan or Germany, doesn't it?" Robert shrewdly remarked. "Not that both countries weren't guilty of creating hell on earth, but it does become difficult to accept official histories when every American is a hero and saint, every German a bloodthirsty Nazi, every Japanese screaming, 'Banzai,' or whatever they are reputed to have screamed. I become dispirited."

"Don't." Harry suddenly smiled. "We're still swallowing lies from the War of the Roses, and that was in the fifteenth century. Never ends. I just nod, smile, and go on my way. But I do try to read original sources and not interpretations when I have time.

Character is fate. Character creates history. That's why I believe, believe like a fanatic, that Tazio did not kill Carla Paulson. It makes no sense in terms of character."

Back in the house, the three musketeers located the tittering. It came from behind a wall in the large room behind the south portico.

"I know you're in there." Pewter slashed her tail back and forth.

"We know you're out there," a deep voice responded.

"Big." Tucker's ears moved as far forward as they could go.

"Show yourself," Mrs. Murphy requested. *"We've seen the work of your ancestors. I suppose you are all FRV, First Rats of Virginia."*

"Of course we are, you silly twits." Another voice answered, this one slightly higher.

"Did you see anyone in here the night of the murder?" Mrs. Murphy got right to the point.

"Three hundred people," the deep voice replied, and then a sleek nose and clean whiskers appeared just underneath the win-

dow west of the door out to the south portico.

Pewter began to wiggle her hind end, but Mrs. Murphy commanded, *"Don't."*

"You can try, fatso," the male rat taunted. *"I'll duck back in here so fast . . ."*

"Sooner or later the humans will find this opening." Tucker peered at the spot.

"Doesn't matter. They'll close it up, we'll chew a new one. We know this place better than they do," he sassed.

"What if they put out rat poison?" Pewter sounded tough.

"What? Kill Mr. Jefferson's rats? Heaven forbid," he joked.

"Was anyone in here? Anyone besides the staff person?" Mrs. Murphy kept to business.

"Melvin spent most of the night with his face pressed to the window—until the murder, that is." The female voice chimed in, and now she stuck her head out.

"Did you see anyone else?" Tucker sounded pleasant.

"No, someone was here, though, because when we went downstairs—we have passages everywhere, you know, we don't have to show ourselves—well, anyway, I

found a cigarette. Fresh. Hadn't been smoked." The female rat was jubilant.

"My wife likes to chew tobacco, and it gets harder to find these days."

"Randolph, they don't have to know that," she chided him, then by way of explanation said, *"Soothes my nerves. You try living with him."*

"You didn't see the person. It could be Melvin's cigarette." Tucker made conversation.

"Oh, no, no one is allowed to smoke in here. Even the workmen have to stop and go outside for a smoke or a chew. Then again, not as many people smoke as they did in Grandma's day." The lady rat, Sarah, sounded sorrowful about that. *"Even Melvin, who smokes, doesn't cheat and smoke in the house when he's here alone."*

"You say you found it downstairs?" Mrs. Murphy asked again.

"Not a puff." She beamed.

"Well, maybe whoever ducked inside knew there was no smoking," Tucker posited.

"Maybe." Pewter's brain started turning over, but she was behind Murphy. *"Then again, maybe they needed to move on and put it aside."*

"Where'd you find it?" Tucker inquired.

"On the floor. It might have been on the table and rolled off. Right by the corner it was, very convenient to snatch up." She came out the whole way now, and she was quite sleek, gray and fat. *"You know, Randolph and I and our ancestors have even more treasures than what they've found in the bedroom wall. They'll never find ours, though. We learned when they started removing walls."*

Mrs. Murphy, surprised at how big the rats were, remembered the conversation Cooper had had in Harry's kitchen. *"Ma'am, do you remember what brand it is?"*

"Virginia Slims."

Little Mim drove down the long, twisting drive of Rose Hill. She liked picking up the mail, delivered in the afternoon, and sorting it. Aunt Tally, awash in magazines, would read them quickly and pass them on to Little Mim and Blair. They need never fill out a subscription form again.

She lifted the rubber-band-bound bundle and tossed it in the car. Then she pulled out that day's magazine haul, which totaled six,

not including one from the National Rifle Association. Although the magazine was improving, it was so thin she thought of it as a colorful pamphlet.

She drove to the main house, put Aunt Tally's magazines on the table in the front main hall, then started sorting the mail.

A blue airmail envelope with her name on it caught her eye. She slit it open with her fingernail and read. Her face turned white, her hands shook, and she stuffed the letter in her pocket.

21

Along the southeastern side of her house, Big Mim had planted hundreds of hydrangeas of all manner in the gardens. Even though they had been long out of fashion, Big Mim loved them, so she planted them. Now that hydrangeas had come back in a big way, people cooed over the massive white, blue, pink, and purple heads.

One of the secrets to her success was that fifteen years ago she'd supervised the digging of narrow trenches, a foot and three-quarters deep. She had placed leaky pipe—piping with tiny holes—there.

Although despite her best efforts it took years for the lawn and the garden to recover from this scarring, the leaky pipe proved a godsend in the long run. Watering was no longer a chore.

She'd dutifully go out and give everything a little spray so the leaves could drink, too, but the leaky pipe was the key.

Standing in the afternoon sun as it washed over her gardens this Monday, she heard a car coming down the drive.

Pressman, her young springer spaniel, heard it first and bounded to the front to greet Little Mim.

Absentmindedly, Little Mim bent down to pet the exuberant dog, who was a beauty.

Little Mim figured her mother, a creature of order, would be in the gardens, since she usually did her weeding, planting, and thinking then. She walked around to the back of the house.

"Aren't they stupendous?" Big Mim swept her arm toward the hydrangeas.

"They are." Little Mim watched a black swallowtail flutter to the massing of butterfly bushes. "Mother, I have to talk to you."

Noting her daughter's grim visage, Big Mim removed her floppy straw hat and said, "Would you like to sit on the bench under the weeping willow? It's so refreshing out this afternoon."

"Yes, fine." Little Mim, glad to be in comfortable espadrilles, took long strides toward the long bench, a copy of an eighteenth-century English one.

"Fight with Blair?"

"No, no, he's an angel." She reached into her skirt pocket, pulling out the blue envelope. "I received this in the mail."

Big Mim used her clear-coated fingernail to tease out the thin paper, same blue as the envelope. She read the two lines:

Put $100,000 in the
Love of Life Fund by this Friday.
If you don't, I'll talk.
Jonathan Bechtal

She dropped her hand, the letter still in her fingers, to her lap. "Have you paid him before?"

The speed of her mother's mind always surprised Little Mim. Her own mind, which was good, very good, couldn't work as quickly as her mother's.

"Yes."

"Before Will Wylde's murder." Big Mim again studied the letter.

"Yes."

"Why didn't you tell me? I would have helped you."

"Mother, it's not about the money."

"Blackmail is always about money—and shame." Her light-brown eyes flickered, a flash of sympathy, for she knew she wasn't a warm person.

She wasn't the easiest person to confide in. She would have kept Little Mim's secret, but her daughter did not feel especially close to her mother emotionally and hadn't opened her heart to her.

Miranda would throw her arms around Little Mim, would comfort her and pray with her, if necessary. Big Mim thought first.

"Well . . ." Little Mim took a deep breath, her bosom heaving upward under her pale-yellow camp shirt. "I had an abortion my sophomore year in college. I couldn't tell you. I couldn't."

Big Mim's voice was soft. "Honey, I was one of those women who fought for reproductive control."

"Mother, somehow I don't think it's the same when it's your own daughter."

"I'm sorry." Big Mim meant it. "I'm sorry you felt you couldn't come to me. How you've carried this all these years."

Tears rolled down Little Mim's cheeks as her mother reached for her hand. "I was stupid." She wiped away the tears with her free left hand. "I got drunk at a fraternity party, and I don't even remember going to bed with my date. Obviously, I did."

"Can you still have children? Sometimes . . ." Her voice trailed off.

Little Mim nodded. "Yes." Then she said, "I never wanted to, because I thought I was a terrible person. First I did what I did, and then I had an abortion. I believe 'slut' is the word. And to Jonathan, I am a murderer."

"You're not."

"Mother, I don't know. Even now when I think about that time, I feel like I've fallen into a cesspool of guilt."

"Darling, I am sorry. I am so, so sorry." She looked down, turned over the envelope. "Marilyn, this wasn't sent from prison."

Little Mim, wiping away more tears, took the envelope from her mother's hand. "22905. That's the Barracks Road Shopping Center post office."

"I assume Will Wylde performed the termination." Big Mim was trying to put the pieces together.

Little Mim sucked in her breath. "Bechtal must have the records." Her right hand flew up to her temple, envelope and paper still in it. "Mother, what can I do?"

"We must see Rick at once."

"This could destroy my political career."

Big Mim removed the letter from her daughter's hand and folded the paper, slipping it back into the envelope. "You have to take that chance. By some great stroke of fortune, this may not be made public."

"I doubt that. I've been in office only two years and already the Democrats poke for any chink in my armor." She smiled ruefully. "I've been good at my work, so they haven't found any, but this, this . . ." She then said, "I kept my mouth shut about the fanatical right wing of the party. That will be my undoing."

"You didn't kiss their ass in Macy's window, excuse the vulgar expression." Big Mim rarely descended to same.

"No, but I sure kept my mouth shut about abortion."

"I don't know what to tell you about that, because I don't feel the way you do."

"You never had one."

"No, I did not, but I think I know myself well enough to know I wouldn't feel guilty. I believe life starts when you emerge from the womb—sentient life, if you will. Anyway, nothing I can say will ever convince the opponents of abortion, nor vice versa, but if I could think of something to say to dispel your malaise, I would."

"Malaise? Mother, it's gold-plated guilt."

"I don't mean to make light of it. Does Blair know?"

Little Mim shook her head again. "No. There was no reason to tell him."

"I think you must."

"I will."

"Are you worried about him?"

"No. I don't expect any man likes to hear about his wife's sex life before him, even if it was in college, but Blair's open-minded. I mean, he's not one to trumpet that double standard."

"Who was it who said that if men could get pregnant, abortion would be a sacrament? Gloria Steinem?" Big Mim studied the postmark again.

"I don't know." Little Mim bent over to read the postmark, too. "Friday, September twenty-sixth. Mother, how did he get these letters out?"

"He didn't. There's a partner on the outside. There has to be." She slapped the envelope on her knee, which made Pressman's head swivel from the cowbird he was watching. "How much have you paid?"

"Nothing."

"No, Marilyn, before this?"

"The threats started three months ago. Each time the demand was for ten thousand dollars. I paid by postal note made out to Jonathan Bechtal. Not even a cashier's check."

"How?"

"I sent it to Jonathan Bechtal, care of Love of Life, P.O. Box Fifteen, Charlottesville, Virginia. That is a legitimate organization."

"So to speak," Big Mim wryly commented.

"What do you mean?"

"You know how I feel about charities. The accounting rules differ from Chapter C corporations, and more to the point, it's so bloody easy to steal in so many ways that someone whose IQ would make a good golf score could easily enrich themselves. I'd be willing to bet ten thousand dollars myself that what you paid dropped into someone's pocket."

"Jonathan Bechtal, but the address was Love of Life?"

"We'll see about that." Big Mim leaned back on the wooden bench, feeling the slats press into her back. "I haven't met Bechtal, but from what Rick and Cooper have said—I peppered them with questions, naturally—he's a true believer. Those kind of puritans rarely are larcenous. I could be wrong." She pressed her forefingers to her temples. "This is strange. What's truly strange is, why is Bechtal taking the fall? Is there more violence to come? Is the money going to fund it? Or is he the dupe?" She began to rub her temples, her mind almost overheating.

"Do you have a headache?"

"I do now." Big Mim smiled, then again reached for her daughter's hand. "We'll get through this. And—I hope you know this—about the Democrats, you know your father has nothing to do with them going after you or what may come next."

"I know. He can't help being a Democrat." Little Mim smiled, a bit of relief flowing into her thanks to her mother's response. "Any more than you can."

"It's a generation mark. My generation would sooner die than register Republican. But in those days a Southern Democrat was a conservative. Well, that's irrelevant. We have to get to the bottom of this. How were you asked for the money before?"

"Same."

"Seems stupid to send a local letter airmail, doesn't it?"

"Does. But I never got a phone call or anything like that. Just three letters and now the fourth."

"When you had the procedure, did anyone else know?"

"Harry and Susan."

"You all were never close. Although you're closer now. How did Harry come to know?"

"Serendipity. It's a long story."

"Did she have an abortion, too?"

Little Mim replied, "No, no. Harry and Susan just happened to be there when I opened the letter with my pregnancy report. They helped me after that. Right now, let's go to Rick Shaw. You're right. I can't go along hoping the worst doesn't happen. I might as well face the music."

Big Mim rose; Pressman followed. "I'll go with you." As they walked toward the house, Big Mim said, "She's solid, that Harry."

"Yes."

"Darling, don't shy away from motherhood. You will find it changes you profoundly. Blair, too. Don't deny yourself that love and, well, all that work, too." She smiled, a small but sweet smile. "I know I wasn't what people would call a loving mother. I'm too reserved, but I did love having you, raising you, watching your first steps, hearing your first words. Do you know what they were?"

"Momma?"

"I've told you," Big Mim answered in a mock scolding tone. "Your very first words were 'nana, nana,' and you were in your daddy's arms down at the stable, looking into a stall. We laughed because we thought you were trying to neigh."

"Bet I was. Well, at least I'm consistent. I'd rather be in the stable than anywhere else."

"Even the governor's mansion?"

"Fat chance of that now. Mother, I love politics, it's in my blood, but if you put a knife to my throat—God, I wish I hadn't just said that."

Big Mim waved the comment away. "Figure of speech."

"I'd rather be in the stable." She paused as they reached her car. "I think I can do some good. I'm practical and I don't give in to fads, pressure."

"Then you will get there. This is a test. You will come through. I don't have to tell you how ugly it may get if Jonathan spills the beans, or if his accomplice does. Stand firm, be clear, and speak the truth. That alone puts you in the minority." She waited a moment as Little Mim opened the driver's door. "Don't pass up motherhood because of a college mistake."

"You just want to be a grandmother." A bit of Little Mim's contrariness was returning, so she was feeling better.

Also, being around Aunt Tally morning, noon, and night had an effect.

"I do, but, darling, I love you. I want you to feel the happiness a child, children, can bring. I know I wasn't a good mother. I was responsible, but I'm not, you know, a Miranda or a BoomBoom or a Susan, where the love bubbles up on the surface and overflows. I'm too rational. I'm sorry. I'm sorry for a lot of things, but I have always loved you, and I love you more now than I ever have. I'm proud of you."

Stunned, Little Mim burst into tears,

reaching for her mother. The two stood there, crying, hugging.

At last, Little Marilyn caught her breath. "Mother, I've always wanted to be like you, but I can't. I'm not as smart as you are. I'm not the woman you are."

"Oh, Marilyn, you are your own woman, and you had to fight me to get there. I'm no example." She released her daughter. Tears ran down both their faces. "And you are smart."

"Mother, your mind flies at the speed of light. I've never met anyone like you. Sometimes you scare me. You scare all of us."

"I don't mean to, darling, truly, I don't. Don't compare yourself to me. My failings would fill the house." She breathed deeply. "Do you have Kleenex in the car?"

Little Marilyn laughed, the laugh of one for whom a great emotion had been resolved. "Yes. Come on. We need to repair our makeup before getting to the sheriff's office."

Pressman hopped in the backseat as the two wiped away their tears and their mascara, too. As Little Mim drove, her mother flipped down the sunshade with the mirror on the back on the passenger side. She didn't have her purse, but Little Mim, well armed, always filled the center console with the necessities of a woman's life.

Big Mim plucked out a long tube of mascara. "You know, I've never tried Lancôme. I'm still using Stendhal. I wonder if they named it for *The Red and the Black*, one of my favorite novels."

"I don't have the patience to use cake mascara—standing there over the sink, wetting the brush, applying it, doing it over two or three times—but it does give your lashes the best look. I know that, but I guess I'm like most other people in the world. I'm getting lazy."

"Overcommitted is more like it." Big Mim liked how smoothly the mascara rolled on her lashes.

"There's blusher in there, too."

"You could do makeup for a film shoot with what you've stashed in there." Big Mim teased her and then that mind clicked on again. "You know, I don't believe you are the only woman to receive those letters."

Little Mim's hands suddenly gripped the steering wheel with added pressure. "I hadn't thought of that. I was so caught up in my own misery."

"My experience is that emotions cloud the mind, although in some rare instances they sharpen the mind and one has epiphanies. Something terrible is going on around us. I don't know what it is. Well, I assume blackmail, but I don't know who. The motive would be clear enough—money, perhaps revenge. But, mmm, do you remember seven years ago when we were down at the stables? Snowed. We knew it was going to snow, but it turned into a blizzard, and we couldn't see the hand in front of our faces."

"Yes, we wanted to get back to the house, and you realized we might not make it, we might wander around in circles. Luckily, you turned me back before even the stable was swallowed up in white, and we weren't ten yards from it."

"You couldn't hear anything but the wind and the snow blowing back into one's ears. Stung. But we managed to get back into the stables and we spent the night there. When we woke up, it was still snowing, but we could see. This is like that. We can't see. We can only hope that, in time, there's a clearing."

"It can't go on."

"Were you ever physically threatened?"

"No. My career was the focus. Like a fool, I was so angry and upset I burned the letters."

"Understandable. Did you check the postmarks?"

"22905. At least I had the presence of mind to do that and remember."

"I hope whoever else is receiving letters will come forward. I doubt their careers are being threatened."

22

"What is it about Mondays?" Cooper sat down at her desk and viewed the pile of paperwork with distaste.

A law-enforcement officer saves lives, pulls injured and dead people out of car wrecks, faces armed men hopped up on crank, endures abuse from angry people over whatever it is that has gone wrong in their lives, and listens to lies, a tidal wave of lies. However, the paperwork, mounting with each year as Americans became ever more dazzled by worthless litigation, seemed much worse than the physical dangers.

"Court appearance." She tossed that aside. "Why do people protest speeding tickets?"

"Because sometimes they win." Rick also

faced a daunting pile. "Big Mim called. She and her daughter are on their way."

"She was just here this morning." Surprise, then resignation, filled her voice. "We can't do a thing about Tazio Chappars. Surely she must understand that. The murder took place in Bedford County."

"What Big Mim wants, Big Mim gets." He smiled wanly. "One way or the other. And she might be on to something about payoffs to our beloved building inspector."

"Ah, yes, Mike McElvoy. Actually, I look forward to poking around in his business."

"I do, too. Something's rotten in Denmark."

"The king dies, the queen dies, Ham dies, they all die." Cooper smiled, remembering the old joke about *Hamlet,* a play she didn't like.

She didn't like Shakespeare, but if she breathed a word of it, Harry, Susan, Alicia, BoomBoom, Big Mim, even Fair, would be scandalized.

"Come on outside with me for a minute. I need a nicotine hit before they get here. I have no idea why I am being treated to Big Mim twice in one day. More curious, she's coming to me."

The two rose, walked down the narrow hall and out the back door. Rick reached into his shirt pocket, fetching a pack of Camels.

"A black pack?"

"Little different coffin nail, so the package is black. Actually, they're pretty good. Want one?"

Coop looked around like a criminal might before breaking and entering. "Yeah. Did I ever tell you about the time I gave Harry a cigarette and she smoked it? Funniest thing I ever saw."

"That was during the monastery case."

"Good memory."

"Susan's great-uncle." He thought a moment. "A good fellow. Shame about how he died. People." He shook his head. "But then, if this were a crime-free world, you and I wouldn't have a job."

"Not one so exciting."

"Except for the paperwork." He winked at her.

"Got that right." She used the old expression with the correct intonation, a Tidewater lyricism.

"This is a good cigarette. Burns too fast, though."

He replied, "Does. If I were a rich man I'd smoke Dunhills and Shepherd's Hotel, but this is a good compromise. Some of the cheap stuff that's out there." He inhaled gratefully. "Don't know how the French can smoke what they do."

"Or eat snails."

"I like snails."

Cooper made a face. "You would. Well, boss, if we start rooting around Mike McElvoy, we'd better do the same with Tony Long. Otherwise, we'll frighten Mike more than we need to, and this way we can make it look like a department check."

"Authorized by whom?" Rick had to face the county commissioners.

"By Carla Paulson's murder. We can say we are working with the Bedford County Sheriff's Department—no lie—and we need to check everything and everybody involved with her."

"Tony Long and Mike take different construction jobs."

"True, but that doesn't mean if Mike were indisposed that Tony wouldn't go out to the site to inspect. So we have to be fair-handed and check both."

"Sounds like a plan." He looked up at the

bright September sky. "Isn't it something how the haze disappears come fall?"

"Love that sky blue, that deep sky blue."

"Looks good on you."

"When did you see me in sky blue?" She was surprised.

"July. You wore a T-shirt that color. I stopped by the farm."

She tried to remember and finally did. "Oh, yeah. The women's magazines say men don't remember clothes, details."

"Wrong. Men remember a lot. All that stuff is bunk. Anyway, I'm a cop. It's my job to remember, and you look good in sky blue." He stubbed out his cigarette. "Which women's magazines?"

Blushing slightly, she answered, "*Cosmopolitan* and *O.*"

He grunted. "Helen reads them all. House is littered with them. I'll give her credit, she reads my *Men's Health* from cover to cover, too." He crunched the cigarette butt again, for he spied a dim glow. "I think I have to accept that I am not going to stop smoking."

"Oh, you might." Cooper put out her Camel. "I stick to one a day."

"From me."

"All right. All right. I'll buy a pack just for

you. After all, I have that five dollars I won from you. Want the black kind?"

"No, I want Dunhills." He grinned.

Cooper's eyebrows lifted. "Well, I do owe you."

A rap came on the door, then the front desk officer stuck his head out and said, "Herself is here, along with Junior."

The two friends and partners looked at each other. Then Rick held out his hand and Cooper swept through the door, as the young officer smiled devilishly.

"Lucky man, boss. Twice in a day."

"Shut up, Dooley." He smacked the young man in the stomach, hard and flat. "Working out."

"Yes, sir."

"Well, try working the brain, too," Rick kidded him.

Cooper said, "Your closed office or the big room?"

"Office."

"Too bad you don't have a floral display. She'd feel more at home."

Rick growled, "Big Mim would be at home in a flooded house in New Orleans or the Taj Mahal. Woman is remarkable."

The two met Big Mim and Little Mim as though this was the highlight of their day.

The cops ushered them into the private office, which Rick kept scrupulously clean mostly because he usually sat outside at a desk in the bullpen. He liked being among his "men"—even though one was a woman—and this way, his glassed-in sheriff's office was tidy.

The sheriff did not sit behind his desk. Mother and daughter sat in two worn but comfortable leather chairs, Rick leaned against his desk facing them, and Cooper sat on a stool.

Wordlessly, Little Mim produced the airmail envelope, handing it to Rick.

As he read, his face betrayed a hint of questioning. He passed it to Cooper.

"Arrived in today's mail." Little Mim started the ball rolling.

Cooper handed the letter and envelope back to Little Mim. "What a scam."

"Exactly," Big Mim spoke at last.

"I've received three letters before this, all before Will was killed. Each asked for ten thousand dollars in a postal order made out to Jonathan Bechtal."

"You paid." Rick knew she had; it was a given.

"I did."

Cooper put her hands on her knees. "What I want to know is, how did he get this letter out of jail? We'd know. He's allowed to write, this isn't a hellhole in the Sudan."

"No hellholes. They're too busy killing one another to bother with incarceration," Big Mim said without sarcasm. "Do you read the letters?"

"I don't, but there is censorship. There has to be, because some of these creeps would write vile stuff to the people they hold responsible for their plight and they'd go right onto someone's blog. So, yes, the letters are read."

"Paid someone off?" Cooper hated the idea.

"I don't think so." Big Mim repeated what she had said to her daughter earlier. "There's someone on the outside."

"Then why send the money orders to Love of Life?" Cooper wasn't discounting the idea, just pondering, as well as realizing Big Mim was one step ahead of her.

"I don't know," Big Mim replied. "It's more than possible that his accomplice is an officer or member of Love of Life. Someone who can access the treasury or bogus accounts. Most charities have a variety of very imaginative slush funds."

Rick and Cooper glanced at each other. They had questioned the officers of the organization as well as those of other right-to-life groups.

Rick spoke. "Who else knows about this?"

"No one. Not even my husband." Little Mim, finding her courage, spilled her story in an abbreviated fashion. "I had an abortion in college. Will was my doctor. The other letters threatened to expose me. So I paid like a stupid—cow."

"For a woman being blackmailed, you've remained sensible." Cooper smiled.

"Coop, I should have come to you right away, but I was ashamed and, even more embarrassing, I put my career first."

Rick exhaled from his nostrils. "Most people who find themselves in your situation pay if they can and hope their tormentor will go away. Naturally, it emboldens the blackmailer." He shifted his weight while he leaned against his desk.

"Mother knew nothing. She didn't even

know I'd had an abortion." Little Mim wanted the two officers to know that her mother hadn't helped her make the payoff. "I'm done with it. I don't look forward to what happens next."

"What do you mean?" Cooper spoke as though this were an ordinary conversation, no hard edge to the questioning.

"They go public and try to ruin me. How they'll do this, I don't know, but the deadline for payment is this Friday."

Cooper reached for the letter again, which Little Mim gave her. "P.O. Box Fifteen, 22905."

"I noticed that, too," Rick mentioned. "We'll have this dusted for fingerprints, test the seal on the envelope to see if whoever did this licked it. You'd think by now people would wear rubber gloves and sponge envelopes shut, but there are still a lot of stupid people out there, thank God."

"I hope so." Little Mim sighed, knowing the hard task would be finding whoever did lick the envelope, DNA notwithstanding.

"I'll keep this, then?" Rick's tone of voice asked more than demanded.

"Of course," Little Mim agreed.

"Do you have the other three letters?" Cooper hoped she did.

"I burned them." Little Mim held her forehead for a moment. "I've been abysmally stupid. I didn't want Blair to find them."

"No phone calls?" Rick pressed.

"No."

"If my daughter has received these letters and the threat is to end her political career, I think we can surmise that other women have received letters, as well. More than likely exposure was promised, too, and for all we know, their lives may be threatened. Prying money out of the unwilling often takes force."

"No one has come forward with any complaint," Rick said.

Cooper, sensitive to the situation, met Rick's eyes. "If a woman can keep paying, she might not come forward. There are good reasons not to, as you know."

"Well, yes," Rick agreed.

"And if Little Mim's medical past is broadcast in some way, that will do one of two things." Coop took a breath. "Drive someone out or drive them further in."

After more discussion, Rick told Big Mim that he would be visiting Tony Long on site tomorrow and Coop would find Mike. "Have to check out both. If Mike is corrupt, no point waving the red flag at him alone."

"Wise." Big Mim rose and put her arm around Little Mim's waist for a moment, then dropped it. As the two were turning to leave, Big Mim said, "I think, Rick, that Carla may have received these letters, too."

Cooper and Rick remained in his office for a few minutes after the two women left.

Coop dialed the Barracks Road Shopping Center to check on Box 15, which was in Bechtal's name. Then she called Love of Life. The lady answering the phone gave their street address. They had no box at the post office, and she was upset that someone had used their name for a P.O. box.

"Well, what a surprise," Rick said, without surprise.

"If they killed Will Wylde, they'll kill again," Cooper said flatly.

"That has crossed my mind. And you can be sure it's crossed Big Mim's, as well. Even if her daughter's political career is smashed, it may be what saves her life." He sighed. "Let's go to the post office and check the paperwork for whoever rented Box Fifteen."

"So you think there are more letters?"

"Yep."

"Me, too."

And there were.

Later that evening, sitting outside in the twilight, Mrs. Murphy, Pewter, and Tucker watched barn swallows dart in for their night's rest. Next the bats came out, their tiny little cries tantalizing to the other animals. The humans could hear a squeak now and then, but the two cats and dog heard the entire concerto, the dominant key being A—at least, they thought so.

Harry and Fair leaned over a paddock fence, watching the three fillies and one colt.

"Time to wean." Harry never liked that chore; the screaming upset her.

"Yes, it is. Won't be long before I'll need to geld the fellow, too." He pointed to Venus, huge and bright above the Blue Ridge. "She's impressive. I like it when Mars is in the sky, too, that pulsating red dot—a dot compared to her, anyway."

"They had an affair, remember?"

"I do. Her husband threw a net over

them." He squeezed her hand. "The myths ring true."

"Powerful stories that reveal to us what we are. Maybe that's why the Christians felt the need to suppress them."

"Didn't work."

"No. The truth will out. That's why I know we can help Tazio."

"Honey, everyone will do their best."

"We have to help Tazio." Mrs. Murphy noticed a small moth zigzag in front of her, then lift straight up.

"Why?" Pewter preferred a more sedentary routine than chasing after culprits.

"For Brinkley." The tiger felt such pity for the yellow lab.

"Oh." Pewter couldn't argue with that. *"But he's with Paul."*

"Not the same," Tucker responded. *"And he knows what's going on. He's got to be wretched. Mrs. Murphy is right. We have to help Tazio."*

"What do we do?" Pewter hoped it wouldn't require too much physical exertion. She didn't mind some exertion, but she preferred it in short bursts, like when she tried to grab the blue jay.

"We go everywhere that Mom goes. We

shoot into her truck before she even picks up her purse." Mrs. Murphy smiled. *"I can always sense when she's fixing to leave."*

"We all can do that," Pewter snidely replied.

"Everywhere she goes, if there's another animal, we ask questions. Did they know Carla? Do they know Jurgen? Have they seen or heard any trouble? You know what to do. The wild animals see things we don't, too, because of their hunting patterns. If we can, we need to talk to them."

"No rats."

Tucker, tongue hanging out slightly, asked, *"And why not?"*

"I didn't think those two at Poplar Forest gave us our proper respect." Pewter huffed some more.

"They're rats, not mice, Pewts." Mrs. Murphy felt a beetle crawl over her tail, which she flicked, and the beetle flew off.

"Still, cats have precedence over rats. It's like a duke over a count, you know."

Mrs. Murphy and Tucker looked at each other and rolled their eyes.

"For Brinkley," the tiger said.

"For Brinkley," Tucker chimed in.

Finally, *"For Brinkley,"* Pewter sighed.

23

Mrs. Murphy, Pewter, and Tucker failed the next morning because Harry, knowing she would be out most of the day, had slipped the sliding door down on the animal door. The two cats and dog remained in the house. Pewter grumbled, then slept. Tucker howled. Mrs. Murphy tore a hotpad to pieces, throwing it all over the kitchen.

Blithely unaware of her hotpad's fate, Harry first stopped by Planned Parenthood to see if Folly Steinhauser was in.

Kylie Kraft, in crisp white, walked into the lobby after Harry had spoken to the receptionist, Anita Cowper. "Harry, how are you?"

"Good. Yourself?"

Kylie's pretty features darkened. "As well as can be expected. Nothing will ever be the same, and none of us knows what will become of Dr. Wylde's practice."

"Are you looking for another job?"

Kylie replied, "Not yet." Then she brightened. "But I am looking for another boyfriend."

"What happened to the one you were with at Poplar Forest?"

She wrinkled her nose, her red curls bright around her face. She spelled it out: "B-o-r-i-n-g."

"You won't have too much trouble finding another one."

"All I want is a young, handsome, funny, sweet man with tons and tons of money. Working isn't all it's cracked up to be."

Harry laughed. "Depends on whether you love your work."

A stout middle-aged lady came out from the back hallway and handed Kylie some flyers. "That ought to hold the office." She turned to Harry. "May I help you?"

"Thank you, no. I asked Anita if Folly was in, and she told me this was her day to be home."

The woman walked back down the hall.

"Harry, if you hear of a good job in another doctor's office, would you let me know? But I don't want to work OB/GYN anymore."

"I'll let you know."

A half hour later, Harry had tracked down Penny Lattimore at Keswick Country Club. She'd started her round of golf early and finished early.

Before Penny could go to the sports-club lunchroom for morning tea with the girls, Harry smiled and asked for a minute of her time.

"Harry, what are you doing out here?"

"Thought I might find Greg Schmidt." She named a prominent equine vet.

"He doesn't play golf, does he?"

"You know, I don't know, but I thought he might stop by for late breakfast or early lunch. How have you been?"

"Fine. Well, it's been terribly upsetting, what with Carla's murder. She really had put her heart and soul into building that house. She often asked me to go over things with her, since I had so recently built mine, plus I had to deal with that slimeball Mike."

"He's not the most popular guy around."

"He'd be pompous if he were smart enough. Instead, he's just ridiculous."

"Penny, I don't want to upset you, but I

must ask if you've ever received letters from Jonathan Bechtal asking for money."

The shock on Penny's face—which she then quickly composed—told Harry what she needed to know.

"No."

"Ah. Should you ever receive any, will you please go to Cynthia Cooper or Rick immediately?"

"Why?" A note of harshness crept into Penny's voice.

"There's good cause to believe that Carla had been receiving threats from him—extortion—before she was killed." Harry fibbed, for that was only conjecture.

Penny's face blanched, but she held firm. "Tazio killed Carla."

"No, she didn't, but it will take time to prove her innocence. The important thing now is that no one else be killed."

"Thank you, Harry. But tell me, why are you coming to me and not Deputy Cooper?"

"She is on the case, but, as you know, the department is shorthanded and there's only one woman. This is best handled between women."

Penny's sandy eyebrows lifted. "Yes, yes, I can understand that."

Her next stop—Elise's grand pile, nestled amid towering pin oaks—proved even less successful. Elise slammed the door in her face.

Harry climbed back in the truck and wondered if Penny had called Elise. It was rare for someone to slam the door in another's face before they even got a word out.

Harry next turned down the long tree-lined drive to Folly Steinhauser's palatial home. She parked to the side of the curving raised stairway.

The huge double doors had brass horsehead knockers. Harry clanged away.

Sienna Rappaport, Folly's female butler—a revolution in itself—answered the door.

"Good morning, Sienna. I don't have an appointment. I was hoping to speak to Mrs. Steinhauser."

"Of course. Wait in the library and I'll see if she's available."

At least she was civilized. Harry sat on a tufted hassock in the extraordinary library, which was temperature-controlled to protect the rare first editions Folly so prized. Within minutes she heard two sets of footfalls. One stopped, heading in another direction. The other came to the library door.

"Harry, what an unexpected pleasure." Folly seemed to mean it.

"Forgive me. I wouldn't have come without calling if it weren't important."

"Would you like something to drink?"

"No, no thank you."

Folly took a seat and motioned for Harry to sit opposite her.

As Harry moved from the hassock to the buttery-soft leather club chair, she noticed a gorgeous red lacquer humidor edged in black and yellow on the end table by Folly's chair.

"What can I do for you?" Folly uttered those lines usually spoken by the person in power.

"First off, I want to thank you for all you did for the Poplar Forest fund-raiser. It was extraordinary, so in keeping with the spirit of the place. The shock of Carla's murder . . . well," Harry threw up her hands, "of all places and all times. The other thing—and I'm at fault for this—I have never thanked you for the burden you're lifting from Herb's shoulders, for all you are doing on our vestry board. Serving with you is teaching me a lot."

"Harry, that's so kind of you."

"I don't have your organizational skills, but I'm trying to soak some up."

"Ah, but, Harry, dear, you have the blood, the connections, and your mind is so very logical."

This surprised Harry. "Thank you." She paused. "I'm here because I'm desperately worried." As Folly's face registered rapt attention, Harry plunged in. "Before Will Wylde's death, a series of women—we don't know whom—received letters from Jonathan Bechtal, ordering them to send money to P.O. Box Fifteen at the Barracks Road Shopping Center post office. If not, he threatened to expose them for having abortions." Harry paused. "There is reason to believe that Carla had received them. Someone I know called me after she received her last one. She finally went to Sheriff Shaw. We are all worried, because there's someone on the outside."

Folly, hand shaking slightly, opened the humidor and plucked out a cigarette. "Smoke?"

"No thank you. I didn't know that you did."

"I hide it, but every now and then I do. Tell me more."

"Well, the early letters asked for ten thousand dollars, which my friend paid. The last one asked for one hundred thousand, which she will not pay. The money is due Friday."

Folly took a long drag, rose, opened a first-edition copy of Cobbett's *Rural Rides* in excellent condition, pulled out an airmail blue envelope, and handed it to Harry. "Like this?"

Harry—hands also shaking, for she never expected this—opened the letter and read it. "God. You aren't going to pay, are you?"

"I don't know."

"Oh, don't, Folly, please. This has got to stop. I truly think Will's murder and Carla's are connected, but I don't know how. The only suspect I can think of on the outside is Mike McElvoy, because he had contact with Carla. But I don't see how he connects to Will's murder. It's a long shot right now."

"They may not be connected. Charlottesville is growing. It's entirely possible that two murders could be committed in short order and not be linked. And there is the problem of Tazio."

"You don't think Tazio killed her, do you?"

"I don't know."

"Folly, you must go to the sheriff about

this. I can understand why you've hidden it."

"Can you?" Her voice rose, she sucked again on the long white cigarette.

"I think I can, and I don't need details. Things happen. We get carried away." She threw up her hands. "Why is it always the woman's fault?"

"Control women and you control men," Folly flatly said. "Therefore we're always supposed to be morally better than men. When a woman fails, it's quite a long way down, even today, Harry, even today."

"It could be worse." Harry tried to lighten the mood. "Could be living under the Taliban."

"We're the only power on earth with the guts to make sure we don't."

Harry didn't reply, because she had a different view although no solution for such extremism. There really are people happy to kill anyone who doesn't believe as they do. "Please promise me you will go if not to Rick then to Cooper. She's a woman. She'll understand. They won't make it public."

"No, they won't, but whoever wrote this letter will."

"Folly, you can fight it."

"Harry, I was young when I married into all this wealth. I am sure it has not escaped you that, middle-aged as I am, my husband is quite a bit older. I was naive about the laws, and I signed a prenuptial agreement stating that if I ever had sex with another man, I would be divorced with no settlement. Harsh. However, I was so in love at the time that I signed it with a flourish."

"Ah." Harry understood, with attendant sorrow.

She smiled wanly. "I discovered that I am human and, well, fragile."

"I understand."

"I can hear Miranda now, telling me not to set my store in earthly treasures. Well, I can't quote the Bible as she can, but you know what I mean. But the truth is, Harry, I love all this. I love the power it gives me, not just to live fantastically well but because I can do some good with the money. He never interferes with my charities."

"If you pay, there will only be more letters."

"I can hope whoever is out there will be caught and killed."

"If they aren't killed but caught, well . . ." Harry turned her hands palms up, a reinforcing gesture. "Folly, go to Cooper. We can always say that you were selected as a victim because of your money. You were so worried about your husband's response and his health"—a slight smiled played across Harry's lips—"that you thought the money was well spent to protect him."

A long pause followed. "I underestimated you, Harry. I promise you I will think about it."

As Harry rose to leave, she noticed when Folly stubbed out her cigarette in a cut-crystal ashtray that it was a Virginia Slims. She would tell Cooper.

As they walked to the mighty double front doors, Harry said, "I am very sorry to upset you, but your welfare is so important, not just to me but to the entire community."

"Who knows you've come to me?"

"No one."

"Thank you for that." Folly kissed her on the cheek.

24

The *slap slap* of the paintbrush provided a rhythmic counterpoint to Mike McElvoy's staccato yap. Orrie Eberhard, applying the second coat to the rococo molding, said nothing.

"Emotional, rude, difficult—I mean, I can work with anybody, but she was a whistling bitch." Mike slapped his clipboard against his thigh.

Orrie fought the urge to dump the bucket of Benjamin Moore paint right on Mike's head. Some would have splashed on Cynthia Cooper, though, and he liked her, so he kept on doing his job.

"Show me the punch list." Cooper reached for the clipboard, ran down the list quickly. "All right, Mike, let's start with the kitchen."

"Fine." He thought he could blow his way through this, but her attention to detail was unnerving.

In the cavernous kitchen he pointed to the outtake-exhaust hole in the ceiling.

"Right. It says here that it needs to be widened by two inches." Coop pulled out a little measuring tape and measured the hole. "Read the code last night. This is code."

"Well," he stammered, "she was bringing in one of those twenty-thousand-dollar stoves, and it needs a larger exhaust pipe."

"That's not what the code says."

"Yes, but the county commissioners will change it soon enough, and she'd have to rip out everything. I was doing her a favor."

"She wouldn't have to rip out anything, Mike. This house met the code when it was built. To date, the building code has not been retroactive." Cooper smiled indulgently, which further discomfited Mike. "All right, the disposal. Let's have a look."

By now he knew she was going to slide under the sink. He also knew he was sinking.

Two hours later, everything had been measured and written in her notebook, plus she'd snapped photos with a disposable camera, which she'd slipped in her shirt pocket. Cooper wallowed in damning detail.

"We've gone through the punch list." Mike, no longer belligerent, wanted to get out of there.

He wanted to call his lawyer.

"Yes, we have, and you've been most helpful. I'm glad Jurgen will finish the house." She looked up from her copy of the list, which she'd also written down while making him wait. Steely-eyed but quiet, she said, "I've kept you from your next appointment. Tell them it was my fault. They can call me if they want to do so." She handed him two cards, one for him, one for the next poor soul building a house.

He read it, slipped it in his back pants pocket. "You still haven't told me why you're doing this. I know the general reason, but this crawl"—he emphasized "crawl"—"seems more than that."

He used "crawl" in the old way, meaning she was crawling over him, not a crawl on a movie screen.

"We're working with Bedford's sheriff department. I know building this caused a lot of stress for Carla and for you. Have to dot the i's and cross the t's."

"Well, I didn't kill her."

She chilled his blood when she said, "I hope not, but everyone is a suspect until we understand the motive. You were at Poplar Forest, and you're on the list of those not at their table during the time of the murder."

"She pushed Tazio Chappars over the edge. Motive enough for me." He flared up.

"And convenient for you, too, Mike." Coop needled him. "It takes strength to cut through the gristle and muscle of someone's neck. Tazio, perhaps, could have sliced through, but I know you could have done it. You're strong enough."

His jaw dropped slightly. He looked at her, mouth agape, then closed it. "Wasn't me."

"I'm glad to hear that."

"I need to go."

"Mim Bainbridge—Little Mim," Cooper added. "You've written down the name and address as well as the date, September thirtieth, Tuesday. The page behind this punch list. You saw me flip it up. Give her my apologies. I kept you too long."

He nodded curtly, closed the front door without slamming it.

Cooper admired Orrie's work. "I knew a lady once named Orrie. Guess it's like Dana or Francis or Douglas. Spelling may be different between the male and female versions, but they sound the same."

"Sidney is another one. A lot of them when you start counting. I was named for my uncle."

"Can you tell me anything about this job?"

"Beautiful house. No shortcuts. Best materials. Best architect."

"From your observation, do you think Tazio could kill someone like Carla? Let me be direct: would she?"

"I don't know about that." Orrie wasn't being evasive but truthful. "I could have killed Carla. She got right under your skin. Raised in a barnyard. No manners. Oh, she had them with people she thought were on her level or above her or she needed, but with the likes of me or Mike or Tazio, she was one hateful bitch."

"I can see you're a fan." Cooper laughed. "How do you feel about Mike?"

"A piece of shit."

"Well," Cooper laughed again, "tell me how you really feel."

"Never liked him. Known him all my life. I was standing on this ladder last Monday when Carla and Mike had their loud creative disagreement—is that the bullshit phrase? Anyway, they were back in the guest room, but I overheard Carla offer him money. She would have paid cold cash to get him the hell out of here, and he refused."

"Of course he did, Orrie, he knew you were on this ladder."

"Thought of that myself, later."

"Think he put the squeeze on people?"

"I never heard any loose talk. On the other hand, he sure buys anything he wants." Orrie carefully wiped the brush on the rim of the paint bucket, then laid it across the top. He climbed down the ladder to be level with Cooper and because he wanted to stretch.

"Cramps?"

"Get tight. Painting ceilings is the worst. I'll keep that crick in my neck for days."

"You've won the contracts for a lot of these new houses, haven't you?"

"I have. We really earned our reputation doing restoration work. I started out with just myself and Nicky Posner. Now I have twenty people working for me plus college kids in the summer. Not good to brag, but me and the boys can do anything."

"How come you're here alone?"

"Most everything is done except for this last bit of trim work. Got a crew at Penny Lattimore's—that's an outside job; wanted to put another coat on the gardening shed. You and I could live in the shed. Another crew is out in Louisa County at a big place. I figured this would give me a few days of quiet. Course, I never expected Carla to be murdered. Still, it has been quiet."

"Jurgen came out?"

"No. He called me and told me to keep going."

"Your jobs—has Mike always been the inspector?"

Orrie fetched a blue bandanna slipped through the loop on the side of his painter's pants. He dabbed his brow.

"Orrie?" Cooper waited.

"Sorry. Mike and Tony about even."

"Is there as much acrimony when Tony's the inspector?"

"No."

"Orrie, if you think of anything that might

be relevant to this case, no matter how trivial it might seem to you, please call." She handed him a card.

"I will." He slipped the bandanna back through the pants' loop. "Don't think Tazio did it, do you?"

"I found her standing over the body with a bloody knife in her hand. I have to go with what I saw. If I were Bedford County's prosecuting attorney, I'd have an open-and-shut case."

"What does your gut tell you?"

"I thought I was supposed to ask the questions," she said in a genial tone.

"I trust my gut more than my brain, what brain I have."

"Actually, I do, too, but it takes years to learn that, and some people never do. Sometimes we know without knowing, and sometimes we know and we can't prove how we know."

"And?"

"My eyes told me she killed Carla. My gut . . ." She shook her head. "I'm not sure, Orrie. Doesn't feel right."

Orrie put his hand on the side of the ladder, paused. "There is something: I never saw Mike have a run-in with a man. Always the woman, when she was in the house without the husband. Don't know if that's important."

"I think it is. Thank you."

Twenty minutes later, Cooper pulled the squad car into the south side of the parking lot at Seminole Square, so named for the trail that led from the Mid-Atlantic states down to Florida. Two tobacco shops were relatively close to each other. One was in Barracks Road Shopping Center, the other here.

Charlottesville lacked a true town center. Someone might say it was Court Square at the county courthouse, but not so, not enough life there. Places like Richmond, or Charleston, South Carolina, or even Oxford, Pennsylvania, had true centers around a town square, but this place did not. Hives of activity dotted Albemarle County, and yet it lacked that one special place where every resident knew the core rested.

The proprietor of the shop, a well-groomed Cuban gentleman of some years, greeted her with a smile. She often accompanied Rick here when he'd splurge for a pack of Dunhills.

"How are you?"

"Good, and you?"

He shook his head. "Violence. So much violence lately."

"Usually the outbursts occur during the sweltering summer days and nights. Can't quite put this together. Well, Dr. Wylde's killer I can."

The gentleman nodded. "No way to solve a problem." He brightened. "I am glad you are here. What can I do for you?"

"I'd like to buy Rick a carton of Dunhills. What would be better, the blue pack, which are mild, or the red, regular?"

"For him, the red. For you, the mild. Have you ever tried the menthol? Clears the sinus."

"No. I tell myself I don't smoke, but I am forever cadging cigarettes off the boss. I owe him a carton."

He bent over, pulled a carton from under the counter.

"Would you mind if I stepped into the humidor? I love the smell."

"Go right ahead." He sprinted out from behind the counter and slid open the glass door. Immediately the place filled with competing, rich aromas.

She stepped inside, looking at all the

pretty cigar boxes. After a few huge inhales, she stepped out.

"Thank you."

"Many ladies smoke cigars."

"I don't think I'm up to it." She smiled.

"Mrs. Steinhauser was in here this morning with Mr. Lattimore. She bought her usual carton of cigarettes. He bought a box of Tito's. Most people don't know the brand. It's not extremely expensive. She bought six Montecristo Petit Edmundos, a very nice cigar. She said she smokes cigars when no one except for Mr. Lattimore is looking." He smiled like the Cheshire cat.

Neither one needed to comment on their friendship, which may well have tipped over into an affair.

Cooper knew Folly's husband was jealous. However, he hadn't stepped in to end the friendship, so maybe it was just that.

"Well, why don't you select a very mild cigar for me and I will try it tonight?"

He came back with a fat, long Montecristo. "Don't worry about the size. The longer, the smoother the draw. Just try it, and don't try to smoke all of it. A few pleasant notes." He smiled while he rang up the bill, throwing in a large box of cigar matches. “From me to you.” He handed her a blue pack of Dunhills. “You will enjoy them.”

“I know I will. Thank you.”

“You always use a match to light your cigarette, no?”

She nodded. “Yes.”

“Good.” His hand swept over the case in the middle of the room. “Expensive, very pretty to hold in the hand, but the tobacco remembers the butane. A match, yes, always use a match. And don’t tell, because I need to sell those lighters.” He laughed.

He was right, too. The oily note of butane could slightly taint the tobacco. Purists always used matches.

She walked out like a kid from the candy store who was given a swirled cherry sucker. She knew that smoking was bad for your health. She truly believed everyone would be better off without it, but in her job she could be dead in a minute. Right now. An alarm could go off in a car in the parking lot or a store. She’d answer the call and the perp could blow her away. The thought of her mortality stayed close. So why not take a nicotine hit? She told herself she wasn’t really a smoker. She only bummed a cigarette a day from Rick.

She opened the car, put the brown paper bag in the passenger seat, and fired the motor. He'd be thrilled with his carton of exquisite cigarettes.

As Cooper drove back to the station, Harry was leaning over a paddock fence with Paul de Silva, looking at the Mineshaft colt, now nine months old. Big Mim produced good results in everything she did. She'd bred her broodmares to a variety of good sires, most of them middle range in price. The Mineshaft colt was anything but middle range, the stud fee being one hundred thousand dollars.

Big Mim had been smart to take her best mare, the one with the best cross, to Mineshaft when she did, because the sire's fee was bound to rise. The top end of the Thoroughbred market was very healthy. The middle and the low end had begun to sag, reflecting economic fear, punishing gas prices, and taxes that would most assuredly rise. The situation in the Mideast hardly engendered economic confidence, either.

"What's she going to do?" Harry admired the dark-bay fellow.

"I think she's going to keep him."

"Really?" This was news.

"Says she hasn't run a horse on the flat in decades." Paul loved the horses, but Tazio's situation had dampened his usual high spirits.

"Heard anything?"

"Ned sees her every day. Even when he's in Richmond. I went down Sunday."

"How did she look?"

"Beautiful." A flash of the courtier returned. "Tired. Worried."

"I thought I'd go down Friday."

"Set bail."

"I heard." Harry folded her hands as she leaned over the top rail.

"Two hundred fifty thousand dollars. For a woman who has never even had a parking ticket."

"Murder One." Harry looked down at her boots. "I'm sorry, Paul. We'll find a way. You know we're all trying."

The cats, Tucker, and Brinkley watched the Mineshaft foal and the others, too.

"I want Mommy." Brinkley's soft brown eyes filled with tears.

"Be strong. She needs you to be strong," Tucker advised. *"We're here to help."*

"I miss her so much. Paul is a nice man, but I miss her scent, her voice. I love her. She loves me. She is my best friend."

"We know how you feel," Pewter commiserated.

For a moment, Mrs. Murphy and Tucker remained silent, for Pewter rarely admitted how much she loved Harry. She pretended to be aloof.

"Brinkley, did your mom ever say anything about Carla? Not how much trouble she was, but if she'd seen her, say, with another man?"

"No. She said that she thought Carla and Mike McElvoy would kill each other if she didn't kill them first. She didn't mean that. It was a figure of speech."

"Can you think of anyone who hated your mom? Hated her enough to set her up?"

"No. Even Carla wouldn't have done that. Carla needed Mom, even if she did treat her ugly." The lab's gorgeous coat appeared almost white in the afternoon sun.

"True." Mrs. Murphy stretched. *"And Tazio needed Carla. It was an important commis-*

sion. She couldn't afford to get a reputation that might turn other people away."

"They'd only have to know Carla to know the truth of that." Brinkley's neck fur ruffled in indignation.

"People have to live here for a while to know those things. New people listen. Actually, even people who aren't new listen. A gossip campaign does damage," Mrs. Murphy sagely noted. *"Humans are prone to it."*

"Remember the Republican primary in South Carolina in 2000?" Tucker followed these things with Harry as they both watched the TV or read the paper. *"They saw that Karl Rove started a whispering campaign about John McCain having an affair with a woman of color. You'd think no one would believe it. Did. Carla's gossip could have hurt Tazio if Tazio had really set her off."*

"Mother didn't kill her, no matter what." Brinkley was adamant.

"Who's growling?" Harry turned from the fence.

Paul did, as well. "Brinkley, be nice."

"I am." Brinkley lay down, putting his head on his paws.

"He's so sad, poor fellow," Paul remarked.

"I'm not much help. I feel . . . I can't even describe how I feel."

Mrs. Murphy rubbed against Brinkley. *"Anything else, anything at all?"*

"No. Mother said that Carla was an emotionally unrestrained person. She considered it irresponsible. After Dr. Wylde was shot, Carla called to cancel her meeting with Mom and Mike, and when Mom put down the phone she said Carla was behaving like an idiot, that you would have thought Dr. Wylde was her lover, the way she was sobbing."

Mrs. Murphy stopped mid-rub. She said nothing, but a tiny piece of this wretched puzzle had fallen into place.

25

There's an old carny trick, successful over the centuries in rural America. A barker called people to the sideshows. He extolled the beauty and weirdness of the bearded lady, the enormous bulk of the fat man, the frightening aspect of the reptile boy, each in their separate tents. Other human oddities filled a row of tents.

When the crowds became large enough, before the tickets were sold, the barker would helpfully tell the crowd—mostly men, since genteel ladies would be too repelled to attend—to protect their money from pickpockets.

Human nature: the men would reach for their wallet to make sure it was still there. They'd pat a breast pocket if wearing a seersucker coat or their hip pocket if in jeans or overalls. Since the pickpockets worked with the barker, giving him a contested percent—he knew they underreported their take—they were in the crowd. Pickpockets noted who patted what, and the rest was easy as pie.

Mike patted his pocket, so to speak, after checking over Little Mim and Blair's plans. He had been uncharacteristically mild, mindful that she was the vice mayor of Crozet.

He drove back to Woolen Mills, where he and Noddy owned a well-kept wooden house. Noddy, being queen of that house, suffered few changes to her way of doing things. Mike had his shed for the lawn mower, gun repair, and tools, and a separate office near the tool room. He could live in there, since he'd tricked it out, put in R-19 insulation, added windows. His small desk held a new computer. A small propane fireplace rested along one wall, and in winter it heated the twelve-by-fourteen-foot office area more than enough. He'd also insulated the floor. First, he'd put down a vapor barrier, then the wooden support slats—two-by-fours, running parallel—and stuffed that with insulation. Next he'd put down a good hardwood floor, having been given some nice oak overflow from a construction site. Under his desk he had a trapdoor concealed by a hard rubber floor covering, so he could roll around on his desk chair without marking up the beautiful stained and waxed oak.

He told Noddy he couldn't stand sitting at a desk in the house when she roared through with the vacuum cleaner, ordering him to lift his feet.

He opened his office door and looked out the windows to see if anyone was around, which they weren't. He pulled the shades just in case. Noddy wouldn't come home from work for another hour, given the traffic. Still, one couldn't be too careful.

He walked into the tool part of the shed, came back with an old towel, put it on the floor, and rolled the chair onto the towel. Mike was as fussy as Noddy. Then he pulled the mat away. Down on his hands and knees, he slipped his forefinger through the recessed brass half ring, which was painted black, and lifted the trapdoor. He stepped down into the small area, not four feet by six feet, which was low but he could stand. Shelves lined the four walls, but only one side of the shelves was filled. He pulled out a key, squatted down, and opened a metal strongbox on the bottom shelf. He counted the cash: sixty-two thousand dollars collected over the years. He examined the jewelry, much of it very valuable. Someday way off in the future he would take the jewelry up to New York and fence it, if he could bear to part with it. Mike appreciated beauty. He shut the small heavy metal door, listening for the sweet click of the automatic lock.

His knees creaked when he stood up. Colored wooden boxes lined the next shelf. He opened one box to gaze at the lace panties within, each one snatched from a conquest—most not terribly willing—over his years as inspector. Smiling broadly, he picked up an emerald-green pair and slipped his hand through a leg opening to gaze at the fine handiwork on the lace. Made by hand, the lace testified that these select undies belonged to a woman of taste and money. Penny Lattimore, in fact. He folded the panties, putting them back in the box.

He loved his victories. He loved the power over women. Hurting a woman wasn't his goal. Mike wasn't a mean man, simply a weak and screwed-up man. He liked making them pay. From some he just took jewelry and money. Others, sex. Still others, both. You never knew in this world, and cash was hard to procure. As for the jewelry, he thought of the ears, necks, wrists, and fingers on which they had sparkled. The panties—now, there lay a prize. Oh, he had to wear them down to get those panties off, but he'd learned over the years that most women had secrets, secrets they wanted kept from their husbands, even a child out of wedlock. He'd learned to read the signs: not much communication with their husbands, obsession with their looks. Being unfulfilled, their energies were directed elsewhere, and sometimes he could catch their nervousness when the subject of sex out of wedlock came up. He made sure it filtered into early conversations with a woman; usually he disguised it as a joke. Finding something wrong in the building code occurred after patient research of the lady of the house.

Noddy bragged to friends how hard Mike worked, how dedicated he was to his job. Little did she know.

26

Claustrophobia gripped Benita Wylde. Not the suffocating kind, where a person becomes terrified in an elevator, but the soft claustrophobia of staying in the house. She needed to get out and do something.

She'd been to the office only once since Will was shot, and that seemed like it had been years ago during the day, seconds ago during the night. Time confused her. Somehow it seemed absurd, marking time. Everything seemed absurd and empty without Will, but she forced herself to not lose those threads that bind a life. Bills will come in and must be paid. Keep on keeping on.

Margaret Westlake sat at the front desk area, which had a sliding-glass window. She looked up from a schedule book, where she had written the names of doctors filling in for Will until a permanent solution could be found.

Surprised to see his widow, she jumped out of her chair and gave Benita a big hug.

"I came by to see how you girls are doing; you've all been so good to come by the house every day."

Hearing Benita's voice, Sophie Denham came out of an examining room, and Kylie Kraft came up the hallway, folders in hand.

After exchanging kisses and some tears, Benita said to the three women, "I thought perhaps I could help with outstanding accounts. I know all of Will's patients were devoted to him, but his passing might encourage a few to delay their payment. So I thought I'd go over those accounts if you have them separated out. If not, I can separate them out. I have a rough idea of the system."

Margaret replied, "You and I are on the same wavelength. I've been working on it."

Benita looked at Kylie and said, "Since there is more time, you might go over the codes. I know the insurance companies send updated discs, if I remember what Will said. Used to make him mad every time they'd jack up a procedural cost . . . well, anyway." She paused because she didn't want to cry again. "Things can get confusing. You might just check from the last updated disc forward to make sure nothing has been misbilled. Is that a real word?"

"Is now." Sophie, glad she was a nurse, had no patience for the bookkeeping aspect of medicine.

Kylie replied, "I'm not the coder. I'm trying to learn it, though."

"Ah, well, you do what you're doing, then," Benita replied. Margaret punched buttons on the computer, then handed Benita the two sheets that printed out.

"Mmm." Benita was surprised at some of the names. "Carla Paulson." She shook her head. "Two hundred one dollars and twenty-nine cents. Margaret, I think best not to bill second notice. I have some idea of what Jurgen is going through."

"That marriage wasn't quite what yours was, Benita."

"I'd heard that." Benita noted that Carla's bill was a simple checkup as well as a mammogram. "Why is the mammogram on our bill?" She touched her forehead. "Forgot. That machine cost more than our house, but it's about paid for itself, hasn't it?"

"People don't want to go to the hospital or even hospital adjuncts. Here they're with their personal physician, trusting him and Sophie. It's faster, more pleasant. He can read the mammogram right in front of them. If something needs to be done, it can be scheduled right then and there. You know Dr. Wylde never dallied if he thought there was any possibility of—how did he always put it—'ugly cells.' " Margaret felt a knot in her voice. "He knew just how to put things so a woman felt confident no matter what."

"He was a sensitive man." Benita put her hand over Margaret's. "We'll get through this. And I will make a decision about this office within a month. You all don't have to worry about anything."

"I know." Margaret cast her eyes down, then up, and looked out the glass partition. "If we stay here, if another doctor buys the practice, we'll work with him, but it will never be the same. Dr. Wylde kept us laughing the whole day. He was the only doctor I know who could tell a woman she had breast cancer or cervical cancer and make her laugh. Very few women left here in tears, and you know how adamant he was about counseling if a woman was going to get a termination."

"Yes, I do."

Will did not discuss his patients' illnesses with his wife, as he was scrupulous about all things pertaining to confidentiality, but they talked about everything else.

Laughter had drawn her to Will in the first place. Both of them came from working-class families, very good families; both were working their way through college with the help of scholarships. Will wasn't the handsomest man, but he was the funniest, kindest man she had ever met. Benita, being beautiful, had college boys running out of every frat house on campus when she'd walk by. But Will won her.

After they completed undergraduate school, she worked to put him through med school. He never once cheated on her, even if he was inclined, because he remembered the sacrifices, her staying up with him when he needed coffee or extra help to study. This struggle brought them so close to each other. It also made Harvey Tillach's accusation all the more unpalatable. They accepted each other's foibles—her blind passion for golf, his irritating habit of thinking he could fix either of the cars if something went wrong. Mostly, they laughed. When the children came, all four of them would be laughing.

She tried to remember the laughter.

"Do you want me to send out a second notice?" Margaret returned to the list.

"Yes. These two patients are way past a second notice."

"Money troubles." Margaret had seen and heard it all.

"Perhaps they could pay over time." Benita's eyebrows lifted a little.

"Worth a try. This one"—she pointed to Star Gurdrun—"is seventeen, and her parents—who agreed, mind you—are punishing us."

"Well, give it a try. You know, with a name like Star, that kid doesn't have a chance."

"I know." Margaret grinned.

Kylie came back in. "What is this? Found it on an examining table."

Margaret slipped on her glasses, which hung from a chain around her neck. "Banamine."

A voice called from the back. "Mine. Left it on the table when I heard Benita's voice."

"Since when are you taking Banamine, Sophie?"

"Since I grew four legs and ate hay." She appeared and snatched the bottle from Kylie, but with humor. "Duke is a little ouchy. He's getting on, you know."

"I know the feeling." Benita smiled. "I haven't seen Duke in forever."

Sophie reached into her smock pocket, withdrawing a photo of a sleek chestnut Thoroughbred. "My baby. You know, Dr. Haristeen said he is the youngest sixteen-year-old he has ever examined."

Benita eyed the large bottle. "I might try some of that myself."

She stayed another hour at the office, going over items with Margaret, who, as her job demanded, was on top of every little detail.

Before leaving, Benita asked, "Margaret, do you and the girls know who has had procedures and who has not?"

Margaret answered, "We do. We don't tell tales out of school. Sometimes I wish I didn't know."

"Fear?"

Margaret shook her head vigorously. "No. The nuts will go after the doctors, not us, until we get organized enough to go after them." Anger filled her voice, but then she quelled it. "When I see someone come in for their third termination, it makes my blood boil. Termination is not birth control. It's a last resort. There are women out there who are so flagrantly irresponsible I want to slap their faces. Like to slap their boyfriends and husbands, too."

"It's an imperfect world, Margaret, filled with imperfect people. I'm one of them, although my imperfections aren't centered around sexual irresponsibility."

Margaret changed the subject. "Isn't it just awful about Tazio?"

"Rather incomprehensible. She's such a nice girl."

"Nice girls can do terrible things."

27

Neither Harry nor Fair ate big suppers. A big breakfast sent them on their way and then a good lunch kept them rolling. All a big supper did was turn to fat because you couldn't work it off.

She'd thrown together a nice salad with small bits of the leftover grilled chicken that was Fair's triumph over the weekend. The scent of grilled chicken sent Pewter into a frenzy.

"Me! Me!" She stood on her hind legs, petting Harry's calves.

"Oink. Oink," Tucker grunted.

"Shut up, tailless wonder." Pewter dropped back on her haunches and swiped at the corgi, who ducked in time.

"Dear God, give me patience, but hurry,"

Harry grumbled, putting some chicken in three separate bowls on the floor.

Pewter whirled toward the bowl, her hind legs skidding out.

Once she gained traction, she sped past Mrs. Murphy and Tucker.

"Amazing how fast that fat cat can move when food's the temptation." Harry put her hands on her hips just as the big vet truck rumbled down the long dirt drive.

As Fair walked through the door, she set a glass of tonic water with a wedge of lime and four ice cubes by his plate; one for her, too. Both of them swore the quinine in the tonic kept them from getting leg cramps. Lately, medical researchers doubted this, but Harry doubted that medical researchers ever put in a full day's work on a farm, especially in punishing heat.

Although it was almost October, the days could simmer but the nights brought relief. Then it would turn in a heartbeat, the mercury hanging in the low sixties, soon to drop into the fifties, and with November the plunge would continue. Nature always granted Virginia a respite with Indian summer, though, a few days or even a week of a return to temperatures in the mid-sixties to seventies. Indian summer, beautiful as it was with the fall foliage, tinged hearts with melancholy. It would soon vanish, to be followed by the hard frosts of winter, denuded trees, and a palette of beige, gray, black, silver, and, finally, white.

"Beautiful girl." He kissed her on the cheek, washed his hands at the sink, and sat down.

Harry took her seat and they ate their salad, caught up on the day's doings. They'd talked about the cigarette butt on the floor of the building adjacent to Will Wylde's, so she told him she'd called Cooper about Folly smoking Virginia Slims. She didn't tell of her conversation with Folly. A secret was a secret with Harry.

"Doesn't it look barren without the sunflowers?" he said after he'd registered her report.

"You know, it really does, but those boys did a good job."

The original plan was for Harry, Fair, and their friends to harvest the sunflowers. Eventually Harry realized that, while they could do the labor, this was only her first crop. Fearing she'd damage those big, rich heads, she broke down and hired a crew recommended to her by Waynesboro Nurseries, the same company that had put in Benita's maples. Granted, labor cut into the profit, but there was very little waste. They got it all up in two days, Monday and today.

"I thought I'd make more." She put down her fork for a minute. "I mean, I would have, but—"

"Harry, you did the right thing. If nothing else, you saved Miranda's back. Our friends are very good to us, but sometimes it's best not to ask for favors."

"You're right, but she's on her hands and knees in her garden, remember. As it is, we made three thousand dollars."

"Whenever you balance the books, if you wind up in the black, that's good." The slightly bitter taste of mesclun burst on his tongue. "These greens are so crisp."

"Fresh out of the garden. The battle with the bugs." She grinned. "I won this year."

"You won because we policed the garden." Pewter lifted her head from her bowl.

"What a liar you are." Tucker laughed. *"All you did was sleep under the walnut tree with your face pointed in the direction of the garden."*

"The barn swallows, tree swallows, and

purple martins ate the bugs," Mrs. Murphy reported. *"Maybe even the blue jay ate a few, worthless though he is."*

"He's funny. He imitates the call of a red-shouldered hawk, scares the other birds, then swoops down to eat, undisturbed. They figure it out, come back, and remonstrate with him." Tucker studied birds, although in a different fashion from the cats, whose motives were murderous.

"People, a lot of them, don't realize that blue jays will mimic other birds. They know that mockingbirds do it, but they forget about the jays. With his versatile voice, he can get close to the hawk notes."

"Voice isn't as smooth. You know, their throats are different from ours. They can make two different sounds at the same time. We can't," Tucker mused.

"Humans can talk out of both sides of their mouth at the same time," Pewter added sarcastically, then looked at Mrs. Murphy's empty bowl. *"You sure ate in a hurry."*

"So you couldn't steal my food," Mrs. Murphy forthrightly replied.

"What is this, assassinate Pewter's reputation day? Tucker calls me a liar, you say I steal food. I ought to box both your ears."

Neither animal took the bait, remaining silent. Miffed, Pewter stuck her face back in her ceramic bowl to lick it since she'd gobbled up everything.

Harry and Fair finished their light supper. As he did the dishes, she turned on the TV in the living room.

"Thought I'd look at the weather before finishing the rest of the chores. Less light now."

"I've been so busy I haven't heard the weather or the news."

"No candidate yet for office manager, chief factotum?"

"No. You know who I'd like to hire is Margaret Westlake. Don't know what will happen to Will's practice, so I thought I'd wait a bit to talk to her."

"Don't you think she'll go with another human doctor?"

"I don't know."

"What about Kylie Kraft?"

"She's a nurse. Might know some office management. Anyway, Kylie goes through boyfriends liked toothpicks. Too much drama and you don't need that in the office."

"That she does." Harry patiently waited for the weather.

"She done them wrong." Fair wiped his hands dry and walked into the living room.

Mrs. Murphy, Pewter, and Tucker also watched the news.

"She's in her late twenties." Harry luke-warmly defended Kylie.

He shook his head. "She's got a mean streak where men are concerned." He dropped his arm over her shoulder. "You crack me up."

"Why?"

"You are out of the gossip loop. By the time I hear it, it's old news, but I hear it."

"I hear some things—but not too much." She watched the world news; a picture of car-bomb debris in Baghdad, bodies every-where, flashed before their eyes. "They can all kill one another for all I care."

"Harry," he chided her gently.

"I mean it. For thousands of years those tribes and religious factions have hated one another. We aren't going to solve it. It's civil war. They'll kill one another until they can't stand it anymore, just like what happened in the English Civil War and just like what hap-pened here. When people become that irrational, only overwhelming pain brings them back to their senses."

He sighed. "I wish you were wrong."

"I wish I were, too." She slipped her arm around his waist. "Hell, we're killing one another, too. Even though I didn't see her, the vision of Carla with blood all over her gown—ugh."

"Isn't it odd that humans will kill over an idea or for money?" Tucker cocked her head to one side.

"They don't," Pewter swiftly replied. *"That's the cover for the real reason."*

"Which is?" Tucker queried.

"The pantry. All wars start in the pantry."

Conversation stopped as the local news came on and there was Little Mim, mikes thrust in front of her.

"My opposition to abortion came from my own experience. I don't regret not sharing that experience. We are all entitled to a private life. Now that mine has been so vilely exposed, I want to go on the record to tell you all, this outing, if you will, and the murder of Dr. Wylde has changed my mind. I will support reproductive control. I will fight this violent fanaticism with all I have in me as Crozet's vice mayor, and I know I can count on the support of the mayor. I want to say to every woman out there who may be considering a termination, think it over. It's one of the biggest decisions you will ever make. If there's any way you can keep the baby, do."

She fielded a few more questions, said, "Thank you," and walked back toward the small city offices to the waiting arms of her husband.

Big Mim stood next to Jim.

The newscaster, Dinny Suga, turned to face the camera, then read from a paper handed to her. She looked into the lens and, rephrasing the bulletin, said, "We have a missing-persons report. Mrs. Penelope Lattimore is reported missing by her husband—"

"What in the hell is going on?" Fair exploded, his voice overriding Suga's report.

"I saw Penny this morning. How can she be missing?"

Fair turned to her. "This morning?"

"Keswick Country Club. I stopped by."

"Harry, usually an adult, unless impaired, has to be missing for at least twenty-four hours before a report is filed. Something is very wrong here."

"You mean if Penny's disappearance made the news, they fear the worst?"

"Yes. Obviously, we're supposed to be on the lookout for her, but she's more than missing, I'm afraid."

28

Harry was shocked at Tazio's appearance when she walked into the area reserved for prison visitors. Unlike big prisons, where people sat on either side of glass, speaking through phones, they sat opposite each other, with a low table between them and a guard at the door.

"Harry." Tazio reached across the table and the two women touched hands.

"Are you all right?"

"I don't know. I can't eat and I can't sleep."

"Is the food that bad?"

"Too much starch, sugar, and salt. I just can't stomach it."

"Brinkley is fine, but he misses you."

Tazio wiped away a tear. "You don't realize how much you love a dog until you're separated from him. Brinkley and I are together all day, every day. He's my shadow, my friend, my best friend, corny as that sounds."

"Not to me it doesn't. Miranda baked gingerbread. The other guard is cutting it up to make sure it doesn't have a saw in it." Harry smiled ruefully. "God knows if you'll get any of it. Smelled so delicious that I almost tore into it myself on the way down here, and you can imagine how undisciplined Pewter was."

"I miss them, too."

"Out in the truck with the windows cracked, although it's coolish today, finally. October is one of my favorite months, but Friday isn't my favorite day." Harry folded her hands, placing them on top of the table.

"Sure puts everyone else in a good mood, because at five, they're off. The weekend starts the minute they leave the job."

"You and I don't have those kind of jobs."

"Miss that, too." She tried to make general conversation. "Why don't you like Fridays?"

"Execution day for the better part of European history. Considered the devil's day."

Harry noted the expression on Tazio's thinning features. "Maybe I shouldn't have said that."

"I am accused of murder." She expelled air with force. "I feel like I'm in a bad dream."

"Big Mim is raising your bail from friends."

She ruefully snorted. "Guess I know what I'm worth."

"A lot, apparently." Harry's voice was soft, then she continued, "Are you being treated okay? Are the other prisoners okay?"

"Harry, they are exactly what you think they are: drug addicts supporting their habits by prostitution. There's no one in here for big crimes, other than myself. And you know what's really weird? I guess it's not so weird, since people always form a pecking order, but the top of the top is considered armed robbery. I'm accused of murder so I'm lower on the totem pole, but the poor girls in there who are strung out on smack, coke, crank, you name it, they're on the bottom. They don't have much to do with me, but they aren't ugly."

"That's a relief."

"I even like some of the women. Poor things, if they didn't have bad luck they wouldn't have any luck at all."

"Good luck will be coming your way. We're working on it."

"Harry, I have replayed that night in my mind over and over again. I can't think of any detail I neglected to report. Ned keeps counseling me to relax, dream a little. He says sometimes stray bits of information might float up. He thinks because of the shock I've blocked things."

"Possible. In fact, I bet he's right."

She shook her head. "I still can't think of anything except that I heard a footfall, steps away from me, but . . ." She shrugged.

"What about odors? Perfume, cologne, liquor, I don't know . . . uh, cigar smoke?"

"The smell of blood was overpowering."

"Plus everything else that comes out of the body."

"That, too. I have thought of one thing, though—not a memory but a note, like a missing note in a line of music." As Harry leaned forward, Tazio said, "The sheriff said that the way Carla's throat was slashed would indicate a right-handed person."

"Uh-huh."

"If the killer came up behind her, grabbed her by the chin, pulled her head back, and exposed her neck, that cut would be left to right. They'd be right-handed." She sighed. "I'm grasping at straws. It really doesn't make any difference."

"Ned said the coroner's report from Bedford County indicated she was slashed from the front and she had made no attempt to defend herself."

"Harry, when someone's throat is cut, the blood shoots out like a fountain. Wouldn't whoever did it be drenched in blood? They couldn't jump aside until the job was done. Blood had to spray over something—clothing, their face, depending on their height."

Harry sat upright. "God."

"So I think whoever approached her—someone she knew or someone innocent-looking—had the knife hidden, perhaps in a towel, a bag, even an instrument case like for a trumpet. If he had a towel, he could have used it to wipe himself off."

"I don't know if it will make a difference, but who knows. Details finally add up to a picture. Have you told Ned?"

"No. I won't see him until tomorrow, Saturday."

"Do you mind if I tell him?"

"No."

"May I tell Coop? She knows more about these things than either of us."

"No, I don't mind. It's curious, isn't it?"

"The men wore white tie, and the blood would be noticeable on the pique front and the tie. Most of the women wore bright dresses; it would show. Might not show on a black dress."

"But you'd smell it."

"I don't know. A lot of folks have lost their sense of smell, thanks to the ragweed and goldenrod plus smoking and pollution, but surely one of us would have gotten a whiff. You're right, Taz, whoever killed Carla had a way to either avoid the blood or clean up."

"Could have gone into a Porta-John."

"Hard to change in there. Not impossible, but the killer would have had to stash his clothes somewhere. He couldn't carry a bundle of clothing under his arm and kill her, go to a john, and hope there wasn't a line. Not likely."

"A person walking to the parking lot wouldn't seem out of place."

"No, they wouldn't. They could have slipped back into the house, though that's less likely with Melvin there."

"So either they changed or got rid of the

bloody towel, if they had one. Stuck it in the car."

"I don't know, but I'll swing back to Poplar Forest and nose around outside. Open to the public, so I can't very well charge inside. Taz, I'm sorry. We'll get you out of here. Another week and I think we'll make bail. You'd be surprised at how many people are chipping in."

Her eyes misted over. "I'm lucky. I have good friends."

"You are a good friend." Harry changed the subject. "Herb's called a vestry-board meeting. Marvin's back but I don't know if he's going to be there, because Penny's been missing since Tuesday. Penny, according to her husband, could go off on a shopping toot and forget to call, but she'd call if she would be late getting home."

Tazio's eyes widened. "Another client of mine. Harry, what's going on? Penny and Carla were friends, sort of."

"I don't know. Could be she's fine or she's not fine. If she had a stroke she might not be able to tell people who she is. What if she fell over at a mall? Someone could have stolen her purse. You never know. Stranger things have happened."

Tazio twisted her fingers together nervously. "She'd be in a hospital. Given the call of her disappearance, someone at the hospital would notify the sheriff. No, Harry, something is wrong."

"Both women used you as their architect."

She leveled her eyes at Harry's. "Both had to put up with Mike McElvoy, too." She sighed. "He's not going to kill anyone. He'd be killed first."

"You never know."

When Harry left, she drove straight to Poplar Forest. On the way she told her four-legged friends of the conversation with Tazio. They appeared interested. At Jefferson's summer home, Robert Taney told Harry she could come inside, but she declined. The killer just couldn't have been that stupid to go back into the house with Melvin Rankin in there. They may have lurked in some part of the house, initially slipping by Melvin when he was elsewhere, but they surely wouldn't go back in after the dirty deed. Harry felt certain about that.

"Let's see if we can find the rats." Mrs.

Murphy bounced across the lawn, tail to the vertical.

The three trotted around the house to the south portico.

Tucker called out in a loud voice, *"Randolph, come on out."*

"Randolph, Sarah." Pewter meowed.

Mrs. Murphy, hearing footsteps above, said, *"They can't come out from the west window. People are up there."*

"Drat!" Tucker sat down, looking around.

A minute later a deep voice called from the west side of the arcade under the south portico. *"You again."*

Two bright dark eyes appeared by the edge of the arcade. Then two more. The rats, half obscured, could duck back in if people walked outside. The last thing they needed was someone squealing about rats. They belonged here more than the humans, those two-legged twits.

"Did you find a bloody towel last Saturday?" Mrs. Murphy drove right to the point.

"What's it to you?" Randolph twitched his whiskers.

"Our mother thinks—well, her friend in prison thinks—maybe the killer used a

towel. The lady in prison is a nice lady. The one killed was nasty. Think of her as rat poison. But if we can't find the real killer, our friend may well spend the rest of her life behind bars."

"You ask a lot of questions, and you don't bring treats." Randolph stalled, sorry that he and Sarah had initially offered information about the cigarette without exacting a price.

"Wait." Mrs. Murphy, lightning-fast, ran to the truck.

The open windows were high, but she jumped into the truck bed, onto the cab roof, then insinuated herself through the open window. She clamped her jaws around a Reese's Peanut Butter Cup, Harry's favorite candy, and leapt out the window onto the ground below.

"Fast," Sarah observed. *"We'd better remember that."*

Randolph boasted, *"We're almost as big as she is."*

Mrs. Murphy dropped the candy before Randolph.

"These are good!" He pushed it toward his spouse. *"Half for you, my sweet. You're sweeter than the candy."*

Pewter looked nauseated at this, but Tucker shot her a "behave" look.

"Your mother doesn't smoke, does she?" Sarah was hopeful.

"No, sorry." Mrs. Murphy prayed the candy would do the trick.

"We found a bloody towel, soaked, under the front steps."

"Could we have it?" Tucker panted expectantly.

Randolph laughed. *"We ate it, you ninny."*

"Tasty. Fresh." Sarah licked her lips as she admired the bright waxed candy wrapper, just waiting to rip into it.

"Ah." Tucker understood. *"We hoped to use it as evidence. It was the murdered woman's blood."*

"You think I don't know that?"

"Randolph, Sarah, are you sure you didn't see anyone?" Mrs. Murphy felt desperate, wanting to help Tazio because she liked the architect but mostly doing this for Brinkley.

"Only other thing we found was the cigarette. We knew someone was in the house besides Melvin. But it's nothing to us. And we have to be careful."

"Yes, you do." Pewter finally opened her mouth.

"Why didn't you tell us about the towel in the first place?"

"I don't put all my cards on the table first time I talk to someone," Randolph sensibly replied.

"Thank you. You've been a big help." Mrs. Murphy meant that, but if Tucker could have carried the towel back to the truck, what a victory that would have been.

It wouldn't have proven Tazio's innocence, but it would have been one more piece to fit into the puzzle.

Once all were back in the truck, Harry closed the windows, turned on the ancient AC since the day had begun to warm, and drove away.

"You know, buddies, Carla and Penny must have had some secrets worth killing for, but I can't think of any beyond paying off Mike. And we don't know that. Think. If he did take money, he wouldn't have put it in the bank. Too obvious. If it was a sex thing, his word against theirs. He knows construction. I wonder if he's hidden things, like the rat stuff Robert Taney showed us when we walked through." She turned on the radio, low. "Maybe I'd better go over

Tazio's blueprints. And then, if there's something in the blueprints that looks promising, maybe I'd better see if I can get into the houses. Course, if you know what you're doing, you can create all kinds of hiding places."

"Why would he hide something at one of their houses?" Pewter, like the others, felt disappointment over the towel.

As if understanding the gray cat, Harry said, "He'd hide it in his truck or, more likely, his home."

Seeing Tazio's state had spurred Harry onward.

"I hope she doesn't break into his house." Tucker's brown eyes showed deep worry.

"For once, I agree with her." Mrs. Murphy watched the road, looking for cats walking about houses or sleeping in windows. *"The stakes are high and Tazio is a friend. Whatever Mom does, I'm doing it with her."*

Harry reached to the center of the bench seat. "Hey, where's my Reese's Peanut Butter Cup?"

No one uttered a peep.

At a stoplight Harry looked on the floor. If the animals had eaten her candy, the wrapper would be shredded. Not a trace. “I can’t believe that. Someone reached into my truck and stole my Reese’s Peanut Butter Cup!”

29

Saturday, October 4, was glorious with sunshine and radiated with the first flush of color, which would peak in about a week. Oaks blushed orange, yellow, russet; maples screamed scarlet. Zinnias stood huge and colorful. Willows bent over in yellow.

Herb called an emergency vestry-board meeting. The spectacular weather provoked him to keep a tight rein on it, because he wanted to be outside himself.

At eight in the morning, Harry, Susan, Folly, BoomBoom, and Nolan Carter showed up, so Herb had his quorum. Mrs. Murphy, Pewter, and Tucker also attended, but the exhaustive discussion of the furnace choices drove the animals down the hall, the thick carpet pleasing underfoot.

Elocution demonstrated how to hit the wall with four feet and do a flip. Cazenovia and Lucy Fur also performed this acrobatic feat, and Mrs. Murphy got the hang of it. Pewter observed but declined the opportunity.

"Come on, Pewts, it's fun." Mrs. Murphy hit the wall again, four clear pawprints on the light-beige paint.

Pawprints covered both sides of the hallway wall, because the three Lutheran cats practiced their skills daily. Herb pretended not to see all the marks, because then he'd have to kneel down to clean them. He could bend down just fine. It was the getting up that ached.

"Nolan, oil's your business. I would expect you to vote for the oil furnace as opposed to a heat pump," Herb genially teased him, although all were preoccupied with recent events.

Nolan, whose waist was expanding but not yet fat, stroked a neat Vandyke, which looked good on him. "Tell you what, there are two sides to this issue. The first is always what is cost-effective over the long run. The second is what provides the most efficient heat." He laid his palm flat on the big report that Tazio had prepared before the Poplar Forest fund-raiser horror. "A heat pump works great until it becomes bitter cold, down in the teens. Then your electric bill skyrockets and, for whatever reason, the heat is insufficient."

BoomBoom interjected, "Plus you feel the air from the vents. It's below body temperature, so it always feels cold."

"Yes, it does." He nodded. "However, how many days does the temperature sink like that?" He held up his hands, questioning. "A total of three weeks in the winter. Granted, you might not be as comfortable as you'd like during those three weeks, but you have fireplaces and that helps."

"Smells great, too." Harry used her fireplaces throughout the cold, plus she had a wood-burning stove in the basement, which worked wonders in keeping costs down. She kept the door to the basement open; the big stove was equipped with a blower, and the warm air curled up the stairs and throughout the house. She kept her thermostat at sixty-seven degrees, but the old frame house remained toasty.

Depend on Harry to find the least expensive way to do something without compromising value.

"What about oil prices?" Susan asked the obvious, pressing question.

"They're going to stay erratic, and it's not just the Middle East." Nolan leaned back on the big sofa. "As long as Nigeria is unstable and they blow up oil fields, it'll cost us. That's a high-grade oil, some of the best in the world. The short answer is: beware."

"Puts you in a spot," Folly said.

"Folly"—he turned to her—"it's more than a spot. I have elderly people on fixed incomes. They won't be able to pay their heating bills. If I don't deliver, they'll freeze. What do I do? Hurt myself or be a good Samaritan? And it's going to get worse."

"You are a good Samaritan, Nolan," Herb praised him.

"I think, at this time, go with the heat pump. The system she's selected here should be good for at least thirty years. By that time there has to be better technology available."

"Nolan, why couldn't we put in the oil furnace and burn ethanol?" BoomBoom liked technical problems.

"No, no." He shook his head. "I know

that's hyped as the answer. Someone touts a new technology as the answer and then it isn't. We've got real problems, and I don't see any shortcuts, despite what the press tells you. Get the heat pump."

Herb scanned the gathered. "What do you think? Shall we vote on it?"

"I move we vote to buy the heat-pump system selected by Tazio," Harry said.

"I second the motion." BoomBoom knew her *Robert's Rules of Order.*

"All in favor signify by raising your right hand and saying, 'Aye.' " Herb knew them, too. "The ayes have it." He chuckled because it was unanimous. "Now for the next question. Do we just do here or do we replace the church system, as well?"

A silence followed this. No one wished to scoot the budget into the red, but all realized if they put it off it would cost more later, possibly as much as twenty-five percent more.

Folly had been quieter than usual, but she did smile warmly at Harry, who was glad that she, herself, didn't carry heavy secrets.

While this discussion unfolded, the cats

and corgi played soccer with a canvas frog jammed full with aromatic catnip.

When Pewter got the frog, she inhaled deeply, her pupils enlarged, then she batted the frog and rolled over.

Tucker liked the catnip aroma, but it didn't have the same effect on her.

After ten minutes of this, the cats were silly. They flopped on their sides and giggled, the frog now between Cazenovia's paws.

The cats' giggling—little puffs of expelled air—made Tucker giggle, too. She expelled air, too, but it came out with a bit more force and sounded like, *"Ho."*

Most people don't think that animals can laugh, but cats, dogs, and horses can.

Elocution, on her side, reached out to snag the frog.

"No you don't." Cazenovia sank her claws in the canvas with a pleasing crunch sound.

"Did I tell you Mom visited Tazio yesterday?" Mrs. Murphy said to Lucy Fur.

"No, how is she?" Lucy asked.

"Going downhill, Mom thinks. Said she looked worn, thin, just drawn out." Pewter supplied the information.

"But the big news is, the two rats that live in Poplar Forest destroyed evidence," Tucker exclaimed.

Mrs. Murphy, Pewter, and Tucker eagerly related how Randolph and Sarah had eaten the bloody towel, as well as how Sarah "smoked" the Virginia Slims.

Lucy Fur licked one paw, then sat up, eyes still large. *"Poppy could be in danger."*

"You're not supposed to tell." Cazenovia sat up, too.

"We can tell. Poppy can't tell."

"What did he do?" Pewter loved Herb, as did they all.

"He didn't do anything," Lucy Fur announced firmly. *"Letters. Some of his parishioners received threatening letters, and when Will was killed they came to him. Others came when Little Mim stepped forward about her own past."*

"Great day." Tucker sighed.

"Why didn't he go to Rick straightaway?" Pewter thought this very strange.

"He can't. He's a minister, and if a person confesses to him, that information is sacred. He has been carrying this around, knowing what could happen." Cazenovia thought her poppy very brave.

"Do you know what was in the letters?" Pewter had a good idea.

"Sure. We all sat there during these tearful confessions. The first letters asked for money, not huge sums, but then the sums escalated. After Will was shot, they really skyrocketed," Lucy Fur informed them.

Elocution, head more clear now, added, *"Greedy."*

Cazenovia, her long calico hair lustrous, worried. *"Penny Lattimore came in Tuesday. Her latest letter from Jonathan Bechtal—supposedly from him, anyway—reminded her she was number two on the list if she didn't pay up. She decided she had to go to Rick and she'd have to tell her husband. She asked Poppy to go with her."*

"Did he?" Mrs. Murphy wanted to be certain of her facts.

"He did. I guess the hard part was telling Marvin that she'd had an affair; the abortion was due to that. Whatever became of that talk, I don't know." Elocution took a deep breath. *"I do know that Rick and Coop have taken her into protective custody. Even Marvin doesn't know where she is. They've put out this story that she's missing to see if*

they can flush out the blackmailer." Lucy Fur eyed the front of the house.

"Well, that might work," Pewter said.

"Might," Cazenovia agreed but qualified it. *"But what we're worried about is, what if the blackmailer figures out that some of his victims have confessed to Poppy? He'll come after him."*

"I hope not." Tucker's voice rose. *"Mom thinks that Mike McElvoy may have killed Carla. But if you think about it, he could be part of this. He's against abortion—Tazio told Mom that—but he presents himself as a reasonable person. So he makes money twice, first through his job, if he has been inventing problems at these construction sites and getting paid off, then through this."*

"I don't know." Mrs. Murphy inhaled, for the catnip scent remained strong. *"Mike would have to have his hands on Will Wylde's records and he'd have had to set up Jonathan Bechtal."*

"Set up? Jonathan confessed." Cazenovia thought that was that.

"I think that Jonathan Bechtal is being used as a cat's paw, forgive the expression." Mrs. Murphy's tiger coat glistened. *"Is he a fanatic? Obviously. Does he expect to get*

out in a few years' time to enjoy whatever money he and whoever have extorted from the patients? Maybe. But even if he isn't in this for the money, I'm willing to bet one of my nine lives that he believes the money goes to Love of Life, all the money. If he finds out otherwise, it could get ugly for whoever is on the outside."

"Mike McElvoy would be that person. And he might have a way into Will's records if he's a computer whiz." Elocution was considering all that had been said.

"He's up to no good, but is it that bad?" Tucker had learned that Mrs. Murphy eventually found the right path.

Cazenovia, thinking about all this and remembering the conversations women had with Poppy, piped up, *"Who was number one if Penny is number two?"*

"Dr. Wylde." Lucy Fur stated this with conviction.

"But he wouldn't have been blackmailed." Mrs. Murphy felt sure of this. *"He'd stood up to death threats before. I don't think he was number one."*

"Little Mim," Pewter declared.

"More likely, but I don't know." Mrs. Murphy flicked the tip of her tail. *"What I do*

know is that the other women who have been paying off have not gone to Rick. Herb knows those of his parish. He can't be the only minister hearing their stories. The other thing is that Harry will blunder right into it. We've got two of our people to protect."

30

"Why don't you buy your own car?" Susan grumbled as she drove her Audi station wagon from the vestry-board meeting. "Here it is Saturday, a perfect day for chores and errands, and I'm hauling your little white butt around."

"Too much money." Harry affected a prudent and pious tone.

"Your husband will buy you a car if you want one."

"It seems . . ." She thought for a moment. "Excessive."

"So I drive out to your farm, pick you up, bring you to St. Luke's, and now we're cruising around because you want to enjoy how great my wagon rides. I've spent three dollars in gas just picking you up."

"I'll pay you." Harry wrinkled her nose.

"Besides, I take you places in my truck. And I just discovered my truck needs a new alternator, so it's in the shop. You can drop me off on the way home."

"Your F-150 that was foaled in 1978? It's not a bad ride. Better than your dually. That thing will rattle your teeth."

Harry nodded. "It may suck up gas, but it hauls the rig, hauls the flatbed. I can do a lot of farm chores with that, and it saves me buying another tractor. Blair lends me his big eighty-horsepower. I thought I might could buy it when he and Little Mim moved to Rose Hill, but he took the tractor. Good thing, because she was still using that old Massey Ferguson from the seventies, the one where the gears would lock up and you'd fly along. Scared the poop out of me when I saw it."

"What is that old Massey Ferguson in horsepower?"

"One twenty."

"Mercy." Even though not a farmer, Susan, like most people in the area, had an appreciation of the equipment, maintenance, skill, and time it took to produce any crop.

Now that she and Harry were partners in

the timber tract, she was learning a lot and she loved it.

"So, what's your gas mileage?"

"I tell you this every time we go out." Susan noticed a maple tree downtown in high orange-red color.

The trees and bushes in town usually peaked before the ones in the country, because town temperature was often five or more degrees higher due to building density, more asphalt roads, and more car and furnace emissions.

"Twenty-five miles to the gallon on the open road. Sometimes twenty-eight," Tucker piped up, since she'd heard it so many times.

Susan patiently repeated these same numbers to Harry.

"Pretty good for an engine this big, machine this heavy."

"You're not old enough to get Alzheimer's; maybe you have Halfzheimer's," Susan teased her.

"I remember. I like to hear you say it," Harry teased her back.

"Funny, Ned took Owen to the office today, and I miss my little guy. We spend most every waking moment together."

"Corgi love." Tucker smiled.

"Don't make me throw up." Pewter faked a gag.

"Hairball! Hairball alert!" Mrs. Murphy jumped away in mock disgust.

"Better than a worm-hanging-out-of-your-butt alert." Pewter's pupils narrowed for a second.

"I have never had a worm emerge from my nether regions." Mrs. Murphy was incensed.

"Oh, puh-leese Louise." Pewter drew out the word. *"I've seen spaghetti strings out of that anus."*

"Never!" Mrs. Murphy cuffed the gray cat, who slapped her right back.

"Get me out of here," Tucker whined as she tried to climb into the passenger seat up front.

"No, Tucker." Harry turned. "You two, stop it. If I have to crawl back there, there will be big trouble in River City. You hear me?"

"I hear you, but I'm not listening." Pewter whacked Mrs. Murphy again.

Mrs. Murphy leapt onto the rotund kitty. Since Susan had put the seats down, the

two now rolled all the way to the hatchback door.

"Susan, if you pull over, I'll settle this."

"Oh, let them have at it."

"You'll have blood in your car."

"Harpy!" Pewter snarled.

"Liar!" Mrs. Murphy scratched.

The lightbulb switched on in Tucker's brain, and she called out above their mutual insults, *"What I want to know, Pewter, is what are you doing studying Mrs. Murphy's anus?"*

This produced the desired effect. Both cats stopped screaming and clawing.

Pewter disentangled herself from the tiger cat, huffed up to full blowfish proportion, and jumped sideways toward the corgi. *"Death to dogs!"*

"Don't think about it." Tucker, bracing herself, snarled.

"Harry will put you in mincemeat pie when I'm done shredding." Her chartreuse eyes, pupils full to the max, glittered with fury.

Mrs. Murphy, who should have known better, leapt on Pewter from behind, and the two rolled back to the hatchback door again.

"All right!" Harry turned to Susan. "Let me settle this."

Susan pulled off High Street into a bank parking lot. "They'll scratch you."

"They'd better not if they know what's good for them."

Harry opened her door. Hearing it slam, the cats perceived the situation. They parted, retreating to opposite sides of the back, and began grooming.

Harry flipped up the hatchback. "Just what in the hell do you two think you're doing?" No feline response brought forth a human torrent. "It's a privilege to ride in this station wagon. It's a privilege to visit Cazenovia, Lucy Fur, and Elocution. And it's a privilege to cruise around town. If I hear one squeak, one snarl, one ugly meow, you two worthless cats are never riding in this station wagon again. Worthless. You haven't caught one mouse in the barn, and I know they are there."

Mrs. Murphy replied, *"We have a deal with the tack-room mice. They aren't destructive. They're—"*

Pewter interrupted. *"She hasn't a clue."*

"You shut up, fatty screw loose. You're the reason we're in this predicament."

"Me! Me!" Pewter stood up.

"Don't you dare." Harry grabbed her by the scruff of the neck, shaking her lightly, the way her feline mother would have done.

Releasing the gray cannonball, Harry peered intently at Mrs. Murphy, pointing her index finger right at her. All three animals knew what that meant. The next gesture would be a little smack on the fanny.

Harry shut the hatchback, returned to the front. "Susan, how do people with children do it? You had two."

"Animals are more intelligent." Susan laughed good-naturedly.

Harry wheeled around as if to catch the cats off guard. "I'm watching you."

Silence.

They drove east on High Street. "How about I turn down by Fifth Street and I'll pick up 64?"

"How about we cruise by Woolen Mills first?"

"What's in Woolen Mills?"

"Mike McElvoy's house." Before Susan could protest, Harry rapidly said, "When we were at the Poplar Forest ball, Mike and Noddy came by. The usual small talk, and she kidded about his work shed. Said he'd spent as much money on that as she did remodeling the kitchen."

"And?"

"She said it's where he buries the bodies."

"Harry, that's a figure of speech."

"Well, we can at least peek in it. Susan, remember Tazio told us he's antiabortion, and might I remind you, Tazio is still in jail. What's a drive by?"

"Nothing I guess, unless you swing the shotgun out the window." She exhaled. "I don't know why I let you talk me into these things."

"Because I'm your best friend. Because you love me."

Susan smiled. "I do, but you drive me crazy."

"Not a far putt."

They both laughed uproariously.

"Yeah, well." Susan shrugged.

"I love you, too." Harry waited a beat, then whirled around again. "I'm watching."

"Two-legged toad. You'll get back trouble before I do," Pewter sassed, but her anger toward Mrs. Murphy ebbed.

"Miss Hemorrhoid," Mrs. Murphy added, a devilish glint to her eyes.

Triumphantly, the gray cat sang out, *"Now who's talking about anuses."*

Mrs. Murphy froze, considered another retaliatory attack, but thought better of it, for Harry meant what she said.

The two-story frame house, painted a Williamsburg blue with white trim, came into view. It was at the end of the street, which afforded a bit more quiet, not that Woolen Mills was particularly noisy. It was a pleasant neighborhood, the only drawback being when the winds changed at the city sewage-treatment plant.

"Hey, those boxwoods are gorgeous." Susan noted the boxwoods lining the walkway to the front porch.

"English. Tight as a tick." Harry craned her neck to see the shed. "Slow down."

"I'm going five miles an hour," Susan dryly replied.

As she turned in the small cul de sac, Harry caught sight of the shed at the rear of the verdant lawn. "Hey, that is nice, and he has a gravel drive up to it. He could do all kinds of things there, and who would notice?"

"Presumably Noddy?"

"Naw." Harry shook her head. "If he's

there working away or using a computer or something, she'd be busy herself."

"Where did I read that Internet porn sites have become a big problem in marriage?" Susan tried to recall the magazine as she drove out of the cul de sac.

"You'd think it would be better than hiring prostitutes."

"That's not the point," Susan, more thoughtful on these matters than Harry, replied. "The point is that instead of communicating with his wife or his girlfriend, a man watches porn sites with those icons of physical perfection. Empty sex."

"That's probably true. I've never seen a porn site." Harry turned to Susan. "Who has the time to sit down and watch a computer or TV? You know, I didn't watch one baseball game all the way through this summer, and I love my Orioles."

"You and I are in the minority. Americans squander millions of hours in front of the TV. I read somewhere that it totals eight years of a life. And then there's the computer screen. It's sad and frightening."

"Here's what I don't get. Why do men watch porn when there's a living, breathing woman in the next room?"

"Because they aren't communicating, like I said. That is one thing I will give Ned. He'll talk. Oh, I might have to goad him into it or charm him, but he will. It's one of the reasons we've weathered some of the storms we have." She picked up speed. "He's a good man."

"That he is." Harry was quiet, looked in the back again with a glare, then returned her attentions to Susan. "Fair communicates better than I do. I don't know. I can't get the words out. Hell, most of the time, I don't even know what I'm feeling."

"I know."

"What do you mean by that?"

"That those of us who know you and love you know that speaking about your emotions isn't your forté. But when you must face them, you do. Course, it takes a damned disaster."

She replied ruefully, "I don't understand how I can be smart in one area and just dumb as a sack of hammers in another."

"We're all like that. You've seen me struggle with math. If it weren't for you, I'd never have gotten through geometry and algebra in high school."

"I love math. There's always an answer."

"Exactly." Susan smiled broadly. "Emotions aren't clear-cut like that. But don't you find, as you get older, that you improve in the area where you're, say, not so gifted?"

"Kinda." Harry changed the subject, since she never could think what to say about her emotional reticence. "If I had the money, do you know what car I would buy? If practicality weren't an issue?"

"A big Mercedes?"

"They are stupendous. But that's still practical. I'd buy a Porsche 911 C4." Animation filled her body. "Oh, that sweet, short throw between gears, the top note of the engine. God, I love it."

"Gearhead."

"I am, but you know, so is BoomBoom."

"Wonder why she never bought a Porsche?"

"She switched to Mercedes because of BMW's iDrive. She likes big cars, so Porsches are too small. But now Mercedes has Command system, just as ridiculous as iDrive. Bet she does buy a Porsche next." Harry shook her head. "The Germans may well be the most intelligent people on the face of the earth when it comes to engineering, music, and I would have to say war, but they do tend to overcomplicate."

"War. How can you say that?"

"Look at what they accomplished since Frederick the Great. Their fatal mistake was not learning the painful lesson of World War One."

"Which was?"

"Germany can't fight a war on two fronts, and Germany can never defeat the United States."

"Ah." Susan liked history, although modern history fascinated her less than the eighteenth century, her favorite time. "But have we learned anything from World War One and World War Two?"

"I think we did. The real question is, did we learn anything from Vietnam?"

"God, Harry, I hope so."

They drove along, thinking about these issues. These two dear friends, born with lively minds, might delight in daily doings and local events, but they could and did consider larger issues. Chances are, the Founding Fathers and Mothers would see in them a vindication of their hopes for an enlightened citizenry. What else the Founding

Fathers and Mothers might think of the times was anybody's guess.

"Susan, I have got to get into that shed." Harry was allowing her desperation to free Tazio and to pin the crimes on Mike to muddy her usually clear head.

"Don't you dare." Susan's voice rose.

"There might be evidence."

"If that man is a killer, you're putting yourself in grave danger, forgive the pun."

"You'd do it for me."

"I'd like to think I would." Susan turned onto the ramp heading west onto 64.

"Tazio deserves it. She's not close like you and I are close, but she deserves help."

"Let Paul do it. Tell him."

"Susan, I can't do that and you know it. Paul wouldn't be any good at something like this."

"You may be right about that, but, Harry, don't even think about it. If you're that worried, send Cooper or Rick there."

"Can't do that without compelling evidence of either corruption or murder or both. I have to find some evidence. We know Carla loathed him. We know he's antiabortion."

"That's hardly enough to convict a man,

and being antiabortion doesn't make him Bechtal's accomplice. I beg you, don't do this."

As they rode in silence, everyone in that Audi station wagon knew that Harry would not listen to Susan's good sense.

31

Sunday, October 5, flourished under the stationary high-pressure system that had ushered in the heartbreakingly beautiful weather of yesterday. The sky, intense blue, domed an emerald-green Virginia quickening to the accelerated pace of fall.

Harry dutifully sat in church with her equally dutiful husband. She soon forgot to be antsy, because Herb gave a sermon based on Mark, Chapter 10, Verse 16.

"And he took them up in his arms, put his hands upon them, and blessed them."

The good reverend expounded on this theme. How do we nurture one another, comfort one another, walk through life together?

She hoped she could remember not just what he said but also how he said it in his deep, resonant voice, because she wanted to repeat it word for word to Miranda. He would return to the sentence from Mark as a refrain. She was pretty sure she could remember that.

As the service ended and the choir sang, the parishioners marched out to where Herb, as was his custom, stood at the front door, shaking everyone's hand, inquiring as to their health and welfare before sending them on their way. Such a simple act—putting his hand upon them—bound them all closer together. When she felt his warm hand shake hers, his left hand touch her shoulder, she realized with a thud that Herb had been practicing what he had been preaching for decades.

She left him, warmed as well as wondering how she could miss something so obvious. She determined to try to be more like Herb. Given her focus on task, this would be a challenge.

"Honey, give me a minute. I have to catch up on Zenaida."

As Fair nodded, turning to talk to other congregants, she raced over to the woman in charge of food for the October 25 St. Luke's reunion. Harry promised four bushels of Silver Queen corn, harvested in August and put in cold storage. She worried it might not be enough and that the corn might not be as tasty as she'd hoped. Silver Queen should be eaten the second it's plucked off the stalk. However, good yellow corn was still being harvested in the southernmost counties of Virginia, and she wondered if she should purchase some as a backup.

Harry noticed while she and Zenaida spoke that Fair, lively and laughing, was talking with Susan and Ned. His countenance changed for a moment, becoming concerned.

He is the most empathetic man, she thought to herself, then returned to corn. "If it has to be Silver Queen, I expect I can get it sent up from Georgia. Florida? Want me to call around?"

"That gets pricey." Zenaida furrowed her gray brows. "Yellow will do."

"I'll pick up a couple of ears from the refrigeration plant and do a test run. With any luck, we might be okay."

"Good. Do that first." Zenaida, easy to work with, smiled underneath her burgundy velvet hat.

Ladies still wore hats to service at St. Luke's. Harry usually plucked whatever complemented her outfit, but if she felt like spiting whoever sat behind her—an un-Christian action—in summer she'd wear a broad-brimmed hat with flowers. Since she spent most of her day wearing a baseball hat, she felt denuded without something on her head.

When she rejoined Fair and they walked back to his truck, she asked, "How are Susan and Ned?"

"Fine. Susan told me how badly our two little girls behaved yesterday."

"They still aren't speaking."

"Ned said they've made bail. Big Mim will have all the money together. He'll go down Tuesday."

"Oh, thank God." Harry's right hand flew to her breast. "Does Paul know?"

"Ned called him this morning before Mass. The paperwork this takes." He furrowed his brow. "Ned was telling me and all I could think of is that it doesn't matter what profession one's in, we're drowning in paperwork."

"Wasteful." She wrinkled her nose.

"It is that, but on the other hand, it creates a lot of paper-pushing jobs, which means fewer people are unemployed, more people are paying mortgages and have a stake in the system, hence political stability."

"Aren't you smart." She reached for his hand and squeezed it.

"Just realistic. He said Little Mim has come through the firestorm and he thinks, although she's lost the support of groups like Love of Life, she's gained more from others. He thinks she can run for governor maybe in six or eight years."

"He wants it first."

"He did, but this first year down in Richmond has been a real eye-opener for him. I would guess any first-timer to politics faces entrenched interests and even more entrenched egos. Given his touch of idealism, it's hard for him."

"There's where Little Mim shines. She inherited her mother's hardness. But Big Mim does have a vision, and I suppose it's progressive. Just no illusions about how you get things done."

"She's an honorable woman, but she knows you crack eggs to make an omelet." He smiled.

"I'm proud of Little Mim." Harry waited as he opened the door for her. "Any word on Penny Lattimore?"

"No." He shook his head. "Ned called Rick, who said they hadn't heard from her."

"I hope she's not dead. This scares me. When someone like Penny disappears, it's . . ." She didn't know how to finish the sentence. Events were spinning out of control, and apart from Tazio's bail, she perceived little progress.

"I don't know how much more of this our little community can stand." He echoed her worry.

32

Monday felt like the freight train that pulls all those cars behind it. Harry stoked the engine. She'd whipped through her basic farm chores like the proverbial tornado and then she gathered up her buddies—the cats still on the outs with each other—cranked up the F-150 enhanced by a new alternator, and drove to Woolen Mills.

At two-thirty in the afternoon, she figured Mike would be on a job site, Noddy would be at the office, and she could sneak into his shed.

Mike could come and go as he pleased, as long as he got to the job sites on his list for that week. She didn't factor his flexible schedule into her plans.

She parked the truck down the street.

Most of the neighbors worked. A few dogs barked, but quiet reigned.

She carefully walked up the front walk, flanked by those beautiful English boxwoods, then ducked between them. As she did, the peculiar odor of the plant rubbed on her. The cats and dogs scooted through, as well.

She walked around the shed, hoping there'd be a door in the back, but there wasn't. She tried the only door. Locked. No surprise.

However, she had a thin file, a cigarette lighter, and a pocketknife. She kept the lighter in the truck, because she'd learned that sometimes you need to light a candle, burn off the end of a rope.

Given that the house sat at the end of the road and the shed reposed on the back of the lawn, she didn't worry about anyone seeing her.

The lock, although simple, resisted her clumsy attempts at picking with the file. Exasperated, she opened the long blade from the pocketknife, wedged it in, and began slowly urging the tongue of the lock to move it back. Sweating, cursing, she finally managed to press it back after fifteen minutes, and she swung open the door, closing it behind her.

"Wow," she exclaimed as she admired the organized work space, tools hung up on Peg-Board, nails in jars, all marked in a row. The gun parts fascinated her. He'd know how to procure a silencer, she was certain, but a hunch wasn't hard evidence. Still, it spurred her on. At the back of the work space rested a large red metal toolbox, about four feet high. She pulled open one drawer. Again, every implement was clean, carefully laid in place.

She walked around the space. Nothing indicated wrongdoing. She tried the door to the office. Fortunately, it was unlocked. The cats scooted in first. Once inside the room, she unlocked the window, in case she needed to make a quick escape.

"She's more curious than we are," Pewter grumbled. *"And not as smart."*

Tucker sat inside by the office door, which Harry had closed, watching, listening with those marvelous ears.

Harry opened Mike's desk drawers, checked the shelves. She checked her watch. Three forty-five. The trip to Woolen Mills from Crozet had taken forty minutes, thanks to traffic. She picked up the pace. She rapped on the walls. She located the studs, but nothing sounded as though it was filled with treasure. She hoped to hear that *thunk.*

She rolled the chair away and pulled back the heavy rubber mat. The trapdoor ring, black, caught her eye. Eagerly, she pulled it upright, tugged, and the door swung up, a musty smell rising with it.

"Aha." She climbed down, the cats readily following her, since they climbed the wall ladder at the barn daily. Harry pulled the string on the overhead light, which revealed rows of boxes. She began opening them.

She found the jewelry, the money, and the panties. "I've got him! I've got him!"

As she put the lids back on, closed up the metal box, too, they heard Tucker barking in the toolshed.

"Dumb dog." Pewter's eyes widened.

Mrs. Murphy quickly said, *"Pewter, jump on a shelf."*

"Why?"

"Just do it."

"Mike!" Tucker warned.

"Shut up, Tucker." Mrs. Murphy commanded, but it was too late.

As Mike ran toward his shed, Harry climbed up the ladder. But before she could reach the window, Mike blasted into the room.

Without a word, he hit her hard across the face.

Tucker jumped out from behind the door and bit his leg. He shook the dog off, grabbed a heavy coffee mug, and slammed Harry on the side of the head.

It didn't knock her out, but it made her woozy. He quickly kicked her down the hole, climbing down after her. Even the cats jumping on his back didn't stop him. He stuffed his handkerchief in her mouth, whipped off his belt, and wrapped it around her hands behind her back.

He climbed back up, slammed the door down, pulled the rubber mat over it, and rolled the chair back on the mat. He had forgotten to switch off the light, although no one would see it.

He tried to catch Tucker, but those long fangs and her quick maneuvers prevented that. Instead, he shut the door behind him, leaving the dog inside.

He hurried back to the house. He didn't know what he was going to do; Noddy would be home soon. She left work at four every day because she went into the office at seven-thirty in the morning.

"Lick her face," Mrs. Murphy ordered Pewter.

The two cats licked, their rough tongues providing what a facialist would term "exfoliation."

Harry's eyes fluttered. She grunted a little. "Damn, my head hurts."

"Tucker," Mrs. Murphy meowed as loudly as she could. *"Only bark if someone comes back."*

They heard the claws click across the boards then soften as the dog walked on the heavy mat.

"I drew blood." Tucker wished she could have reached his throat.

"So did he," Pewter called up.

"Is she all right?"

"Cut on her forehead and temple. A lump is coming up, but she's all right. We have to get the handkerchief out of her mouth so she doesn't choke on it."

"I will, Murphy, I will," Pewter said.

The mighty little dog sat down, deeply worried. Their only prayer was that Mike wouldn't shoot. Too many people in the neighborhood would hear him, even if he closed the trapdoor. A gun makes a smart report. He probably wouldn't slash her throat in his shed, because of the mess. He would have to get Harry out after Noddy was asleep.

All three of the animals figured that out, and so did Harry.

She struggled to free her hands from the belt. The cats bit on it. They might be able to bite through enough of it to weaken it, but it would take maybe a half hour, maybe an hour.

Fair called her cell. She didn't answer. He called home. He called the barn. Finally, he called Susan.

"Susan, is Harry with you?"

"No."

"It's four-thirty. She's a creature of habit, and on Mondays she'd be putting back bedding in the stalls she stripped and aired out yesterday. I think she's done what you predicted. She's not answering her cell. Something's wrong."

"I'll call Coop."

"Good. I'm going to Mike's."

Susan gave him directions, and it took him until five-thirty to get there, because of rush-hour traffic. Fortunately, most of it was heading west, but there was enough to make him truly worry.

Fair saw Harry's truck parked on the street, and he hoped he was in time. He was so scared he wasn't even mad at her.

He parked, hurried out, but didn't go up the walk, because Susan had told him where the shed was.

Tucker barked, *"Fair! It's Fair."*

Dogs and cats can identify footfalls and tire sounds, but humans can't.

Hearing the corgi, Fair ran. The door was locked. He slammed his shoulder against it and broke it down.

Mike heard the dog, then saw Fair. Noddy ran to the back kitchen window, too.

"What is Fair Haristeen doing?" She put her hand on the doorknob.

He covered her hand. "You stay here."

He ran outside just as Fair, who now could hear his wife and the cats, reached the desk. Frantically, Fair kicked the chair back, pulled the mat off, and flipped up the trapdoor as Mike barreled through the shed door.

Tucker cunningly hid behind the office door. As Mike opened the door, ready to brain Fair with a crowbar he'd snatched off his workroom wall, the corgi sank his fangs all the way into Mike's calf.

Fair spun on his heels and hit Mike with a right cross, using all his weight and six feet five inches. Mike's eyes rolled back in his head and he fell clean backward, half out the door.

The crowbar hit the floor with a heavy clunk.

Noddy ran in after him, shocked at what she saw.

"Noddy, stay right there." Fair scared her. "The police will be here in a minute. Don't try to run."

"Why?" She hadn't a clue.

Fair slid down the ladder like a fireman and quickly undid the belt, which the cats had worked on.

"He was going to kill me," Harry, shaken, gasped, but she kept possession of herself.

Fair spied the handkerchief on the floor and knew what Mike had done. "How'd you get the handkerchief out of your mouth?"

"The cats pulled it out, or I'd be dead. It was slipping back in my throat."

Fair picked up Mrs. Murphy in one arm, Pewter in the other, and kissed their heads, then kissed his wife. Noddy had crept to the opened trapdoor and knelt down.

"Don't shut that, Noddy."

"I didn't even know it was here," she, bug-eyed, answered Fair.

"Help her out, will you?" Fair boosted Harry up.

Noddy gently lifted her out.

Mike rolled over, shook his head, spit out some teeth, just as Fair came up behind Harry.

Lightning-fast, Fair put his knee on Mike's back, yanked his arms behind him, and used his own belt to tie him up. Then he kicked him over, as Noddy grimaced.

"You killed Carla, and Penny, too, didn't you?"

"They found Penny?" Noddy slumped in the office chair.

"No," Fair told her. "Not yet."

Even though her head was splitting, Harry thought she had never heard a sound so sweet as Cooper's squad-car siren, followed by another.

Within minutes Cooper and Rick hurried into the shed.

"Down there." Harry pointed to the opened trapdoor.

"Penny?" Noddy feared the worst.

"No. No bodies, Noddy, but enough to send your husband down the river for a long, long time."

She put her head in her hands and wept.

"Did you know?" Fair asked.

She shook her head no, as Rick bent over and dropped down into the space.

Cooper read Mike his rights.

Another squad car arrived, and the officer stood patiently in the office doorway.

Rick's head popped up, his hands on the floor. "Doak, cordon the place off. I want everything photographed, cataloged, tabulated. There's enough here to convict him."

"For murder?" Dooley hoped.

"For theft, extortion, and maybe even rape. With luck, murder will follow."

"Rape," Noddy wailed.

"I didn't kill anybody!" Mike's broken teeth made him suck in air. He shut his mouth in a hurry after he spoke.

"That's what they all say." Cooper wanted to kick the rest of his teeth in.

After Harry provided what information she could, she and Fair left.

"Ride with me. We can come back for your truck tomorrow."

A grateful and chastened Harry cuddled the cats and dog. As Fair drove them home, she said in a small voice, "I'm sorry. If you hadn't saved me he would have killed me tonight."

"Susan told me about your drive by. It didn't take a rocket scientist to figure out where you were. She called Coop."

"I'm sure he's Bechtal's outside man. I just know. Crazy ass, to do what he did to those women. He had money, he had jewels, you wouldn't believe what he had down there."

"He almost had you."

"I thought about that, too." She rubbed her temple, then winced. "You know, these cats and dog would have died to save me."

"I know." Tears came into Fair's eyes.

"I was a fool."

"Yes," he quietly said. "And you were very, very lucky."

"Well, maybe we can celebrate that." She sighed, feeling both guilty and vindicated.

Not quite.

33

"Mother!" Brinkley put his paws on Tazio's shoulders and kissed her face as she bent her knees slightly to greet him.

Paul had wanted to go to the prison with Ned, and Big Mim thought that was fine. She could do with a day in the stables herself.

However, through Ned, Tazio had asked that Paul stay at work. She wanted to wash the stink of the prison off her, fix her hair, girly herself up.

Ned brought Brinkley.

On the drive home, Ned provided all the details he had of Mike McElvoy's arrest.

"Did he confess to the murders?"

"No. He swears he's innocent." Ned couldn't help the irritation that crept into his voice. "So, kid, we're still not out of the woods yet, and it will be expensive."

"At least I'm out of jail. How can I ever thank Big Mim for going to people and raising bail?"

"By being yourself. She likes you. Well, she'd have to, wouldn't she?" He smiled. "There is one thing."

"What? A building?"

"Big Mim has wanted to create an orangery for years. Never got around to it. Perhaps you might surprise her with plans."

Her eyes brightened, for Tazio had never designed an orangery.

Always up to a new challenge, she said, "I will. Wonder if I can create a misting system that won't be intrusive."

Ned smiled broadly this time, because he knew Tazio was on her way back to the Tazio they all knew. This experience had bruised a sensitive soul.

Given what she considered her state of ugliness, it took Tazio two full hours to prepare herself. Then she hopped in her wheels—with Brinkley, the happiest dog in America, in the passenger seat—and drove to the stables.

Paul, in a back paddock, heard the engine. He quietly slipped the halter off the yearling, closed the gate, and burned the wind running to the parking lot, the halter flapping all the while, for he had forgotten to hang it up.

Tazio had no sooner taken three steps from the car than Paul smothered her in an embrace. Then she cried and cried. She'd known she loved him, even though she'd kept that to herself. But she hadn't known how much.

He cried, too.

Brinkley, respectfully seated, wagged his tail because he knew they weren't sad tears.

"I love you," Tazio simply said.

Big Mim, who had just come out of the house to walk into the garden, saw them out of the corner of her eye. She thought she'd wait a little before going down there, but she did see Paul drop to one knee, take Tazio's right hand in his. She looked up to heaven and thought, truly the Lord works in mysterious ways, His wonders to perform.

After Tazio agreed to marry Paul, the two of them, holding hands, walked up from the stables to the big house. Tazio wanted to thank Big Mim.

Big Mim waved from the garden as she saw them coming, took off her gardening apron, and opened her arms.

"Thank you. Thank you," Tazio cried again.

Paul did, too.

Big Mim managed to hold it in, but she swallowed hard. "You'll be cleared. Wait until you read today's papers."

Paul wiped his eyes with his hand, straightened his shoulders, and spoke with his seductive accent. "Mrs. Sanburne, Tazio has granted me the honor to become my wife."

"Marvelous!" Big Mim kissed Tazio and Paul. "You couldn't have chosen a better partner, nor a more beautiful woman. You are a lucky man."

Paul beamed and Tazio said, "I'm pretty lucky, too."

Big Mim held Tazio's hands in hers, enthusiasm in her voice. "I know you two have a lot to do, people to call, but, Tazio, you have got to read this. Come on."

In the kitchen, Tazio sat down and Gretchen made her coffee. Big Mim put the front page in front of Tazio as Paul sat next to her.

"Oh, my God." Tazio enunciated each

word slowly. “Oh, my God.” As she read, her breathing grew stronger and she couldn’t stop interjecting phrases throughout.

“Isn’t that the most incredible thing you have ever read?” Paul said as she put the paper down and picked up the coffee cup.

“Harry could have been murdered.”

“Would have.” Big Mim enjoyed her third cup today—one too many, but what the hell.

“He’s claiming innocence. That will slow the process, but how many murderers confess?” Gretchen couldn’t help but throw that in.

“State prosecutor will get him.” Big Mim hoped so, anyway. “Sixty-two thousand dollars in cash and all that jewelry. And he cataloged every single woman he had taken money, jewelry, and panties from. It’s so bizarre. Why catalog?”

“Possession.” Tazio, with insight, said, “He still felt he possessed them.”

“The panties. How can anyone live that down?” Gretchen laughed.

“He’ll be living it down in jail. And maybe this time he’ll be the victim.” Tazio felt a flash of genuine hate for Mike.

“Noddy will bring him soap on a rope

so he doesn't have to bend over in the shower." Gretchen laughed.

"Gretchen." Big Mim pretended to be scandalized.

"Noddy will divorce him if she has a grain of sense." Tazio shook her head.

"I can't imagine the humiliation she feels." Paul glanced at the article again.

"He was probably complicit in Will's murder, but it will take a great deal of work to prove it. The rub is proving he killed Carla. He was absent from his table, but so were others." Big Mim folded her hands on her lap. "Rick will crack it. I have faith in him."

34

Mike McElvoy, in the cell next to Jonathan Bechtal's, talked to him over the days. When he was talking to him, he listened to Jonathan's delusions about being the hammer arm of God.

Neither man particularly liked the other.

A week had passed since Mike's arrest. Noddy refused to visit him. The guard gave him the daily papers. Each day his shame deepened—not guilt but shame.

"You're cooked." Jonathan cheerfully read the papers, too.

"Shut up."

"Don't tell me to shut up, you pervert. What do you do with those panties? Jerk off into them?" Mike ignored this. "Couldn't get enough from your wife. She's dumped you, too."

"Shut up. No one visits you."

Jonathan's face darkened. His beard, now straggly since he wasn't allowed any grooming implements, made him look fiercer. "My angel can't visit me. No one must know."

"Married, is she?" Mike crossed his arms over his chest.

"You shut your filthy mouth. She's a pure, sweet angel. She's not married. She'll never marry. She's married to our great cause of saving lives. They'll kill me eventually, but I die a martyr. I die for the unborn."

"She'll open her legs before your body is cold." Mike could give as good as he got.

Jonathan slammed up against the cell bars between them. "I'll strangle you if you get near enough."

"Yeah. Yeah."

As it was Monday, the usual medley of drunks from the weekend had been released. Only the two of them were incarcerated.

Jonathan, clever in his way, lowered his anger and his voice. "Why didn't you take the money and the jewelry and run?"

Mike got up, pacing. "Never thought I'd be caught. Every one of those women had something to hide. Affairs. Drinking or drug problems. The usual. I'd drop a few knowing hints, looks, and wait for a guilty flush. You'd be surprised how easy it can be. And you know, a few wanted it. Bored with their husbands."

"You shouldn't sleep with a woman if you don't love her, if you don't marry her." Jonathan truly was a Puritan.

"You say. You miss a lot, buddy." Mike smiled sarcastically. "Why didn't you run? You might have gotten away with it. Killed more doctors."

"I wanted to be caught. I wanted to be heard."

"People think you're nuts."

Jonathan's anger welled up again; he forced it down. "Saving lives, that's crazy now. You said you were a member of Love of Life. What's the matter with you?"

"I do think it's murder." Mike paused. "And I didn't kill anyone."

"I did," Jonathan solemnly declared. "Vengeance is mine, saith the Lord."

"You helped it along." Mike started to say, "And you hurt our cause," but he didn't, because they'd had that discussion before, at high decibel level.

"I'd do it again. We planned it. We gathered a lot of money for the cause, and my angel is keeping it. Love of Life doesn't know of our great plan to shut down every abortion clinic and doctor in America. Those were my letters after I was in jail. I'd written them before. My angel thought of that so we'd get even more money for our cause. Killing Will would open their bank accounts to us. It would scare the money right out of them. We'd get everything out of those murdering women."

"One of them turned out to be braver than you thought." Mike meant Little Mim.

"God will take care of her in His own way and in His own time." Jonathan, at first elated that a fellow traveler was in the cell next to him, had soured as he got to know Mike. "He'll take care of you, too."

"When you go before St. Peter, you'll have bigger sins to confess than I do. I didn't kill anybody. And now that Penny Lattimore has come out of hiding, I hope she'll tell the sheriff that, yes, I put the touch on her, but I never threatened to kill her. I underestimated the sheriff. Pretending that Penny had disappeared scared some of the other women you'd blackmailed into going to him. At least that's what I think. And I never, ever, threatened to kill Carla or Penny."

"She'll die." Jonathan tightened his lips.

"We'll all die."

"She's number two."

Mike, stupid in some ways and no fool in others, pretended not to be galvanized by this information. "Carla was number one."

"Was?"

"Refused to pay?"

"She paid, but after I was in jail she got hysterical. Carla got hysterical when Will was shot. My angel said you would have thought Carla'd been shot. Murdering woman."

"Your angel?"

"My angel is doing God's work. God speaks to me and I speak to her. As you know, God doesn't speak to women. Carla had an abortion. She was a murdering woman. The only way these killers can atone for their monstrous sins is to give money to our cause so we can save more children. If they don't, they die. My angel took care of Carla."

"Why does your angel keep the money?" Mike pretended not to care that he'd just heard who killed Carla, even though he could not identify the woman.

"Idiot! How would it look if large sums of cash were handed to the treasurer? Love of Life won't put the doctors out of business. Too scared. No real fire for the task. We need the money to complete our work. I'll die, and my angel will have her revenge."

Mike leaned back on his bunk. How could he get to Rick without Jonathan knowing? The man never seemed to sleep. If Mike asked the guard anything, Jonathan would know. But he'd heard from this fanatic's own lips that his angel/accomplice had killed Carla.

There wasn't but so much Mike could do about his crimes, but he could at least clear himself of murder. In an odd way he was glad he'd been caught, because he would have killed Harry. And killing was never his intention.

35

Rick walked with Coop across Jackson Park toward the courthouse downtown on Thursday, October 16. "What do you make of it?"

"He's trying to save his skin."

"Yes, but it is plausible."

"Then we'd better put security on Penny Lattimore."

"Marvin is rich enough to hire his own. I'll call him. Remember, if we go over budget I have to face the commissioners; you don't."

"If I did, I'd wear a low-cut dress and show cleavage. Works every time."

Rick laughed. "How would I know? I've never had the privilege."

She laughed, too. "Really. They've done studies to show that when men think of sex they can't think."

"They needed to do studies for that?"

"Is pretty silly, isn't it? How many thousands of years have we known what we are?"

Rick pulled out a cigarette, stopping to light it. He handed it to her for a puff. "Best damned things."

"I used the five dollars I won from you when Jonathan Bechtal turned himself in."

"You used more than that." He took it back, inhaling deeply. "Murder is a sin and a crime, but I'll be forced, on Judgment Day, to answer for leading you to cigarettes."

"I smoke one a day."

"You'll smoke more." He closed his eyes in pleasure after another long, long drag. "Well, we have a fascinating situation on our hands."

"What's funny is that Mike's panty fetish has people more in an uproar than the murders."

"New news." Then Rick smiled wryly. "And it's all about sex. That's a lot more interesting than crimes committed over ideology, money, property. Sex makes everyone perk up."

"Does, doesn't it?"

"Lorenzo must have called."

"You know," she paused, "he did. I've seen him once for lunch, on my day off, and I like him. More than that I don't know."

"But you know if you're attracted to him. You can't invent that. Either it's there or it isn't."

"Sex." Coop smiled. "I think that's why it's so difficult for women to understand men like Mike. Intellectually we know why he did what he did, but emotionally it doesn't compute. Never will."

"Let me let you in on a little secret: it doesn't compute with a lot of men, either. I find Mike more disgusting than Jonathan Bechtal. Bechtal is a fanatic, a lunatic. Mike abused public trust as well as abusing women. He's a liar, a thief, in my mind a rapist, and a corrupt official. Anything that breaks down trust in government, to me, is a sin. And God knows, there's a lot of it out there."

"I agree. Without trust you have nothing in any kind of relationship. You know what I see now that I didn't see before? I see the trust that Harry has with her pets and they have with her. Those animals may well have saved her life."

"They did." Rick's cell rang and he flipped

it open, listened intently, flipped it shut. "Come on, partner."

She followed him at a run.

Closing the squad car door behind her, Coop breathlessly asked, "Penny?"

"No." He hit the sirens and roared off. "Mike."

They reached the jail. Mike's crumpled body lay on its side in the outdoor exercise area. His bloodshot eyes testified to strangulation even before Rick knelt down to examine the bruises on his neck.

The guard, Sam Demotta, stood helplessly next to the body. "I turned my back for a minute. Chief, honestly. I heard a gurgle and Jonathan had his hands around his throat. I couldn't stop him. I blew my whistle. By the time Tom got here, Mike was toast."

"Snitch," was all Rick said as he rose, heading toward the cell block.

Coop followed.

No need to explain the judgment reserved for snitches in prison, or the armed forces, for that matter.

Smugly sitting on his bunk, Jonathan did not rise to greet them.

Rick said, "You kill him?"

"I did."

"Would you like to give me a reason?"

"Oh," Jonathan airily commented, "I tossed him a few morsels, knowing he'd run to you when he could, and that way I had reason to kill him. He was a pervert. He deserved to die."

Coop said, "Couldn't you have killed him without tossing him morsels?"

"I could." Jonathan spoke patiently, as though to a dim-witted child. "But it's boring in here. This helped pass the time, and he deserved to die. It's God's will, you know."

The two law-enforcement officers walked outside the cell block, shutting the door behind them.

"Jesus Christ, he's crazy. He'll get off because he's crazy!" Coop uttered in total despair.

"He knows it, too. He'll be spared the death sentence and spend the rest of his worthless life in a high-security mental ward." Rick appreciated the twisted prisoner's intelligence. "And there's not a damned thing we can do about it. But I am going to do something he doesn't like, even if we have to strap him down, and I bet we will."

He did, too. One hour later, Sam Demotta had the honor of cutting off Jonathan's beard, then shaving him. Tom had to hold his jaw tight, but they did it. A few cuts appeared on Jonathan's good-looking face.

"I should have done that when we first arrested him," Rick declared. "All right. I want photographs and, Sam, the best one better be in tomorrow's paper. I'll call them right now."

"They won't run it," Coop told him as they hurried to the jail office. "Newspapers always use their own photographer."

"They'll use this, because I am going to tell them that the prisoner is far too dangerous for anyone to be near him and he has killed again."

The next day, Friday, October 17, the newspapers, the television news, and the radio carried the story of Mike McElvoy's murder.

The photo in the paper startled Benita Wylde. She remembered where she'd seen Jonathan Bechtal.

36

Benita, good with names and faces, remembered that she had once seen someone who looked like Jonathan Bechtal talking to Kylie Kraft outside Will's office. Benita had gone by to drop off a salad for Will since he was being careful about his eating habits.

She also remembered that when Kylie came back into the office after only minutes outside, she made a crack about men not understanding that no means no. Given Kylie's ever-changing string of boyfriends, Benita had discounted it.

However, Kylie had seen the photo in the paper, too. Taking no chances, she was at the airport one half hour after seeing the picture.

• • •

By the time Rick and Cooper reached Kylie's apartment, she was gone. Her clothes and furniture remained. Cooper checked the bathroom; her makeup bag was gone.

Cooper found a pack of Virginia Slims, which they put in a plastic bag.

They put an alert out for her car, which was found at the Charlottesville Airport parking lot. However, her name did not appear on any flights.

Either she had been picked up by a friend or she stole a car from the parking lot. That wouldn't be evident until the owner returned to an empty space days or maybe weeks later.

At nine-fifteen that morning, Rick and Cooper interrogated Jonathan Bechtal.

"Do you know Kylie Kraft?"

"No."

"Did she tell you to kill Dr. Wylde?"

"No," he answered Rick.

"Was Dr. Wylde on to her stealing the records?"

"How would I know?"

The only flicker of emotion in Bechtal's face came when Rick said, "She left town in a hurry with all the money you'd raised."

Rick didn't know that. He was baiting Bechtal. But he was reasonably certain it was true.

When Bechtal said nothing, Cooper slyly mentioned, "She will continue your work."

A beatific look infused his face. Again he said nothing.

Rick and Cooper ended their interrogation and left the jail. Once in the car, Rick started the motor. Before he pulled out, he reached into a dash cubbyhole, extracting two dollars and fifty cents. "Here."

"What's this for?"

"Half and half. I bet a woman. You bet a man."

She smiled. "We'll get her."

"Might take years, but she'll make a mistake. They always do."

"Do you think she's a true believer?"

He pulled out of the parking lot. "I don't know. If she is, she's in some ways more frightening than he is. And smarter."

"True."

"Still," he smiled, "I have this vision of her

in a beautiful hacienda in Uruguay or an opulent seaside house in Chile, living high on the hog."

"And?"

"There's a revolution." He laughed.

"Probably not in those two countries, but she'll tip her hand and we'll get her. She killed a woman; she orchestrated the death of a doctor."

"And she's a nurse. You know, I never connected with that. Carla was killed by someone who understood anatomy, understood what happens when you slit a jugular. Somehow, she got out of the way of that mighty gusher."

"I'd like to know how." Cooper stared out the window at clouds massing up in the west.

"Well, when she turns up, wherever she turns up, we'll find out."

"At least Mike didn't kill Carla. That's some comfort to his widow."

"Cold comfort," Rick grunted.

Cooper turned to look at his profile. "If nothing else, this showed Little Mim's mettle, and I bet there are women—we'll never know who—who talked to their husbands or friends and resolved their burden about their past. Some good came of it."

"We can hope."

"Smoke?" she asked.

"Have you ever known me to refuse?"

She reached for the hardpack she'd slid in her front pocket, fishing out a long cigarette. "Coffin nail, just for you."

He quickly glanced at it. "Dunhill Mild."

"It's true, you're corrupting me."

"Damn," was all he said, as she held a match for him when they reached a stoplight.

"If you have no objection, I'll drive out to Harry's and give her the scoop."

"That is one lucky woman." He inhaled. "What are we going to do about her? She's a damned nuisance, and one of these days she's going to get herself or one of us killed, I swear."

"Ask her to join the force."

Rick laughed. "That will be the day. I'd sooner ask Mrs. Murphy, Pewter, and Tucker. In fact, they demonstrate more sense than she does."

"They've saved her on more than one occasion."

He rode along, silent for a while. "We use German shepherds. Why not a corgi and two cats?"

Cooper related this to Harry as she cleaned tack in the barn.

"Guess he's mad at me."

"Do you blame him?" Cooper's eyebrows raised.

"I did find a criminal. Okay, Mike wasn't the killer, but he sure was guilty of plenty of other stuff."

"Paid for it," Cooper tersely replied. "Harry, you've got to be more careful. You can't just go do these things on a whim."

"It wasn't a whim. Well, okay. It was."

"I can't believe she admitted it!" Pewter listened to the mice behind the tack trunk.

"There. That's finished." Harry hung the tack on the half-round bridle holder on the wall. "Come on in the house. I'll make you some Silver Queen."

"Where'd you get Silver Queen in October?"

"I bought four bushels in August and put them in cold storage—you know the refrigeration plant downtown? Anyway, we tested two last night and they're still really good."

"Four bushels?" Cooper asked as they left the barn, Simon looking out from the open top barn door in the hayloft.

"For the St. Luke's reunion."

Mrs. Murphy, Pewter, and Tucker tagged along.

"Saturday after this; that's always such a wonderful day, isn't it?" Cooper smiled.

As they passed under the wide branches of the walnut tree, Matilda, swinging by her tail, dropped.

She just missed Harry, who was walking behind Cooper, and landed right on Pewter.

"Death from the skies," Matilda hissed.

Pewter screamed so loudly that everyone jumped. Matilda slithered toward the barn. Time to go in, because she knew in her bones that tonight would be the first frost.

"God!" Cooper exclaimed.

"She was going to wrap herself around my throat. She's a wicked, wicked snake." Pewter, beside herself, babbled on.

"Every now and then she does that," Harry laconically replied.

"Why is she in the tree?"

"Birds' eggs in the spring and summer—birds, period. She's fast when she wants to be. Look how fast she's heading toward the barn."

Harry knelt down to pet Pewter, who was recovering.

"Big baby." Mrs. Murphy giggled.

"Shut up." Pewter crawled into Harry's arms, allowing herself to be carried into the house.

The women chatted as the corn boiled.

"Sometimes things do fall out of the sky. Sometimes we miss things." Cooper was still surprised at Matilda's bomber act. "If we hadn't shaved Bechtal, who knows? And we should have done that right away. We only had a high-school photograph of him, no beard. He'd erased most everything about his life."

"Criminals fall into two camps: dumber than posts or extremely intelligent."

"Yep."

"I'm reasonably intelligent, but . . ." Harry didn't finish.

"You'd be lost without us." Mrs. Murphy smiled, then hopped on the kitchen counter to gaze out the window.

Mrs. Murphy knew they'd been very lucky this time. She and Pewter had used up one of their nine lives, and it was uppermost in her mind that Harry had only one.

Dear Reader,

I keep forgetting to mention that four books equal one year. Each mystery represents a season. I thought it was obvious, which it is to cats, but I overestimate human intelligence sometimes. You'd think after all these years with my typist that I'd figure out how dim they are.

I will give my human credit for a green thumb. She can grow anything and I reward her for her crop of fresh catnip by not shredding the furniture.

This isn't to say I don't love my human and like some others. I do, but the poor things are so limited. Can't see in the dark for squat. No claws. No fangs. Slow as molasses when running. Climb with difficulty. Besotted with ideologies that don't correspond to reality. It's a wonder they've survived, and really, they only began to flourish after we cats chose to assist them. Think what would have happened to the granaries of Rome if cats hadn't guarded them? But as usual, humans are so drastically self-centered, they ignore what we've done. They ignore dog contributions, too, although we all know dogs aren't as intelligent as cats. In some ways they are well suited to be companions to humans since dogs believe what humans tell them.

Not me. I know the emperor has no clothes; a pity, since naked humans are ghastly!

Ta Ta,

Sneaky Pie

Dear Reader,

She really is insufferable!

About the Authors

RITA MAE BROWN is the bestselling author of several books. An Emmy-nominated screenwriter and poet, she lives in Afton, Virginia. Her website is www.ritamaebrown.com.

SNEAKY PIE BROWN, a tiger cat born somewhere in Albemarle County, Virginia, was discovered by Rita Mae Brown at her local SPCA. They have collaborated on fifteen previous Mrs. Murphy mysteries: *Wish You Were Here; Rest in Pieces; Murder at Monticello; Pay Dirt; Murder, She Meowed; Murder on the Prowl; Cat on the Scent; Pawing Through the Past; Claws and Effect; Catch as Cat Can; The Tail of the Tip-Off; Whisker of Evil; Cat's Eyewitness; Sour Puss*; and *Puss 'n Cahoots,* in addition to *Sneaky Pie's Cookbook for Mystery Lovers.*